"Do you ever think about your baby?"

Darcy's question took Paige by surprise. She said nothing.

Her friend reached out and squeezed her hand. "It can't be easy," Darcy continued. "I'm surprised that you agreed to work at the clinic. Where," she added meaningfully, "you'll be dealing with girls who'll remind you of how things were at Serenity House." She paused and lowered her voice. "*Girls with babies.*"

Paige swallowed hard. She never talked about this. "I deal with babies every day."

"You know what I mean."

Suddenly Paige's throat felt parched. "You mean girls who made a different choice than I did?"

"Yes." Darcy hesitated a moment, then asked, "Do you ever think about her?"

Her? Paige's head began to swim. Her eyes burned. *Her!* The baby she'd given birth to fifteen years ago had been a *daughter*.

A fact she'd never known.

Dear Reader,

Welcome to SERENITY HOUSE—a trilogy of stories about women who spent some of their adolescent years in a group home for troubled girls. Each story explores what effect their dysfunctional backgrounds had on them. As you might guess, trust—not being able to trust—is a big issue for all of them. But with the help of those who love them, each woman overcomes her difficult beginnings and becomes the person she was meant to be.

The series opens with Paige Kendrick, a pediatrician, who likes life the way it is. Enter Ian Chandler, gorgeous OB-GYN, who turns her world upside down and makes her face parts of her past that Paige would rather keep buried. As with most of my books, this one deals with serious issues: troubled teenagers, the effects of a dysfunctional past, adoption and taking the risk of depending on someone else. It also has personal relevance for me: it's set in upstate New York in a town similar to where I grew up, it deals with some issues that I had to deal with growing up and the girls of Serenity House are very much like the students I work with every day as a high school teacher.

I hope you enjoy reading about these women's struggles to put the past behind them, take their rightful place in society, find love and happiness with the right man and make the world a little better than the one they grew up in.

As always, with my series books, this one stands alone, but I hope you'll read the other two scheduled books, A Place To Belong (Darcy's story) and Against the Odds (Anabelle's story).

Please write and let me know what you think. I answer all reader mail. Send letters to Kathryn Shay, P.O. Box 24288, Rochester, New York, 14624-0288 or e-mail me at kshayweb@rochester.rr.com. Also visit my Web sites at http://www.kathrynshay.com and http://www.superauthors.com.

Kathryn Shay

Practice Makes Perfect

Kathryn Shay

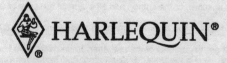

HARLEQUIN®

TORONTO • NEW YORK • LONDON
AMSTERDAM • PARIS • SYDNEY • HAMBURG
STOCKHOLM • ATHENS • TOKYO • MILAN • MADRID
PRAGUE • WARSAW • BUDAPEST • AUCKLAND

To the following teachers and school counselors, who work with girls like those of Serenity House, and who provided the inspiration for this book: Martha Buseck, Candy Carlo, Jo Ann Coffey, Allyn Dasta, Sandy Foley, Julie Gangai, Stacy Killings, Stacey Lauricella, Patricia Marx, Joan Stevens and Laurie Tooley-Jeffers.

ISBN 0-373-71066-6

PRACTICE MAKES PERFECT

This edition published by arrangement with Harlequin Books S.A.

® and TM are trademarks of the publisher. Trademarks indicated with ® are registered in the United States Patent and Trademark Office, the Canadian Trade Marks Office and in other countries.

Visit us at www.eHarlequin.com

Printed in U.S.A.

CAST OF CHARACTERS

Serenity House	**A group home for teenage girls in Hyde Point, New York.**
Jade Kendrick Anderson	Paige's sister, one of the original residents of Serenity House
Jewel Anderson	Jade's daughter
Mary Ellen Barone	Current resident of S.H.
Ian Chandler	Obstetrician
Lynne Chandler	Ian's birth mother
Anabelle Crane	Police officer, one of the original residents of S.H.
Charly Smith Donovan	Social worker, one of the original residents of S.H.
Nathan Hyde	Congressman, son of the town's founding father
Paige Kendrick	Pediatrician, one of the original residents of S.H.
Elsa and Tom Moore	Ian's adoptive parents
Taylor Vaughn Morelli	One of the original S.H. residents
Nick Morelli	Taylor's husband
Darcy O'Malley	One of the original S.H. residents, now runs a day care
Meli and Claire O'Malley	Darcy's daughters
Nora Nolan	Founder and house mother of S.H.
Scalpel	Ian Chandler's dog—and best friend
Hunter Sloan	Local boy, friend of Dan Whitman's
Dan Whitman	Police chief, fiancé of Nora Nolan

PROLOGUE

April 1987
Hyde Point, New York

NORA NOLAN struggled to stay calm as she climbed the stairs of Serenity House, Hyde Point's new home for troubled girls. Behind her were Sergeant Chief Dan Whitman and Jade Kendrick, one of the resident teenagers. They hurried to the first room on the left.

Paige, Jade's sister, was sprawled across the bed, wearing oversize boxers and an oversize T-shirt to cover her huge stomach; she peered up from her book, *The First Nine Months of Life*. "What's wrong?" She spotted her sister. "Jade? What're you doing home in the middle of the day?" Her eyes narrowed. "Did you get in trouble again at school?"

Bursting into the room, Jade climbed onto the bed with Paige. "No, Dan came and got me." She sidled in close. "Something's wrong."

Paige's eyes widened; she slipped her hand into Jade's and looked up at the adults. "What happened?"

"I need to talk to you both." Nora tried to keep her tone even as she came into the room, followed by Dan. She inched Paige and Jade over and sat on the bed. "I just got a call from the state police. I'm so sorry, girls. There's been an accident." Her voice cracked, and Dan put a hand on her shoulder. "Your parents were on a motorcycle. They were killed instantly."

For a minute everything seemed suspended in time. No one moved. Then tears welled in Jade's eyes, and she turned her face into Paige's shoulder. Paige shifted and encircled Jade with her arms. But her own eyes stayed dry. "It's okay, sis, I'll take care of you." Swallowing back emotion, she looked at Nora. "H-how did it happen?"

"They crashed into a utility pole on the way here." No need to tell them yet that Sam and Sari Kendrick, who had just been released from rehab, had visited their dealer and had been high as kites when they drove their motorcycle off the road.

"No, no," Jade sobbed, almost hysterical. "They were coming to take us home this weekend."

"I know they were." Nora reached out to soothe Jade's shoulder.

Paige's hand went to her stomach. "What'll we do now, Nora?"

"We'll decide that later," Nora said, tucking back a strand of Paige's hair. "Sweetie, it's all right to cry."

Shaking her head, Paige lifted her chin. "No, I have to figure this out. We're alone now. I'll have to take care of Jade. I'll have to…" Her face tightened, then blanched. "I, um, don't feel good."

Nora cocked her head. "The baby?"

"No. Just…a little sick to my stomach. I gotta go to the bathroom." She tried to ease away from Jade.

Her sister clung to her. "No, Paige," Jade said brokenly. "Don't go."

Nora pried the younger girl loose. "Let go, Jade. She'll be right back." She wrapped Jade in her arms and Paige bolted off the bed and headed to the door. Just as she

reached it, she stopped short. "Nora, Nora, my...I..."
She looked down at the wet splotches on her boxers.

Nora drew in a breath. "Your water broke."

"That means the baby's coming." Paige gripped the
jamb. "It's a month early." Her face contorted and she
hunched over. "Oh."

Dan reached her first. "Easy now." He grasped her
shoulder, just before she crumpled. Swinging her up into
his arms, he crossed to the bed and set her down. "Nora,
call the ambulance."

"No, Nora, don't go." Paige grabbed for Nora's arm.
"Don't go. The baby's *coming*."

"Okay. I'll make the call." Hurriedly, Dan left the
room.

"Nora, it's coming *now*."

"Well," Nora said with a calm she didn't feel. "I have
some medical training. And Dan's an EMT, so if the
medics don't get here in time, you're still in good
hands."

Paige's grip on Nora's arm intensified. She moaned as
a contraction slammed into her. "Ohhh..."

"Breathe in, Paige. Like we learned in class. Let the
air out slowly."

The contraction crested, but another seemed to hit immediately. It was too soon for them to be coming so fast.

Dan returned. "The medics'll be delayed. The only
ambulance is on another call." Nora tried to hide her
concern. Serenity House was located on the outskirts of
town; under the best of circumstances, it took at least
fifteen minutes to drive out here.

Another contraction. When it finally subsided, Paige
whimpered, "I want my mother."

"I know you do, sweetie, I know."

"Oh, God, it hurts."

"Nora," Dan said, "get some towels and sterilize a pair of scissors." His voice was confident, cutting through Nora's panic. "It won't be long."

Nora did as Dan asked. By the time she returned, Paige was soaked in sweat and breathing hard. Dan and Jade were at her side. Nora took Dan's place on the bed, and he went to wash up.

After a fierce contraction, Paige drew in a deep breath and grabbed Nora's hand. "They're really dead."

"Yes, sweetie."

"Mom said I could keep the baby. That they'd help. They can't now, right?"

"No, they can't now. But—"

"Then I don't want it."

"Oh, Paige. You don't have to decide now."

"I don't want it." She lifted her shoulders off the bed, and tightened her hold on Nora's hand. "Promise me, you'll take it right away. I don't even wanna know what it is."

"Sweetie, now's not the time—"

"Promise me!"

"All right, I promise. I'll take it away until you have time to think about it."

"I don't want to know…" Another contraction. "I don't want to know anything."

Dan returned, and forty-five minutes later, Nora watched as the tiny infant slipped into his hands. Sirens blared in the background. Paige turned her face to the wall. "Take it away," was all she said.

Nora's throat clogged and her eyes blurred, but she wrapped the baby in a blanket and stood holding it by the bed.

"Take it away!" Paige screamed.

Slowly, cradling the newborn to her chest, Nora turned and walked out the door.

CHAPTER ONE

April 2002

PAIGE FLOATED *facedown on a raft in the kidney-shaped pool on the Princess Cruise Liner docked just off the coast of Jamaica. The tropical sun warmed her back and almost lulled her to sleep. Suddenly, incongruously, a ringing pierced the air—a bell of some kind. She moaned and tried to block out the noise, but it persisted. Damned if it didn't sound like a phone...*

"Arrgh..." Paige buried her face in her pillow. Blindly she reached out her arm, fumbling for the intrusive instrument. "Hello."

"Dr. Kendrick?"

"Yes, this is Dr. Kendrick." She kept her eyes shut, hoping the call would take only a few minutes and she could go back to Jamaica.

"Just a moment, please. Dr. Chandler would like to speak to you." Muffled sounds. The woman giggled as she spoke away from the receiver.

A deep, morning-after voice came over the phone. "Hi, Paige."

"This better be good, Ian."

A throaty chuckle. "Hmm. Last time a woman said that to me..." The man was a notorious flirt. She remembered that now.

"Cut it out." Her words were slurred by the pillow.

"Sorry to wake you, Sleeping Beauty. I wouldn't have called, but one of your fan club just delivered, and she said *you* said she could call any time—"

Paige's head cleared instantly. "Kari Linstrom?" Her heartbeat quickened. If the pediatrician was being called in the middle of the night... She glanced at the clock. *Okay. Calm down. It's 5 a.m. Not the middle of the night.* And she *had* told the teenager she could call at any time. "Is the baby all right?" Paige asked.

"Little Alyssa Paige is fine. But she has a hemangioma on her left cheek, and Kari won't believe me when I tell her it's just a vascular birthmark and will go away. She wants you."

Sliding out of bed, Paige crossed to her closet. "I'll be right there."

"Just talk to Kari on the phone," Ian told her. "It's early. You can catch some more sleep."

"No, I want to come down."

"Fine. I'll tell her you're on your way."

"Ian? Did the delivery go smoothly?"

"The second one is usually easier."

"Spoken like a man."

Again a sensual chuckle on the other end. God, did he take sexy pills? "See you soon."

She pulled on navy pants, a white blouse and a light sweater, stuck her feet into a pair of Birkenstocks, and was out the door of her twelve-room house on Spencer Hill and into her silver BMW in less than five minutes. She reached the sprawling Hyde Point General Hospital in record time and arrived at the Birthing Center a mere twenty minutes after being snatched from her Caribbean cruise.

Ian met her outside one of the birthing rooms. Despite

the early hour, he managed to look irritatingly handsome in green scrubs, with his long hair the color of mink framing a face that turned grown women into simpering idiots. "What did you do, fly?" he asked.

"Wish I could. It would save time."

He nodded to the first door. "Sorry about this, but it's your own fault. All the mothers of your little patients think you're *their* mother."

Mother. She ignored the twinge, though it was hard when she remembered today's date. And hard, too, because Kari, like Paige, had been a resident of Serenity House when her first child—a son—had been born. Which was why, at Nora Nolan's request, Paige had agreed to be the Linstrom children's pediatrician. She said to Ian, "Your patients think you're Dr. Kildare, so we're even."

"Who's he?" Ian called out to her retreating back; she brushed past him and into the first room without answering.

Kari Linstrom sat on a bed with yellow-covered pillows and sheets, cradling her child. Paige dropped her purse on a table. "Hi, Kari. So she came early?"

The girl's face glowed, though it was etched with exhaustion—and something else. "Yes." Her voice quavered. "Dr. Paige Kendrick meet Alyssa Paige Linstrom."

Paige smiled warmly at her. "I'm honored." She crossed to the sink. "Let me wash up." Scrubbing, she asked, "Everything go okay?"

"It hurt."

"I know, sweetie."

"But she's worth it." Kari was looking down at the child when Paige approached the bed. Bending over, Paige moved the blanket away from the infant's face.

Sprouts of red hair, the exact shade of Kari's, peeked out from under the gauzy pink cap. Little fingers flexed, and Paige stuck her own pinky into the baby's hand. Alyssa grasped it and Paige chuckled. "Well, hello there, little one. Welcome to the world."

Kari whispered, "Dr. Kendrick, look at her face."

Though the baby's skin was typical newborn red, a tiny purplish blotch did indeed mar her cheek. "It looks like a fairy's handprint," she said, recalling the description in Nathaniel Hawthorne's story "The Birthmark." "But Dr. Chandler was right. It's a hemangioma, also known as a strawberry mark."

Tears clouded Kari's eyes. "She has it because I'm not married."

"What?"

"My father said God would curse the baby because I'm not married. Just like Jimmy's feet." Kari's son had been born with club feet and had gone through painful surgery and a full year of casting to correct the deformity.

The young mother began to cry in earnest. Paige sat down on the bed and pulled Kari and the baby into her arms. "Shh, Kari. It's all right. God hasn't cursed your baby."

Damn society. Nineteen-year-old Kari Linstrom had grown up in the projects on the north side of Hyde Point and had spent a year at Serenity House—just as Paige had done. After she'd moved back home, Kari's very rigid father never let her forget her unwed status.

Paige ran a soothing hand down Kari's hair. "Listen to me, Kari. Children are often born with these kinds of marks. They mean nothing, and most of them go away within the first two years of life. If they don't disappear, laser surgery can easily remove them."

"R-really?"

"Really. But understand this, honey. Even if that wasn't the case, like with Jimmy's feet, birthmarks are flukes of nature, not acts of God."

Kari raised her eyes to Paige. They were still swimming with tears. "My priest doesn't believe that."

"Your priest sees things from a more narrow perspective, Kari. I see them in a broader sense." *And more sanely.* "Now, I don't want to hear any more of that bunk about little Alyssa's pretty face."

When Kari still looked skeptical, Paige added, "You have to have faith in me. I would never lie to you."

"I know." Kari gulped back her tears. "I do have faith in you. Thanks."

Paige reached for the baby. "Now, hand her over, kid. I want to count my namesake's fingers and toes."

Kari glanced past Paige's shoulder. "I'm sorry I didn't believe you, Dr. Chandler."

Paige's head snapped around. She'd been unaware of their audience and was vaguely discomfited. "I didn't hear you come in."

"I didn't want to disturb you." He gave her a killer grin.

She scowled back.

"I was wondering if I could see you after you're done here."

For a moment Paige hesitated. A shudder of something went through her. *Like someone walking over my grave,* was how Nora always described similar feelings. Paige shook the notion off. "Sure, I'll be about half an hour."

"I'll be in the doctors' lounge on this floor."

"Fine." She turned her back on Ian. Best to concentrate on the baby. "Now, let me have her."

As she cradled the child in her arms, Paige felt the

same sense of well-being she experienced every time she held a newborn. It was one of the reasons she'd chosen to specialize in pediatrics. She loved all children, but babies especially. And she had "the touch," her mentor, Elsa Moore, used to tell her.

Smiling, she lay the little girl on the bed and unwrapped the blanket.

"CAN I MAKE fresh coffee for you before I go on duty?" The petite blond nurse—Sabrina Sherman—smiled at Ian through heavily made-up eyes.

"No thanks, ma'am. My ma learned me good." He winked at her, and saw those eyes widen. Uh-oh. His brother, Derek, constantly teased him about his effect on women. His mother had other admonitions. *Be careful with that charm, young man. God gave it to you to use, not abuse.* "Thanks, anyway. I can do it."

Sidling close to him, Sabrina gave him an I'm yours-if-you-want-me smile, then left.

Women. They were the joy and bane of his existence. He chuckled as he washed the pot and assembled the coffee. Take Paige Kendrick. He never would have guessed she could be Ms. Warm and Sensitive. True, he hadn't seen her work directly with patients in her exclusive practice on the hill, but he did run into her at Hyde Point General, the only hospital in the small upstate New York town; he was an ob/gyn and she was a pediatrician, and they'd consulted a few times, too.

As the aroma of coffee filled the air, he crossed to the table and dropped onto a chair to fiddle with one of the jigsaw puzzles that he routinely brought in here. He didn't dare sit still or he'd fall instantly to sleep.

Soon Paige walked in. "What are you doing?" she asked, checking her watch. "At 6 a.m.?"

"A jigsaw puzzle so I don't doze off."

Paige looked thoughtful. "You ever get used to this?"

"Calls in the middle of the night? Nope. My dad said you never get used to it."

"Your father was an obstetrician?"

"Yes." Standing, Ian crossed to pour coffee for both of them. The pain of his parents' death a year ago was still there, and when he was tired like this, the wound felt raw. "Before he retired, he'd cut back on his practice and was teaching at Elmwood Medical School."

"Elmwood? I went there."

"Yes, I know." He turned and handed her a cup. "Black, right?"

Nodding, she took it from him and glanced at her watch again. "What did you want to talk to me about?"

So much for small talk. It was the one criticism her colleagues had about her. She was cold and standoffish— all business. Some nurses joked that they needed to wear a sweater when they worked with her. Quite a contrast to what he'd just witnessed in the birthing room.

"Come sit down." He moved past her and sank onto the lumpy cushions of the couch. "You can keep me awake."

She didn't smile. Nor did she act as though his every word was a come-on, which frankly he was pleased about; she sat a respectable distance away and sipped her coffee. "Shoot."

"I want you to join us at the center I'm establishing for young mothers and children." This was Ian's pet project—a facility to treat unwed mothers and other young mothers who couldn't afford medical care for themselves or their children. Pregnant girls from Serenity House would receive pre- and post-natal care, though they would give birth at the hospital.

Paige's soft-brown eyebrows arched. She didn't pluck them, he noticed. They were thick and full, like her lashes, which framed eyes the color of the sky in spring. "I thought you were ready to open next month. You have all your personnel, don't you?"

"We did. But Diane Conklin backed out." He managed to say it without wincing. He'd had no idea the young doctor had joined for...spurious reasons. "Her husband took a job in Cleveland and she's going with him." After Ian had made it clear he didn't sleep with married women.

"That's too bad. Diane's terrific with kids."

"So are you."

Paige frowned. "I didn't respond to your memo the first time, Ian, because I'm too busy with my private practice."

"Ah, yes. But I wanted you, you know."

It was subtle, just a slight shifting, but she inched away from him. "Really? Well, nothing's changed since last year when you sent it around. If anything, I'm busier."

He drank his coffee; the caffeine was kick-starting his system, and he could think more clearly. "I've been assessing your practice, Paige." He studied her. "You don't have a lot of underprivileged patients. Your practice is pretty upscale."

"That's none of your business." Her tone was glacial.

"Well, I'm making it my business. The Center is for young mothers who can't afford good medical care for themselves or their kids. Don't you think you should give back to a society that's gotten you where you are?"

"That society did me a lot more harm than good, Dr. Chandler." She sent him a don't-mess-with-me look. "Not that it's really your concern. In any case, I'm simply too busy to help you out."

Hmm. She was prickly about this. For some reason, it challenged him. "Sounds pretty self-centered to me."

"Ian, I mean it. What I choose to do isn't any of your business."

"Maybe not. It's just that you've been so good with Kari's kids."

The genuine compliment seemed to melt her iciness a bit.

"Look," she said, "I have this resident working with me until the end of the month. As far as I know, he's not committed after his rotation. You can ask him."

"I don't want a resident. You could start by giving us one day," he said coaxingly. Ian knew that one of his faults was that he was like a pit bull when he wanted something. "Or is it that you don't agree with the concept?"

"No, of course I agree with the concept." Her eyes blazed blue fire. "Hyde Point needs good medical care for young girls and their babies. I admire you for doing it." She frowned. "I just don't want to be a part of it."

"Why?"

"God, Ian, are you always such a bulldozer?"

"Only when I need to be."

"I don't want to do it."

She stood, moved to the counter and rinsed her cup in the sink. He watched her, noting the way her pants hugged her curves. He'd rarely seen her in slacks, and he stopped himself before he could tell her how good she looked in them. He wanted to woo her into his center, not his bed. Time for the big guns. The manipulation he was about to engage in caused him a momentary twinge of conscience, but he went ahead, anyway. "Paige, do you know the name of the new center?"

Pivoting, she threaded her fingers through her light-brown hair. Lank and silky, it swung around her shoulders. "No. Does it matter?"

"It might to you. It'll be christened the Elsa Moore Center."

Paige gripped the cup. "How do you know Elsa Moore? You didn't go to Elmwood, did you?"

"No, I went to med school out West." He gave her his best grin. "But I knew Elsa Moore very well. She was my mother."

A VISION OF ELSA—small, slender and delicate—swam before Paige's eyes; Elsa was so unlike the tall, muscular man with linebacker shoulders who was sprawled on the couch. For a moment Paige was speechless. He must look like his father, she thought. "Elsa was your mother? Really?"

"Yes."

Paige knew Elsa was married to Tom Moore. She'd met him in Elsa's office, of course. She'd never met Elsa's sons, although she'd seen scattered photos of two small boys around the office. "I remember her telling me her sons' names were Derek and Tommy?"

"I'm Tommy. Named after my father. Thomas Ian. It got confusing and Dad and my friends started calling me Ian, but Mom liked Tommy."

Her brows knitted. "You don't have your parents' last name."

"No. It's a long story."

It didn't add up. "The only pictures I ever saw of you were when you were little. Elsa had those on her desk."

Gray eyes were briefly shadowed with hurt. "Yes. She said that I was still her little boy even though I'd grown up."

Paige leaned against the counter. "I never knew." Her

insides knotted. God, she hated surprises. "Ian, I've known you for four years. Why didn't you ever tell me this?"

"For the same reason you never came to our house, spent time with our family, even though you worked for my mother all through medical school."

Paige had a brief flash of Elsa's invitations. *We're having a picnic this Memorial Day, dear... You and your sister are welcome to spend Christmas with us, Paige... My husband and sons would love to finally meet you... It's Tommy's graduation...*

"Paige, are you all right?"

"This is a shock to me." Her eyes narrowed on him. "What do you mean, for the same reason I never came to your house?"

"My mother said you were a very private person who didn't want to mix your personal life with your professional one." He waited a minute. "It's why you never saw much of her once you opened your own practice."

"She retired to Florida soon after that." Paige's tone was defensive.

"They came up to Keuka Lake every spring and summer."

"Well, you're right, really. I still don't like to mix my personal and professional lives."

"Yes, everybody knows that about you."

Paige stiffened.

"Don't get your back up. I didn't mean it was the subject of gossip."

Paige thought of something else and straightened immediately. "Ian, I was doing that physician-exchange program in England when Elsa and Tom died. That's why I didn't make it to their funeral."

His throat worked convulsively. "I know, we got your note." It had been addressed to "The Moores."

"I would have said something to you personally had I known you were her son." When he didn't respond, she added, "I'm so sorry I missed the funeral. I got back a month afterward." She hesitated. "I went to the cemetery." Actually she'd visited more than once.

"She would have liked that." Ian stood and stretched. The scrubs strained across his chest. Paige was tall, but he loomed over her. "In any case, I'm naming the center after Mom for a couple of reasons. One is personal. But mostly I'm doing it because she was a brilliant doctor who donated her time to worthy causes like this."

"She worked magic with kids." Paige had learned the tricks of her trade from Elsa, who'd always accepted non-paying patients and showed by example how doctors could help society in many ways.

"The touch, she called it. You have it, too. She'd said that, but I never saw you in action before tonight. Watching you was like watching my mother treat patients."

Paige shook off the compliment, though it warmed her. "I'm dumbfounded." And…upset that she'd known Ian for years but hadn't known he was Elsa's son.

"Good. I'm catching you in a weak moment. Join us, Paige, at the Center."

"I—"

He raised his hand and she stepped back, afraid he was going to touch her.

"Don't say no again. Think about it."

He was something else, but he was starting to get to her. And the last thing she wanted was to work regularly with unwed mothers who reminded her of her own past. Just dealing with the few Serenity House patients as a favor to Nora was difficult. It was why she'd chosen to practice on the Hill—usually the moms were older, married and more established. So she said more firmly, "I don't have to think about it, Ian." She crossed to the exit.

"Wait, Paige."

She halted at the door and faced him. He was, after all, Elsa's son.

"My mother would have loved to see you working with disadvantaged children."

Exasperated, she said, "Do you always resort to emotional blackmail to get your way?"

"Only when I have to."

"It won't work this time."

"Hmm," was all he said. But the smug grin on his face unnerved her.

IT WAS SEVEN that evening before Paige let herself think about Ian's proposal—and one of his comments, in particular.

My mother would have loved to see you working with disadvantaged children.

She sat in her car, outside Serenity House, where she'd driven as soon as her day—which had begun so early—was over.

She studied Serenity House in the twilight. The gabled three-story structure, set on a hill, had changed over the past fifteen years. It had been painted gray and new steps had been installed. The saplings Dan Whitman had planted that first spring were towering red maples now.

Everything had grown up at Serenity House, including her. She and her sister, Jade had been placed in Serenity House when their too-wild parents had been ordered into rehab by the courts. Then, on the day they were released, they were killed in a motorcycle accident on their way to pick up their daughters. Paige and Jade had stayed at Serenity for a year, until Paige turned eighteen and was legally able to take care of her sister.

Ian Chandler had rocked her world today, and here she was, reflecting on her life. She closed her eyes and thought about that night exactly fifteen years ago when she'd given birth to her own child. Dan had delivered it. The medics hadn't arrived in time; there was no good care for the girls all those years ago.

Paige had asked for so little back then. That she get through the baby's birth and give it up for adoption. And know nothing about it—not even whether she'd had a girl or a boy. Complete withdrawal was the only way she could get through the whole ordeal.

And she never would have survived and made something of herself if it hadn't been for Nora Nolan and later, Elsa Moore. Both women had given her lifelines: Nora, the nurturing she'd needed to give birth and endure the aftermath, and Elsa, the professional opportunities to become a doctor despite her deprived childhood.

She winced at the recollection of Ian's words, *Don't you think you should give back to a society that's gotten you where you are?*

A gentle tap on the window drew her from her musings. She recognized the visitor and buzzed down the window.

Nora Nolan's smile was as warm as the noontime sun. "Hey, sweetie. What are you doing out here?"

"Thinking."

"Want some company?"

"Only yours."

Nora slid into the front seat. Just fifty, she had strands of gray in her light brown hair now, which tonight was pulled up girlishly in a short ponytail.

"Have a bad day?" Nora asked. "It's April sixth."

Paige sighed. "I survived."

"You always do, dear."

"Nora, do you think I'm selfish? Having the kind of practice I do?"

"You are one of the most unselfish people—doctors—I've ever known. What on earth gave you that idea?"

"Nothing. I'm just feeling maudlin today, I guess. Tell me what's new with you."

For a moment Nora watched her, probably trying to read whether Paige had meant what she'd said. "Well, I was going to call you later about something." Nora held out her hand, where a diamond ring sparkled.

"Oh, my God." Paige's gaze flew to Nora's face. "From Dan?"

A dreamy smile lit her face. "Yes, of course."

Paige grinned broadly. Nora Nolan had loved Dan Whitman for years. It had been a favorite topic of the girls of Serenity House. But Dan had been married, his wife an invalid, and his and Nora's relationship had remained platonic because they were both people of honor. Mary Whitman had died a year ago February.

Like Jane Eyre and Mr. Rochester, Dan and Nora could be together now. The girls had watched the classic movie on TV back then, along with many of the old TV shows.

Like *Dr. Kildare*. Reruns that Ian, obviously, had never seen.

Though gestures of affection were hard for her, Paige reached over and hugged Nora. "I'm so happy for you."

Nora returned the embrace. "I'm going to hold you girls to your promise all those years ago."

Paige drew back and stared at Nora. The original residents of Serenity House—the first six girls to live there in 1987, the year it opened—had pledged that they'd all come back to Hyde Point no matter where they were in the world when Nora got married. Typical of group-home residents, Paige had not kept in touch with her former house sisters. Darcy Shannon O'Malley, the wild redhead with a devil-may-care attitude, had returned to Hyde Point two years ago, and only then had Paige struck up a friendship with her. "I see Darcy occasionally. Do you know where everybody else is?" she asked.

"Yes. Anabelle's kept in touch." The youngest and shyest resident, Anabelle had left town, and no one but Dan and Nora had heard from her again.

"And I hear from Taylor and Charly all the time. They live in Elmwood."

Though Paige wasn't friends with either of them, she did bump into Charly and Taylor around town occasionally. Charly had become a social worker like Nora and had married an older man. Taylor, who'd come to Serenity House after being found beaten by the side of the road with no memory of who she was, was happily married with three children.

"That just leaves your sister," Nora said softly.

"I know where Jade is." Paige couldn't keep the chill out of her voice.

"She still won't see you?"

"Nope. Just talks to me occasionally on the phone." Paige shook her head. "I don't get it."

"Well, you can ask her when she comes for the wedding. It's going to be in July."

"That should be enough notice for everybody."

"What's more, I'm asking all you girls to come a few days early. I want to see how my first flock's doing."

Paige breathed in deeply. More surprises. Nora's wedding. Contact with the other Serenity House residents.

And maybe seeing her sister for the first time in more than three years. Add that to Ian Chandler's little bomb—that he was Elsa Moore's son and that he wanted Paige to work in the center he'd named for his mother—and it had been quite a day.

Paige wished like hell she really was on that Caribbean cruise.

CHAPTER TWO

"WILL YOU INTRODUCE me to Linus, Casey?" Paige smiled down at the six-year-old girl, warmed by the trust she saw in the child's big brown eyes. Paige ignored the quiet gasp from Casey's mother, who sat in a chair across the room.

"'Kay." Casey had scooted over on the examining table to make room for her imaginary friend. "Linus, this is Dr. Kendrick. She's nice."

"Hello, Linus," Paige said easily. "How are you feeling today?"

"He says good."

Paige smiled. "Well, fine." After a bit more conversation designed to gain information about Linus, she picked up Casey and carried her to the sticker box. "Why don't you choose a sticker for yourself and one for Linus?"

Her chubby hands around Paige's neck, the girl said, "He likes cats."

"Well, there's a kitty one there."

"Can I look at them all?"

Paige smoothed Casey's hair. "Sure." She smiled. "I like the Casper the Ghost one best."

Ignoring the restless shifting behind them from Casey's mother, Paige read the words on each sticker to the child.

After the big decision was made, Paige set Casey

down. Then she nodded to her nurse, Marla. "Now, why don't you and Linus go with Ms. Simmons and let me talk to your mom."

"Okay, Dr. Kendrick." Casey threw her arms around Paige's waist and hugged her. The affection soothed Paige, as always. It made up, in part, for having to deal with the child's mother.

When Casey was gone, Paige turned to Mrs. Riley. "As I said on the phone, it's not unusual for young children to have imaginary friends."

The woman threw back her shoulders. "My husband says it's unhealthy."

"On the contrary, it's a way of fitting in. I've advised you before to get Casey into some kind of social group. TenderTime Day Care has a terrific Saturday-morning program for six-year-olds."

Mrs. Riley sniffed. Paige knew that sniff, from dealing with other yuppie parents. "*Day care?* We don't use day care. We even home-school Casey."

Which is part of the problem. Paige assumed her own haughty-queen demeanor. "And because you do, Casey needs friends. She doesn't have them, or even acquaintances to interact with every day, so she makes them up." Paige arched an eyebrow. "Enter Linus."

Mrs. Riley stared at Paige; Paige folded her arms across her chest and stared back. A knock on the door broke the stalemate. "Come in," Paige said coolly.

Marla Simmons peeked in. "Dr. Kendrick, I know you don't like to be disturbed, but there's an emergency of sorts in examining room three."

She spared her nurse a glance, said, "We're finished here," then recaptured the other woman's stare. "Think about what I said, Mrs. Riley. Darcy O'Malley runs a top-notch program at TenderTime." Pivoting, Paige walked out the door.

"I'm sorry, Paige," Marla apologized.

Preoccupied, she looked at Marla. "It's fine. What's going on?"

"Rob Roberts is having trouble with Jimmy Linstrom. The boy's due for a booster shot."

"Doctors—even residents—don't give shots."

"Dr. Roberts decided to do this one because Jimmy hates shots."

Paige shook her head. Thankfully she only had a few more days of working with Rob Roberts. The current resident rotation finished May 10; it couldn't come soon enough.

Would he be off to work in the Elsa Moore Center? Ian had tried several times over the past few weeks to get Paige to change her mind about working at the Center. She'd continued to refuse. There were rumors that he was thinking about asking Rob to take the position. She'd recommended the guy, after all. Hell, Rob was a superb physician; he just needed to work on his bedside manner.

Pushing away the disturbing thought, she knocked brusquely on the door to examining room three and walked in. At the far end of the room, Kari Linstrom held little Alyssa on her lap. The young mother's eyes were wide and fearful.

"Jimmy." Rob towered over the examining table, a syringe in his hand, a clip in his voice. "Come out from under there and be a little man."

Paige shook her head. If that was Rob's idea of coaxing… The kid was four. "Can I help?" she asked, purposely easing herself between Jimmy and the resident.

Rob said from behind, "No need. Jimmy here just needs a shot."

Jimmy wailed. The shrill probably could be heard downtown.

Paige kicked off her shoes and knelt down. The space under the examining table was about four by five, and Jimmy was huddled inside. "Hey, buddy, what's going on?"

Hiccups. A tearstained face. His blond curls were damp. "No shot."

"Scoot over."

Jimmy complied.

Folding up as small as she could, she crawled into his cocoon. "You know, my sister and I used to hide in cupboards at our house like this."

"Make a tent," Jimmy said.

"Uh-huh. It's like making a tent."

She talked some more about tents, remembering how she and Jade had always felt safer tucked away like this, particularly when their parents had been on one of their binges. When Jimmy calmed, she asked, "Remember the last time you had a shot, Jimmy?"

Tears again. She drew him closer, put her arm around him.

"I know it hurt. But you were so good." She stroked his hair, kissed the top of his head. "I gave you an 'I'm Brave' sticker."

From beneath the table, she could see Kari's sneakered feet under the chair, hear her calming the baby. She could also see Rob's wingtips tapping impatiently. "I've got a new sticker. It's says 'Shots Make You Feel Good'."

Still Jimmy shook his head.

"They do, buddy. Later on, shots keep you from getting sick. Remember, we talked about that."

It took her a few more minutes to coax Jimmy out from under the table. Five more minutes were needed to talk him into letting her give him the injection. By the time she was done, she was running half an hour behind schedule. But she made the time to find Rob before she tended to her next patient. She counted to ten as she approached the office where he was tackling paperwork. "I'd like to talk to you."

He glanced at his watch. "Sure."

"You didn't handle Jimmy very well."

He arched a brow. "You don't think so?"

"No, I don't."

"It seems to me Jimmy's a troublemaker. Most kids from the projects are. It might be best to curb their tendencies now before they get into school." He crossed his arms over his chest. "Save his teachers a lot of grief."

"It's not the job of a pediatrician to save the teachers grief. Our job is to give the best care we can to young children."

"Look, Dr. Kendrick, I know I'm not a people person. But I'm working on it."

"You need to work harder."

He stiffened a bit. "One of the reasons I asked to do this rotation with you was because I was aware of your no-nonsense, all-business reputation in medicine. That and the nature of the clientele you deal with." He grinned. "Along with the hefty fees you charge."

"Is that why you chose medicine?"

"No, I like medicine, though I might go into research eventually. Besides, the HMOs have pretty much stopped us from becoming millionaires. I do think you're savvy to charge fees above and beyond regular medical coverage."

Paige ignored the sting of his assessment. She'd deliberately joined a practice that charged more than most insurance coverage so she could avoid women—and their babies—who'd grown up like her. The memories they evoked were too painful.

"I have to admit, I'm surprised you accept patients like the Linstroms."

She closed her eyes, mentally working out his evaluation. Lacks sensitivity in dealing with children *and* is a snob.

"It's okay to be no-nonsense and all-business sometimes," she finally said. "But when it comes to the kids, you have to be human, Rob."

His back became even more rigid. But he tried to hide his displeasure from her.

"We've discussed this before," she said. "You lack sensitivity."

"All right. I'll keep that in mind." Then, as if he couldn't help himself, he added, "However, Ian Chandler thinks I'm doing a fine job. He's already talked to me about his new care center."

Most kids from the projects are troublemakers. "Did he offer you the job?"

"Not yet. But he will. I'll probably do that for a few months, until I can find something better. Something more like your practice." Rob angled his head and gave her his best charming look. "You don't want a junior partner, by chance, do you?"

Not in a million years. "No." She didn't want to work with Rob. She didn't want to work with Ian, either. Damn these men.

TWO DAYS LATER, Paige headed for Ian Chandler's offices in the doctors' building attached to the hospital. He'd called and asked to talk to her today. Since she had a patient in the neonatal care unit, she'd agreed to stop by his office. It was six o'clock and the receptionist had gone for the day. She made her way into the back rooms, hoping Ian hadn't left yet. And in some ways, hoping he had. She suspected he'd hatched some new ploy to try to entice her into his center.

When she reached his office, she found the door open. Ian was on the phone, his back to her. His feet were propped on his desk, and he leaned precariously back in his padded chair. He wore knife-creased slacks and a steel gray shirt to match. "Hi, Sal. I was wondering if you had Martha Jones's results yet." Ian laughed, a deep chuckle. "I know. But I couldn't wait."

Something from the other end of the line.

"Oh, no." Ian dropped his feet to the floor, sat forward and listened. His shirt pulled across his shoulders as he tensed. "Damn it."

A response.

"Yeah, it sucks." He ran a hand through his collar-length hair, mussing it. "I know. Thanks." Hanging up the phone, Ian stared at it a moment; then he shocked Paige by hurling the file in front of him across the room.

"Ian?"

He whirled around. His classic features were drawn, and his gray eyes were the color of storm clouds. "I didn't know you were here."

"I didn't mean to eavesdrop." She nodded to the file. "Problem?"

Again the sadness. He was always in such a good mood, flirty, smiling, that she was surprised to see this side of him. "An older patient. The mother of a friend." He glanced down to where he'd thrown the file. "She has uterine cancer."

"I'm sorry." Paige stepped inside. "I know how hard this kind of thing can be."

He studied her, making her uncomfortable. She'd

thought about him this week, wondered about the things he'd told her. Why didn't he have the same surname as his parents? And why was he so interested in starting the care center? Combined with how he was looking at her...

She straightened. "You wanted to talk to me about something?"

"Why do you do that?"

"What?"

"Withdraw? Shut down?"

Because it's safer to withdraw. "You don't know me well enough to ask that."

"Maybe we could fix that." The flirt was back.

"No, thanks." She sat in an adjacent chair and crossed her legs, pulling down the shantung skirt she wore with a tailored silk blouse. "What did you want to talk to me about?"

"Dr. Cold and Calculating."

"Who?"

"Your resident."

When she realized what he meant, she couldn't keep from smiling. She had no idea Ian used nicknames, too. Like she did. "If you think that, why are you asking him to join your center?"

"I haven't asked him yet."

"He's sure you're going to."

"The boy should really work on his self-confidence."

Again she smiled. "Seriously, can't you find someone else?"

"I had a lead on two other doctors. Both fell through." He gave her a lush grin. "That's, of course, after the best of the best refused me."

She sighed. "Cut the charm."

"Fine. Since you recommended Roberts, I thought

maybe you could give me an indication of his good points.''

Most kids from the projects are troublemakers. ''He isn't the best choice, Ian.''

''I know that, Paige. But I'm running out of options.''

Staring at him, she thought of his mother, who had given her so much. When Paige had gotten the work-study program in medical school to help out Dr. Elsa Moore as an office aide, Elsa not only made sure Paige worked enough hours to support herself and Jade, but she encouraged Paige to accompany her on rounds and showed her how to treat the little ones and soothe the parents. Overall, Elsa had taught her what it meant to be a good doctor. Then Paige thought about Nora and her unending selflessness at Serenity House. Finally she reflected on Rob Roberts's boorish attitude—and Kari Linstrom's kids, whom Paige loved working with.

What the hell.

''All right. I'll be your baby doctor. On my day off, and two other afternoons if I can clear my schedule. Will that be enough?''

''Yes, we're all working part-time till we see how things go.''

She stood. ''So we're set.'' She began to walk away.

He swiveled in his chair and grasped her arm. His big hand squeezed, making her edgy. ''Thanks. I appreciate this.''

She didn't know what to do with his sincerity. Sitting there, he stared up at her with those gray eyes; she'd never been close enough to see the black ring around the irises. His jaw was square cut and his mouth could only be described as sensual. She felt a jolt of awareness go through her. So she shrugged off his hand and said glibly,

"Don't be too appreciative. I'm not doing this for free. We still have to negotiate salary."

And then, disturbed by the uneven tattoo of her heart, she left before she had any other untenable reactions to Dr. Hot and Hunky.

CONGRESSMAN NATHAN HYDE III came from the founding family of Hyde Point. Grandson of town patriarch Nathan Hyde I, he sat behind his desk in his big office and studied Ian. "What can I do for you, Ian?"

"I just wanted to show you the final roster for our care center."

"*Our* center." Nathan adjusted the cuffs of his designer suit. "That has a nice ring to it."

"Hyde money made the Center possible. At least part of it." Part had come from the inheritance Ian's parents left him, and the rest from federal grants. "That's why you're conducting the opening ceremonies in a few weeks."

Leaning over, Nathan took the folder from Ian. "I like the thought of helping troubled girls." There was a catch in the congressman's voice. Since he'd been working on this project with Nathan, Ian had suspected there was more than philanthropic interest behind Nathan's support of the Center. And of Serenity House, which also received significant Hyde money.

"Can I ask you something?" Ian asked.

Nathan looked up from the folder. "Of course."

"Is there a reason you're so interested in this venture? I get the feeling you have…an ulterior motive."

"Other than wanting to be reelected to Congress?" Nathan was running again for the district seat in the House of Representatives.

"Yeah. Other than that."

Nathan was quiet for a moment. "A long time ago something happened to me that…" He shook his head. "I'd rather not discuss it."

Ian shrugged. "No problem. I just want your cash, anyway," he joked to ease the moment.

As Nathan read the folder, his eyes widened. "I can't believe you got Paige Kendrick for the pediatric position."

Ian chuckled. It was quite a coup. So what if he'd had to resort to a little spying and blackmail? Marla Simmons had come through with just the right nugget of information to make Paige reconsider joining the Center. Though Ian felt vaguely guilty—he would never have hired Rob Roberts—he'd gotten the best doctor for the Elsa Moore Center. "Yeah, me neither. Must be my legendary charm."

"From what I hear, she's immune to charm."

"You tried yours on her, Hyde?"

Nathan held up his hands. "I'm an engaged man, remember? Which reminds me, Barbara thought it might be fun if we had dinner together sometime, the two of us and you and a date."

For some reason, visions of light-brown hair and snapping blue eyes came to mind. "I'd like that." They made arrangements for golf and dinner on Sunday at the Hyde Point Country Club.

As Ian left the office and drove home, he thought about who to ask. Nathan's fiancée, Barbara Benton, was a sophisticated lawyer for the town's main industry, Hyde Point Electronics. Would Paige get along with her? Not that Paige would go out with him, anyway. Not that he'd want her to. Damn, where was his mind going these days? He didn't even particularly like the woman.

He pulled into his driveway in South Hyde Point, got

out of the car and opened the condo door, only to be attacked by ninety pounds of black Lab. "Hey, Scalpel, how ya doin', buddy?" The dog barked his greeting and licked him mercilessly until Ian sank to the floor and wrestled with him. "Come on, I'll take you outside. Let me change first."

They were running along the Chemung River—without the leash, which Scalpel hated—when Ian thought of Paige again. He'd seen her once or twice at the country club. "Does she play golf, Scalpel? What do you think?"

Trotting alongside him, Scalpel shook his head. Ian laughed. Sometimes the dog seemed human.

"Does she date?"

The dog growled.

What kind of guy did she like? Ian wondered. He knew it wouldn't be someone like him. Maybe someone more like Nathan, who kept his feelings to himself.

Scalpel nudged Ian's pocket, where he kept a ball, then ran ahead. "Okay, okay," he grumbled, and tossed it to the dog for a little throw and fetch. As he played with his pet, he told himself it didn't matter what kind of guy Paige Kendrick liked. All that mattered was that she'd be working in the care center.

The Elsa Moore Center.

Small world!

PAIGE WAS THINKING what a small world it was when she stepped up to the eighteenth tee and caught a glimpse of the foursome behind them. Two men and two women were approaching the last hole.

"Oh, look, Dan, it's Nathan and Barbara." Nora shaded her eyes with her hand. "Who's that with them?"

"Ian Chandler and some woman I've never seen before." Dan locked his hand around Nora's neck and she leaned into him. The loving gesture made Paige's insides go soft. "We've slowed them down, I guess," Dan added.

"Let them play through." Paige stepped back. Golf was still too new to her to have an audience; she didn't like not being competent at an activity. Especially with Dr. Good at Everything watching. She'd heard her colleagues talking about Ian's terrific golf game. Jeez, did the man excel at everything?

When the foursome came closer, Nathan and Dan Whitman hugged.

"Good to see you, buddy." Dan held on to Nathan's arms. Paige knew Dan had been best friends with Nathan's older brother, who'd been killed when he was young. In addition to being a father figure to all the girls at Serenity House, Dan had been a surrogate son to the Hydes and brother to Nathan, who was going to be best man in his and Nora's wedding.

Nathan grinned. "Good to see you, too." He leaned over and kissed Nora's cheek. Introductions were made all around. Ian's friend was Missy Columbo, a teacher at the high school.

As Nathan, Dan and the women made small talk, Ian turned to Paige. "I didn't know you golfed, Paige."

"I'm learning."

Missy Columbo, beautiful enough to be Miss America, cuddled closer. "Me, too. Ian's a seven handicap."

"Well, play through, then." Paige nodded to the tee. "We're taking our time." She winced inwardly at her curt tone. Though she'd never win the Miss Congeniality award, she was usually more gracious. Even Nora gave her an odd look.

Paige stood back and watched Ian, dressed in a navy golf shirt and khaki slacks, stride up to the tee. He chose a driver from his bag and winked at Dan. "Old Nate and I have a bet on who makes the longest drive. The loser pays for dinner."

Barbara leaned into Nathan. "Old Nate, huh?"

Ian's date giggled adoringly. Nora rested her hand on Dan's arm. Paige felt unaccountably lonely as she watched Ian, head down, face fierce with concentration, swing the club. The ball soared out of sight.

Nathan snorted. "I'll be paying." He turned to Dan. "Join us for dinner?"

"We were eating here, anyway." Dan looked to the women. Nora nodded.

Paige balked. For some reason the thought of watching Miss America fawn over Ian all night had ruined her appetite. "Why don't you two go ahead. I've got some work—"

Nora frowned. "Oh, no, you said you'd have dinner with us. I was looking forward to it."

"I—"

Ian slid his club into his golf bag. "I'll think it's because of me that you're opting out." His charm was oozing today.

"No, of course it's not." *Liar.*

He gave her a boyish grin. "Well, then?"

"Fine, I'll stay."

Purposely she turned away and turned off the unfamiliar emotion she was experiencing by mentally planning her week ahead. Work was always a good distraction when she didn't like what she was feeling.

IT WAS AT DINNER that an odd thing happened. They'd just ordered their meals—Ian and Paige both picked the stuffed flounder and a light chardonnay—when Nathan proposed a toast. "To the Elsa Moore Center. And the two doctors who are going to make it work."

In the process of reaching for her wineglass, Nora repeated, "*Two* doctors?" Obviously startled, she knocked over her drink. Dan, openmouthed, began mopping it up. Something had clearly surprised the older couple.

"Paige?" Nora said. "Are *you* going to work there?"

"Where?" Missy asked.

"At the Center for young mothers and their babies," Ian announced proudly. "We have a physician's assistant, an internist, me, of course, and Paige has agreed to be our pediatrician."

"The Center is Ian's pet project," Nathan explained.

"Yes, I realize that." Nora's voice was grave. "But I didn't know... Paige, dear, when did you become involved?"

Ian glanced at Paige, noticed the grim set of her lips.

"Ian charmed her into it, most likely," Nathan put in.

"I did." Ian sensed Nora's unease. "You seem surprised, Nora."

She looked at Dan.

"It's just that Paige is always so busy," Dan said, rescuing his fiancée.

"Don't give her ideas." Nathan scowled. "Ian needs her."

Ian was still pondering their strange reaction when the harried-looking manager rushed to their table. "Dr. Kendrick? Dr. Chandler? We need your help. There was a fire in the kitchen and..."

Paige and Ian exchanged a quick look and were out of their seats before the manager finished.

Paige said, "Let's go." On the way she asked, "Who was hurt?"

"Two of our staff were burned. They don't want to go to the hospital but—"

"We'll determine that," Ian said easily.

In tandem, Paige and Ian strode through the dining room toward the back of the club. "Any expertise in burns?" Ian asked.

"A lot. Kids are like moths to flames."

"Good. I'm a rookie in burn treatment. Pregnant women stay away from fires."

Inside, amidst the scents of cooking meat and baking bread, the kitchen was hushed. "They don't want to go to the hospital," the manager repeated.

"Let's have a look," Ian said, ushering Paige in front of him.

Stepping up to the male victim, Paige said, "Take the ice off the burn immediately."

"I told you to use butter," a woman on the side muttered and reached for the tub.

Ian stopped her. "No butter, either. Ice can cause tissue damage and any ointment or butter traps heat in the burn."

Paige inspected the man's arms. Both were red and mottled. "You need to go to emergency. These look like second-degree burns, but I can't be sure they're not third. In any case, they need treatment." She reached for his wrist. "I'm going to take off your watch." Slowly she removed it. The man moaned; she swathed both arms in the clean linen she'd asked a waitress to bring.

Paige looked at Ian. He was inspecting a younger woman whose hands were burned. "Palms and fingers, looks like second or third degree to me." He smiled at the girl. "You need to go, too, young lady."

"Is there any sterile gauze here?" Paige asked.

Someone produced a first-aid kit. She undid the gauze

pads and inserted them between the girl's fingers. Then she wrapped both hands in more fresh linen.

Together she and Ian gave a few instructions and in less than ten minutes, the victims were on their way to the hospital, driven by the club manager.

As they stepped out of the kitchen, Ian slid his arm around Paige. It felt…good. "See, Paige, honey, we make a great team. We're going to be dynamite together at the Center."

She drew away. Obviously she didn't like the sound of that.

Frankly, Ian was surprised that he did.

THE PORCH SWING creaked as Nora gave it a push with her foot. A soft light at the door bathed her and Dan in its mellow glow, and the spring air enveloped them. Nora sighed against his shoulder.

"Something wrong, love?" he asked, kissing her hair.

She still couldn't get used to his open affection. Oh, she'd known for years that he loved her, though he'd never spoken the words until Mary died. But to have him touch her, pamper her, appreciate her as a woman was like a gift from God.

She squeezed his hand, inched closer. "Not wrong, exactly."

"You're worried about Paige."

Nora nodded. "Why would she agree to work at the Elsa Moore Center?"

"She's a pediatrician, Nora. She works with children all the time."

"I know. I was concerned about her choice of career in the first place, but this? The girls she'll be treating will remind her of her own past. It will open old wounds."

Dan was silent for a moment. She loved the way he

thought before he spoke. She loved everything about him. Moonlight turned his angled features soft, and she couldn't see the gray that liberally sprinkled his hair now. Finally he said, "Maybe old wounds need to be opened, Nora. Lanced. I worried that giving up her baby would come back to haunt Paige at some point."

"Because she never dealt with it? Never talked about it?"

"Uh-huh." He pushed the swing again. "You tried to get her to open up."

"That didn't work. I don't think she's ever discussed it with anyone. Not even Jade."

They were silent. The crickets chirped loudly and the swing swayed. Dan said, "You can't protect her, honey."

"I know. I just hope Ian didn't bulldoze her into doing something that's going to cause her pain."

Dan smiled. "I like that boy."

"I like that he cares so deeply about things."

"They're very different, aren't they?"

"Paige cares," Nora said defensively. "She just hides it better than most of us."

"I know she does," Dan said gently. "I just meant she doesn't show her feelings."

"She's cautious. She doesn't trust easily."

"Why would she, after the hand she was dealt?" Again the quiet. "We'll keep an eye on her," Dan finally said. "Like we've always done." In a swift and surprising move, he tugged Nora onto his lap. "Now kiss me, woman. I've waited years for you and now I can't get enough."

"What about the—" She didn't finish. Her mouth got busy and her mind turned to mush. She forgot about the girls upstairs in Serenity House. She forgot about Paige. For now, anyway.

CHAPTER THREE

A WEEK AWAY from opening, construction on the Elsa Moore Center was just shy of being finished. As the four doctors and one physician's assistant met in the small conference area, hammers pounded in the background, and the smell of paint wafted down the corridor.

Paige watched as Ian ran the meeting. His color was high and his smile wide as he talked about schedules and supplies and the mechanics of operating his new center. "Since we've agreed to use as much of the available space as possible for patients, we'll double up on offices, if that's all right."

Marcus Volpe, a semiretired internist, asked, "Who gets the pretty ladies?"

At the end of the table, staff psychologist Elliot Emerson smiled.

The physician's assistant, Carol Camp, rolled her eyes. "Marcus, don't you know, in this day and age, that comment could be construed as sexual harassment?"

He winked at her. "At my age, my dear, that would be the highest of compliments."

A mother of four who was interested in working a couple of days a week, Carol said, "I'll share with Marcus."

Ian glanced at Paige. "That leaves you and me, Paige."

She felt a blush creep up her neck. "Really? I just assumed as director you'd have your own office."

"Nope."

"What about Elliot?" She'd been trying very hard to ignore the psychologist. She hadn't known one was going to be on board.

"Elliot will have a separate space for counseling. He'll keep his desk and records in there."

Paige bit her tongue, literally.

"Paige?" Elliot asked. "Is something wrong?"

Busying herself with the yellow legal pad in front of her, she asked, "Wrong? No, why?"

"Well, quite frankly, you scowled when I was introduced, and you seem…unhappy about my being here."

Ah, the joys of working with Dr. Freud. "I'm fully aware of your reputation at Elmwood, Elliot. You do good work educating medical students in psychology."

Elliot's green-eyed gaze bored into her. His dark-blond hair was cut perfectly in a short professional style. Quite a contrast to Ian's mane. On anybody else, Ian's style would be feminine. Instead, he looked like Samson in a white lab coat.

"But something's bothering you about me, Paige, I can tell."

Okay, she'd voice her opinion. "Truthfully I was surprised a psychologist was asked to join the Center. Young mothers, even unwed ones, aren't necessarily screwed up."

Ian braced his arms on the table in front of him, a man defending his child. "No one's saying that, Paige. It's just common sense. If the women who come here can't afford medical care, something's not working in their lives. Elliot has done a great deal of aptitude testing, job counseling and career seminars, as well as being Elmwood's finest psychologist.''

Again Paige forced herself to relax. Her problem really had nothing to do with Elliot. It was personal and had to do with comparing herself to the patients who would be coming to the Center. That was, after all, why she'd balked at taking the job. ''I wasn't criticizing Elliot. I was just making an observation.'' She smiled at the other doctor. ''I agree that we're lucky to get you.''

He settled back, but seemed to study her like a patient with an ailment he couldn't diagnose.

Ian dealt with logistics, talked about the opening and generally played cheerleader for the Center. ''I guess that's it,'' he said finally. ''I look forward to working with all of you, and again, thanks for becoming part of the team.''

Standing, he signaled the meeting was over. He walked Carol and Marcus out. Quickly Paige gathered her things. Discomfited by Elliot's observation, she wanted some time alone to collect herself. But she turned to find that the psychologist had come up behind her. ''I hope you meant what you said, Paige.''

''Of course I did.'' She gave him a warmer smile this time.

His return smile was a sexy one. ''I'm looking forward to working with you.'' He extended his hand. ''And getting to know you better.''

''Me, too.'' She accepted his handshake.

He let go and turned; Paige saw Ian standing in the doorway.

''Good night, Ian,'' Elliot said, on his way out.

''He's married, you know,'' Ian said when they were alone.

''Excuse me?''

"Dr. Mesmerizing Eyes is married. He took quite an interest in you. You might be wise to stay away from him."

"First off," Paige practically sputtered, "I don't need to be warned against getting involved with a married man."

"Have you been? Involved with a married man?"

Her mouth dropped open. "That is so none of your business."

"Answer it, anyway."

She narrowed her eyes on him. "No!"

"No, you won't answer it, or no you haven't been?"

"Both."

He smiled at having flustered her enough to give him the information he sought.

"And second," she said, "I won't have you poking into my personal life."

"Sorry." He didn't sound sorry at all. "But office romances interfere with work. I'm just being cautious."

"You have nothing to worry about, Ian. There won't be any office romances here."

Again the interested look. It made her want to bolt. "Tell me something else."

"What?" The exasperation in her voice was evident even to her own ears.

"Elliot was right. You were upset to find him on staff, I could tell. Why?"

Because Paige didn't like to lie, she'd become a master at evasion. "Look, Ian, I agreed to work with you, not be your friend. I think this center is a worthwhile endeavor, but I don't like to get close to my colleagues. If there's a reason I'm uneasy about Elliot being here, it's not something I want to talk about."

"I don't understand that kind of thinking. Life's so

short. And relationships are the most important thing.'' He studied her. ''But they aren't to you, are they.''

Unnerved, she fumbled with her bag. They used to be. Until she lost her child's father. And her own parents. And then Jade. ''No, they aren't.''

''What is?''

''My job. Helping people. Being the best—'' She stopped.

''Being the best at what? Everything?''

Yes. ''Just my job. That's why I agreed to work here. Not to find new friends.''

He hitched one hip onto the table. Today he wore slate-blue slacks and a blue pin-striped shirt under a taupe blazer. ''You don't trust many people, do you?''

No. Well, maybe Nora. And Elsa. ''I trusted your mother,'' she said softly.

He looked like someone had given him the moon. ''That's a wonderful thing to say.''

She smiled.

''You trusted my mother. My mother trusted me. Maybe you could make that leap.''

''Ian, as I said the other day, we don't know each other well enough—''

''And as I said, I'd like to change that.''

She shook her head. ''You got me to work here. Be happy with that. Any relationship other than professional isn't going to happen.'' Shrugging into the jacket of her red linen suit, she picked up her bag. ''The Center is a wonderful and much-needed facility, Ian. I'm happy to be a part of it.'' Which wasn't exactly true. ''But that's all.'' Quickly she headed out.

She could feel his eyes on her back as she disappeared through the door.

THE SETTING SUN, a pink, fiery ball, still burned brightly. Paige was relaxing on her raft in her kidney-shaped pool. This wasn't the Caribbean cruise she longed for, but it was a little bit of paradise in her own backyard, and she treasured the time she spent here.

The day had been eventful—scores of sick children, as usual, and a few cases of strep. She'd also gotten a list of patients she'd be seeing at the Center, and one was from Serenity House. Mary Ellen Barone was due to deliver in a few months, and Paige would be her baby's pediatrician. Six degrees of separation was more like two. Everything seemed closely connected—the Center, Elsa Moore's son, patients from Serenity House. How on earth had she become involved in all this?

Well, that was easy. Dr. I Always Get What I Want had engineered it. *You trusted my mother. My mother trusted me. Maybe you could make that leap.* Jeez, didn't Ian Chandler ever give up on anything?

Paige heard a thump at the west end of the yard. A five-foot wooden fence circled the pool, but she could see a glint of copper-penny red hair through the slats. She'd recognize it anywhere. "Is that Miss Meli I see peeking into my yard?" she called out.

A skinny arm shot up straight above the fence and waved. Paige chuckled.

"Come on in, sweetie. Say hello."

"Mama said not to bother you." Paige could hear Meli but only see her hand.

"You won't be bothering me. I'm lonely. Come keep me company." There was some truth to that statement. Tomorrow was her day off—the last for a while, since the Center was opening soon—and she had no plans to see anyone.

Paige paddled the raft to the side of the pool, climbed

off and crossed to open the gate. Outside was three feet ten inches of terror. Seven-year-old Meli O'Malley, one of Darcy Shannon O'Malley's daughters. Meli's bright red T-shirt and shorts were smudged with dirt. Skeins of red hair hung down her back and over her shoulders. Under the hair, big brown eyes peeked out of a freckled face. In her hands she held a baseball and glove.

"You look hot and sweaty," Paige said to the little girl.

"Uh-huh." Meli gazed longingly at the pool.

"Would you like to swim, Meli?"

"Mama said not to bother you," she repeated solemnly.

"I told your mom that you guys could use the pool any time, whether I was here or not. As long as an adult comes with you."

"We swimmed in it Saturday when you were working."

"I'm so glad. The pool doesn't get enough use."

Meli nodded enthusiastic agreement.

Paige said, "Why don't you go back to your grandma's and get your sister, Claire." Darcy lived with her two daughters in the carriage house on her mother and stepfather's grounds, right across the street from Paige. "Get your mom, too. You can all come for a dip."

"Mama'll be mad. Grandma, too."

Paige cocked her head. Meli's grandmother, Darcy's mother, was not one of her favorite people. In turn, the woman seemed uncomfortable with Paige, probably because Paige reminded her of Darcy's days in Serenity House. But most likely Meli wouldn't get to swim without Paige's intervention. "How about if I walk over with you and invite them myself?"

Meli's eyes danced, and she nodded vigorously.

Paige took a moment to slip into her Birkenstocks and throw a white lacy cover-up over her tangerine "tankini," then she grabbed Meli's hand. As they headed across Paige's yard, Paige was treated to a delightful report on the merits of the Yankees over the Dodgers this year. They'd just reached the curb when Meli said, "Car's comin'. Gotta wait."

Paige smiled and squeezed the girl's hand in approval.

A yellow Corvette was climbing Spencer Hill at a respectable speed. Paige admired the sleek lines of the convertible as it tooled up the slope. She was shocked when it came to a halt in front of them. She was thrown even more off balance when she recognized the driver's wind-whipped hair and big shoulders. He pulled off his sunglasses and gave her and Meli his toothpaste-commercial smile. "Well, well, well, who do we have here?" Ian took in Meli's red hair and clothing. "Little Red Riding Hood?" He darted a glance at Paige's outfit. "This certainly isn't Grandma."

No, but you'd qualify as the wolf.

"I'm Meli O'Malley, and this is Dr. Kendrick."

Ian's grin widened. His white shirt highlighted his dark hair, and his eyes twinkled as he said, "Hi, Meli. I'm Ian Chandler." His gaze moved over Paige's neck and chest, partially exposed beneath the cover-up, to her bare legs. Briefly, discreetly, male interest flared in his eyes. "Hi, Dr. Kendrick. You're looking mighty fine tonight."

"We're going swimming at Dr. Kendrick's," Meli said happily.

Ian stared past her shoulder at the attractive glass, stone and wood house she'd bought two years ago. The fenced-in backyard was barely visible from the road. "Sounds great." He glanced down at his clothes. Paige followed the direction of his eyes, noting the white shorts he wore. "It's too hot for tennis," he said.

"Tennis?" Paige asked. She tried to think of who on the hill had courts. A couple of eligible beauty queens. Just Ian's type. "Well, we'll think of you when we're playing Marco Polo."

"Hmm. Think of me. I like that." His gaze focused on Meli. "Nice to meet you, Meli."

"See ya," she said, tugging at Paige's hand.

"Go around the front of my car." He glanced in the rearview mirror. "There's no traffic now."

Meli pulled Paige around the hood. She felt as if she was on display, but quickly followed the child to the other side. A horn beeped as Ian roared off to his tennis date.

They had just reached the edge of the lawn when Darcy met them. "Melanie Anne O'Malley! What did I tell you about bothering people?" Darcy's petite frame, freckles and red hair down to her waist didn't detract from the sternness of her voice.

"I didn't bother Dr. Kendrick, Mama, honest."

Raising green eyes full of apology to Paige, Darcy said, "I'm sorry. Just what you need is more kids after putting in a whole day with them."

"Don't apologize. I came over to ask you and Claire to join Mel and me in the pool. It's hotter than blazes." Too hot for tennis.

"Paige, really—"

"Darce, I'd love the company." She crossed her arms over her chest. "When have you known me to say something I don't mean?"

Darcy grinned, and Paige was reminded of the imp who'd lived at Serenity House with her. Very different from the respectable director of TenderTime Day Care and a member of the Hyde Point Small Business Association who stood in front of Paige now. Even Darcy's clothes—knee-length khaki shorts and a tailored white blouse—were a far cry from the old Darcy's penchant for bright colors and funky jewelry.

Memories of Serenity House made Paige nostalgic. Darcy was the closest thing to a friend Paige had. "Please come. I want you to."

Darcy studied her a moment. "All right." She glanced back at the house. "Thank you. Claire would like it, too. I'll be right over." She looked to Meli. "Come on, honey, let's get your suit."

The little girl pulled up her T-shirt, revealing a zebra-print suit. "Got it on already."

Darcy shook her head, Paige laughed, and suddenly the night seemed a lot brighter.

A half hour later—the sun was dipping well into the horizon now—she and Darcy were sharing lemonade at one of her outdoor tables, watching Meli try to convince Claire to dunk her head underwater. Though Claire was four years older than Meli, she was much more timid. "I worry about Claire's cautiousness," Darcy said.

"We talked about this, Darce. She's just not as willing to jump into things the way you and Mel are. Nothing wrong with that."

"I know. But she misses her daddy something fierce. I think because she was older, his leaving hit her harder. That's part of why she's so withdrawn."

"I agree." The girl lacked trust because of a man who'd simply abandoned his wife and daughters three years ago and hadn't been heard from since. Paige and Darcy both knew all about parental abandonment. "She's getting better. Look."

The women watched as Claire held her nose and put

her head underwater. Her long red hair—just like her mom's and sister's—fanned out on the surface of the water. When she came up for air, both girls giggled.

"So," Darcy said, "what do you think of Nora and Dan's news?"

"I think it's great." Paige chuckled. "Remember how their unfulfilled love seemed so romantic, just like Jane Eyre and Mr. Rochester?"

Darcy nodded. "Little did we know that unfulfilled love was anything but romantic."

Paige agreed.

"Speaking of Serenity House, Paige, I was surprised to hear you're going to work at the new care facility for young mothers."

Maybe because Darcy had shared the tidbit about her ex or maybe because Paige was feeling unaccountably lonely tonight and couldn't help wondering what it would be like to spend the evening with a man like Ian Chandler, she said, "They needed help. I'm available. They're opening in two days."

"Yes, I know. I'm hosting the reception."

"Really, why?"

"I've just been appointed president of Hyde Point's Small Business Association. It's good PR for us."

"Congratulations."

Darcy sipped her lemonade. "As I said, I was surprised you agreed to work at the Center."

"Because of my background?"

Darcy reached out and squeezed Paige's hand. "It can't be easy. You'll deal with girls who'll remind you of us when we were at Serenity House." Then she added meaningfully, "Girls with babies."

Paige swallowed hard. "I deal with babies every day."

"You know what I mean."

Her throat suddenly felt parched. "With girls who made a different choice than I did?"

"Yes."

Paige watched Meli coax Claire underwater again.

Darcy asked, "Do you ever think about her?"

"Her?"

"Your baby."

"Her?" Paige's head began to swim. Her eyes burned. *"Her?"*

"Paige," Darcy said, staring at her, "are you all right? I know you don't like talking about this, but—"

Paige threw the chair back and stood. "No, Darce, I don't. I don't—" She had to move. Quickly she shed her cover-up, crossed blindly to the edge of the pool and dived in; the water was bracing.

It didn't help.

It didn't help take her mind off the startling revelation that, fifteen years ago, she had given birth to a daughter.

A fact she had never known.

WHEN SHE ENTERED the Elsa Moore Center for the reception following the outdoor opening ceremonies, Paige was still on edge from Darcy's revelation of two days ago. She hadn't been sleeping well and felt the effects of her fatigue. Though she knew this wasn't a big deal, she'd been ambushed by information she'd specifically asked never to be told. She tried not to think about the past, not to dwell on it, but she couldn't control her thoughts.

She'd had a baby girl.

Ian approached her as soon as she stepped inside. He was dressed today in a suit of charcoal gray with a pristine white shirt and a red paisley tie. He looked like John

Q. Businessman, even with the long hair. "Paige, I—"
He stopped short. "What's wrong?"

"Nothing." She fidgeted with a button on the short
yellow jacket of the suit she wore. She'd dressed brightly
today to cheer herself up.

Studying her a moment longer, he took her arm and
ushered her into a small room off to the side.

"Ian, what are you doing?"

"Something's wrong."

"I just said there wasn't anything wrong."

"Your bloodshot eyes say otherwise. Were you on call
last night?"

"No."

He frowned. "Is it something personal? Look, if it's
about a guy, I'm a good listener. I might be able to help."

She had to smile. The man thought he could take on
the world, solve everybody's problems. "I wouldn't lose
sleep over a guy, Ian."

He rolled his eyes. "Then you've been dating the
wrong men, lady." He sobered. "What *are* you losing
sleep over?"

"Someone surprised me with something. I don't like
surprises."

"I'll remember that."

Carol Camp poked her head in. "Ian, there's a reporter
looking for you for a picture." Her gaze landed on Paige.
"You, too, Paige. They want all the staff in the front of
the reception area."

Paige kept herself from sighing. She wanted to be part
of a photo shoot about as much as she wanted to deal
with an outbreak of chicken pox. But at least it would
stop Ian's badgering. "We'll come right now." Without
looking at Ian, she followed Carol into the reception area.

The place was packed. About fifty people had gathered

to celebrate the opening of the new facility. Darcy was behind the reception table, looking cool and efficient in a slim suit, her hair drawn back in a soft chignon. Last night her hair had dangled down her back in wet strands, and her eyes had been troubled...

Paige had stayed in the water a while, but Darcy was waiting when she climbed out. "Paige, I'm sorry. I know you don't like to talk about the baby. I shouldn't have brought it up."

Dripping wet, drying her face in a towel, she'd said, "No, it's okay. I just..."

"What?"

Unnerved, Paige had blurted, "I never knew it was a girl."

Darcy's eyes had filled immediately. "I'm so sorry, Paige. I didn't know. Or if I did, I forgot."

"That's all right. Really. It's no big deal..."

Paige felt someone take her arm. "Come on, you need a baby-sitter today," Ian said, pulling her with him. "You stopped right in the middle of the room."

"Ian, really, I'm fine."

"Yeah, and the sky is bright green." They drew up close to the others. "Here we are." He stepped into the group and brought Paige with him. She pasted on a smile for the camera.

Later she talked to the reporter from the *Hyde Point Herald* about how glad she was to be part of the Center. Again it felt like a lie. After the interview she studied the literature for patients stacked on a table to the side, all the while wondering what the hell she was doing here. Birth-control pamphlets. Caring for a newborn. New mother's health. On the bulletin board was an entire section of job opportunities available in and around Hyde Point.

Her gaze landed on a discreet notice tucked in the corner. It advertised an organization called Right to Know or RTK. She read it. RTK was an adoption clearinghouse on the Internet, whose purpose was to unite birth parents with the children they'd given up. Paige sighed as she turned away from it. Damn, this place was full of reminders of her past. Glancing at her watch, she decided to leave. She'd been here for an adequate amount of time.

Scanning the room, she saw Ian in the corner talking to a woman. About five-eight and dark haired, she wore a lovely Liz Claiborne dress—Paige recognized it—and a navy hat. She was gazing up at Ian, occasionally touching his arm, smiling as if he'd hung the moon. He gestured wildly as he told a story and laughed periodically.

Paige crossed to them. "I'm sorry, I don't mean to interrupt, but I'm leaving now, Ian. Thanks. This was a great kickoff."

"Just a sec. I want to introduce you to someone."

The woman turned. Classic features were paired with beautiful gray eyes.

Familiar gray eyes.

"Paige Kendrick, this is Lynne Chandler. Lynne, this is my baby doctor."

Chandler? Was Ian married? No, of course not. He openly dated. "Oh, you must be Ian's sister." That would account for the resemblance.

Lynne smiled. "No, but thanks for the compliment." The woman's gaze darted to Ian, as if to check out his reaction.

Paige was puzzled.

Casually Ian slid his arm around Lynne's shoulders and tugged her close. "This is my mother, Paige."

"Your mother? I thought…" She glanced over at the

picture of Elsa Moore hung prominently on the wall. "You said Elsa was your mother."

"She is," Ian told her. "Lynne is my birth mother. I was adopted by my parents just after I was born."

"You…" Paige cleared her throat. "You've kept in touch?"

"Yes. It was an open adoption. Lynne's been a part of my life right from the day I was born."

Paige remembered some of his cryptic remarks.

You don't have their name.

No, it's a long story why.

There are other personal reasons I'm opening the Center.

Once again Paige was surprised.

Once again she didn't like it.

CHAPTER FOUR

SCALPEL NOSED Ian's hand as he reached for the piece of cloud; Ian stared down at the puzzle. "Yeah, boy, I think that's the right one, too." Studying the jigsaw, he remembered how Paige Kendrick's face had turned the color of those clouds when he'd introduced her to Lynne. A moment later she'd regained her legendary cool, but Ian had caught the surprise, then the uneasiness, in her eyes. What was going on with the good Dr. Kendrick?

Fitting the puzzle piece into its position, Ian sighed and looked out over the river; the sun had turned the surface of the water a honey-gold, a view he always enjoyed from his condo's screened-in porch. Earthy scents of water and grass filtered in. But tonight he was unaccountably restless. And melancholy. He reached out and stroked the dog, who inched closer. "What's going on in my head, do you think? Is it the opening of the clinic? Did it remind me too much of Mom and Dad?" It had been a whole year since they'd died. He shouldn't still be so affected.

The dog settled his chin on Ian's bare leg. He'd taken Scalpel for a run and hadn't changed out of his gym shorts. Maybe he needed a beer. Standing, he walked into the kitchen through triple sliding glass doors; Scalpel's claws clicked on the terra-cotta tile behind him. Ian glanced at the clock. Hmm. Time for dinner. The refrigerator offered nothing interesting. He opened the freezer. "How about steaks?"

Scalpel barked enthusiastically, recognizing the word. Ian reached for a frozen sirloin. There were two stuck together. "Is this a sign to ask somebody over, buddy? Some pretty woman to take my mind off whatever's bothering me?" He smiled down at the dog.

Scalpel barked in response. Ian took out the two steaks and thought about whom to call. Missy Columbo with the great golf swing and even greater... Nah. She was a little too interested, too soon. Marla Simmons? He owed her big time for giving him the skinny on Rob Roberts, which had been enough to get Paige to work at the Center.

Paige. Did she like steak? Did she like him?

Is there a woman who doesn't? his mother once asked.

"Your grandma liked Paige, didn't she, boy? She'd want me to be friends with her."

Where *was* Paige tonight?

It was unlike Ian to be so preoccupied with a woman, but the fact was, he'd been thinking about Paige a lot. Maybe because of his mother's relationship with her. Maybe that was why he...wanted to be with her. "What the hell," he said to the dog. "Let's give it a shot."

Forgoing the phone—he'd need his in-person charm to convince her to have dinner with him—he grabbed the steaks, stopped off in the dining area to snare a bottle of merlot from the wine rack and picked up the dog's leash. "Come on, Scalpel, what do we have to lose?"

With the top down and the Beach Boys blaring at high volume, he drove into the city and took the turn to Spencer Hill. Paige lived in an expensive section of Hyde Point. It was nice up here. Tree-lined, quiet, except for the occasional rumble of a lawn mower. The sweet scent of flowers surrounded him. He preferred the ambience of the river, but this was picturesque.

He reached her house in less than fifteen minutes; he was relieved when he saw her BMW in the driveway. Holding the leash and wine in one hand, and the sack of steaks in the other, he leaped out over the side of the car. With Scalpel at his heels, he went up the curved stone steps up the front incline of her cedar-sided contemporary.

Man, what did one person do rambling around in that house by herself?

Maybe she wasn't by herself much.

He didn't like the notion. "Ring the bell, buddy."

Scalpel jumped up to rest his front paws on the wall beside the door and pressed his nose on the bell. No answer. They repeated the procedure a few times, and Ian felt a sinking sensation in his chest, which surprised him.

Then he remembered something. *We're going swimming at Dr. Kendrick's,* the little girl had said the other night. Paige had a pool. Maybe she was in it now. He frowned. She shouldn't be swimming alone. Then a thought struck him. Maybe she wasn't alone.

Well, there was no other car in sight, so he headed toward the back, passing bushes of hydrangeas and a few lilacs. When he reached the rear of the house, he could hear someone in the water. Peering over the top of the wooden fence, he saw her—as sleek as a mermaid—swimming laps. Goggles on, her face was submerged, except when she turned it to the side to take a breath.

Slowly he eased open the gate and moved into the pool area. "Shh," he whispered to Scalpel. "Don't bark." Ian crossed the slate patio and stopped beside a table with a forest-green umbrella over it and four chairs, the cushions in a geometric print.

He scanned the yard. The slate area was huge and circled the pool. There was a sizable patch of grass inside here, too. Several lounge chairs were scattered around. Two more umbrella tables. Potted plants. The whole place could have been a scene from *Outdoor Decorating,* a magazine his mother used to read. Had Paige shared that interest with her mentor? Again Ian wondered if he was here because of his mother, because of Paige's connection to her.

Scalpel jerked on his leash. Dropping his stuff on the table, Ian unfettered the dog and stretched out on a chaise. It felt good to be off his feet. He'd looked forward to the opening of the Center today, but emotionally it had drained him. He watched Paige cut through the water. She had a disciplined, even stroke. No surprise there. Everything about the woman seemed disciplined. He smiled. And began to count. Hell, didn't she ever get winded? He was up to twenty-five laps. God knew how many she'd done before he got here. The rhythmic motions lulled him. Content, with the dog at his side, he relaxed and let his eyes close.

PAIGE'S ARMS ACHED and her lungs burned, telling her it was time to stop swimming. She did a few more easy laps, then flipped over on her back. Eyes still closed, she floated until her breathing slowed. In the shallow end, she stood up, grasped the side of the pool, pulled off her goggles, opened her eyes—and came nose to nose with the black face of a monstrous beast. She screamed and fell back into the water; the thing began to bark bloody murder.

Out of nowhere a man materialized, grabbing the animal by the collar. "Quiet, Scalpel."

The brute quieted immediately, but Paige's heart stampeded in her chest. It was a few moments before she could speak. "What the hell is that dog doing here?" She looked up at Ian. "And you?"

He bestowed a meant-to-melt grin on her. She scowled.

"No big deal. Scalpel and I just stopped by to see you." His gaze landed on the water. "We caught you playing the Little Mermaid. I didn't want to interrupt, so I sat down." He shrugged. "I fell asleep."

Doctors got tired enough to doze off anywhere, but Paige wasn't feeling any too friendly toward the guy. "Do you always make yourself at home in a stranger's house?"

"We're not strangers, Paige." At her stern look he said, "I'm not Goldilocks, though you're sure acting like one of the three bears."

He had nerve. After all, he'd barged into *her* backyard. "Why are you here?"

"I came to see if you wanted company."

"Why would I want company?"

"You seemed disconcerted today." She didn't like the fact that he'd noticed. "And I'm at loose ends. I thought we might spend some time together."

"Don't you believe in phones?"

"You wouldn't have heard it."

"You didn't know I was swimming." Tired of craning her neck up at him, she climbed the three steps out of the pool and crossed to the towel bin near the built-in bench. Though his dog had scared her half to death, she was actually glad to see Ian, and she didn't like that feeling at all. She dried her face, wrapped the towel around her one-piece black Speedo and turned. "Ian, don't you think this is a bit intrusive?"

"Are you busy?"

"A person doesn't have to be busy to be intruded upon."

He scanned the area and took a quick glance at the house. "Anybody here?"

"No."

"'Cept me and my dog, ma'am." Again the grin. It was almost impossible to resist.

Her gaze dropped to the big black Labrador retriever. The dog's mouth was open, and she could swear he was grinning, too. "He scared me."

"He doesn't like it when pretty ladies scream at him."

She ignored the compliment. "I wouldn't have screamed if I hadn't come face-to-face with the Creature from the Black Lagoon as soon as I came out of the water." She scowled at the dog.

Ian frowned, and Scalpel hung his head and made a mewing sound. "It's okay, buddy, she didn't mean that."

The dog's mouth practically scraped the deck.

Paige bit back a laugh.

"Now, you're just gonna have to let us cook up the meat we brought on that fancy barbecue over there to soothe Scalpel's hurt feelings."

Paige studied the animal. "He's beautiful." She caught herself. "But he seems as pushy as his master."

"He is. You might as well give in gracefully and let us stay for dinner."

For some reason she liked the idea. "I was going to make a salad."

"Good. It'll go great with dinner. Make a lot."

"He doesn't eat greens, does he?"

"No rabbit food for my best buddy here. Just steak."

Scalpel perked up and barked.

Paige rolled her eyes. "All right. You can stay." She glanced at the table. "Wine, too?"

"Uh-huh. You like merlot?"

She did. "It's fine." She turned to the house. "I'll bring you a corkscrew."

Paige entered through the downstairs bath/changing area and threw on a terry-cloth cover-up and sandals. She refused to change her clothes because Ian Chandler had suddenly dropped by acting like God's gift to women. But she did take a peek in the mirror. Her hair was tangled and hung around her face. Shrugging, she picked up a comb and did some quick damage control. Then she snuck a lipstick out of the makeup bag. Chiding herself for fussing as she dabbed it on, she finished quickly and walked down the hallway to the kitchen. She'd just retrieved wineglasses, cutlery and plates when she glanced out the window.

Ian's back was to her. He was standing and staring at the water, his arms folded over his chest, his hands tucked in his armpits. Though he flirted and was outrageously presumptuous, she sensed strain in his wide shoulders and a coiled tension in his stance.

Today must have been hard for him. Elsa Moore had meant a lot to him, even though she wasn't his biological mother. That thought sent some tension through Paige's own body, but she dismissed it. Was Ian feeling bad? Was that why he'd sought her out?

Quickly filling a tray with glasses, place mats and settings for dinner, she decided to make the salad later and hurried out to the patio. "Ian?"

He turned. His face was taut and his mouth tight.

"Are you all right?" she asked.

"Just dandy."

She studied him for a moment, then went to the table, set the tray down and picked up the bottle of merlot.

He crossed to her immediately and took it out of her grasp. "I'll do it."

She shook her head, but didn't tease him about his autocracy. Instead, she sat on a chair. The dog came up and perched right by her legs, staring up at her in apparent adoration. When Ian opened and poured the wine, he stood above her and clinked their glasses. "To a good start," he said, smiling and looking more his usual self.

"To the Center."

His eyes sparkled. "Mmm." He sank onto a chair. The dog sidled over and dropped at his feet. As Ian sipped his wine, his eyes drifted to the water again. He said with the seriousness of a funeral director, "You shouldn't swim alone, Paige."

She started to bristle. "I…" Then she remembered his parents' boating accident. "You're right. It's just that I'd never get to use the pool if I had to wait for company."

They drank in silence, though she noticed Ian only sipped a little, probably because he was driving.

"Today was hard for you, wasn't it," she finally said.

Drawing in a deep breath, his eyes got bleaker than an overcast sky. "I didn't expect it."

"They've only been gone a year. What *did* you expect?"

"For it to hurt less by now."

"There's no time limit on grief. Go easy on yourself." She smiled. "Elsa would have loved the Center."

He grinned. "More than you would have guessed." His eyes focused on her. "That I was adopted came as a surprise to you?"

"Yes."

"You never knew?"

"No, of course not. Elsa and I didn't share many personal things. Sometimes, when I was worried about Jade, I couldn't help confiding in her. Asking for her advice. But I never wanted to be a burden."

"Helping your friends isn't a burden." She said nothing more. "Who's Jade?"

"My sister."

His eyebrows arched. "I didn't know you had one."

"She lives in New York City."

"Why did you need to talk to Mom about her?"

"I raised her till she was eighteen."

"What about your parents?"

The coldness seeped in. *There's no time limit on grief.* "They're dead. They died when I was seventeen and Jade was fourteen."

"I'm sorry." He waited. "It must be hard having your sister live so far away. I wouldn't like it if my brother wasn't nearby."

Trying to conceal her interest, she asked, "Is he..."

"Adopted? Yes. Derek wasn't Lynne's child, though. Mom and Dad got him through another one of Dad's patients."

"Excuse me?"

"Lynne and Derek's mother were my father's patients."

"Oh."

"It's not that unusual. Doctors sometimes arrange private adoptions."

"Is that why the process was open?"

"No. My dad was a big believer in openness and honesty about everything. He thought this way would be best for everybody."

"Was it?"

"Yes. My life has been far richer with Lynne Chandler in it." He gazed at the water again. "Especially now."

"It's a little unusual to keep the birth mother's name, isn't it?"

"I guess. Mom and Dad said they had so much of me, they could give her that one little piece."

"That's nice, Ian. I'm glad it worked out for you."

"But you don't agree with open adoption, do you?"

"Why would you say that?"

"Your reaction when I introduced Lynne. And now you seem tense."

Paige did not want to discuss this. "I think young mothers have to decide for themselves what's best. What works for one girl, or family, isn't necessarily the best thing for everyone."

"No, of course not."

His perusal of her made her uncomfortable. Or maybe it was just the topic.

"In any case, it worked for me," he told her.

"And Elsa, she was all right with it?"

"She was a gem." He cleared his throat. "In more ways than one."

Again, images of her mentor surfaced: Elsa demonstrating how to give shots with a minimum of trauma; Elsa staying all night by a little boy's bedside, teaching dedication by example. She *was* a gem professionally, and from what Ian said, in her personal life, too.

Paige's stomach growled, and she was thankful for the distraction. "I'm hungry. Shall we put the steaks on?"

Scalpel barked.

"Looks like everybody wants to eat," Ian said.

An hour later the remains of rare steak, a huge green salad and hot crusty bread that Paige had bought on the way home—Ian had called it manna from heaven—was spread out before them. Ian closed his eyes as he put his feet up on the chair opposite him and sighed. "What more could a man ask for?"

Scalpel lay at Paige's feet. She wasn't used to having dogs around, but this one's endearing personality had her slipping him scraps. Scratching his head, she feared she'd made a friend for life. She stretched out like Ian and stared up at the sky. It had turned dark and stars twinkled overhead. Crickets began their nightly chorus from the trees.

After a while Ian said, "How about dessert?"

"Did you bring that, too?"

"No, we could go to Abbott's for ice cream. You can ride in Scalpel's seat, can't she, buddy? You'll give it up for a pretty lady, won't you?"

Once again, Scalpel barked.

At Paige's shake of her head, Ian said, "What? You have to teach them manners, you know."

She laughed.

"So, ice cream?"

"Hmm, I don't think so, Ian."

"Aw, come on, live a little."

The dog began to whimper, almost as if he was begging.

Paige laughed again. She realized she was enjoying them both.

But...

"You're scowling, woman. Don't you like creamy, sinfully rich chocolate ice cream? Or better yet, black raspberry?"

She loved chocolate. But...

"Come on, Paige, this was fun. You don't have enough fun in your life."

"Ian, you have no way of knowing something like that."

"Well, have some tonight. Come on. Let me spoil you."

Paige drew in a breath. She didn't like the sound of that. She valued her independence and didn't need men to spoil her. Particularly sexy men with dictatorial tendencies. Ian was the type who'd take over her world if she let him. Paige preferred less-aggressive men. "I don't think so, Ian. I'm tired." She glanced at her watch. "It's almost midnight."

"And Cinderella doesn't want the prince to take her in his chariot for a little ice cream?"

"No, but thanks."

"All right, I won't press my luck." He stood. "Until the next time."

"Ian, don't misunderstand tonight. This isn't the start of something."

He leaned over, and she was afraid he was going to kiss her. Instead, he ran a finger down her cheek. Just a light caress, but it made her insides quiver. "We'll see, Ms. Cool and Cautious." He straightened. "Say good night, Scalpel."

The dog, of course, barked on cue, and nuzzled her hand.

Then she watched them both disappear out the gate and into the starlit darkness.

CHAPTER FIVE

"GOOD MORNING." Ian flashed a smile from his seat at the small conference table where he waited for his meeting with Paige to begin.

"Good morning." Paige hadn't seen him since Thursday, when he'd come to visit—unexpected and uninvited. Today was Monday—their first day at the Center.

"How are you?"

She took a seat one down from him. "I'm fine."

He eyed the navy-blue sundress underneath her lab coat. "You look good." He studied her face. "Rested," he added as if he deserved credit for it.

"Thanks." Despite the fact that Ian and his almost-human dog had unnerved her, she *had* slept better. And she felt more at ease about working with him after that evening they'd spent together. "So, how do we proceed today?"

"I'm fine, Paige, thanks for asking."

She looked directly at him. Today he wore a cocoa-brown silk T-shirt and dress pants of the same color. A leather-strapped watch wrapped around his wrist, and a gold chain peeked out from the neck of his shirt. "How are you today, Dr. Chandler?"

"Just fine. Scalpel sends his regards."

She laughed. She couldn't help herself. "Now can we talk business?"

"Of course." He picked up a sheet of paper and

scanned it. "All the patients have been cleared financially."

She frowned. "Don't you hate it that they have to reveal their financial circumstances to get treatment?"

"Yeah, I do," he replied seriously. "But most of them get welfare when they need it." He shrugged and handed her a file. "We're meeting with this patient in a few minutes."

"Do you do the clearance, too?"

"No, some of the grant money we get from the federal government is earmarked for a part-time office manager to do that."

Paige opened the folder. "Mary Ellen Barone."

"Yes. She's due in about two months. Nora Nolan's bringing her in from Serenity House."

Careful to keep her face blank, Paige read the file. "She's having twins."

"Uh-huh. A boy and a girl."

"Hmm. A ready-made family."

From the corner of her eye, she saw Ian lean back in his chair. "You want kids someday, Paige?"

"Maybe someday."

"Any man in the picture? I thought about watching my back after I left your house the other night."

She looked at him. He was sprawled in the chair, arms folded over his chest, staring at her. Smiling. Flirting.

"There's no man in the picture right now, so you can sleep easy." Her dry tone changed. "I told you not to misunderstand that evening, Ian. I don't mix business with pleasure."

"Pleasure," he whispered. One hand curled briefly as if he wanted to touch something. Her?

There was a knock on the open door. Nora stepped in with a dark-haired, very pregnant girl of about seventeen.

"Hi, we're here. The nurse told us to come on back."
Nora smiled. The girl did, too, shyly. Nora said, "Mary
Ellen, this is Dr. Kendrick. And of course, Dr. Chandler's
been treating you throughout your pregnancy."

Paige hadn't known that. Did he work directly with
Serenity House? she wondered. "Hi, Mary Ellen."

"Come in and sit down." Ian stood and pulled out
chairs for the two women.

Nora and Mary Ellen came farther into the room. The
girl was about Paige's height, and the advanced pregnancy made her waddle. For a moment Paige remembered the strange sensation of being off balance, of feeling that basketball in front take over. Briefly her hand
dropped to her stomach.

Mary Ellen sat. Nora squeezed Paige's shoulder—a
gesture of support—and flanked the girl. Ian smiled at
them and took a seat on the other side of the table. "How
are you feeling today, Mary Ellen?"

"Like a hippo. I can't believe I still have two more
months to go."

"Hmm. Only a hippo, huh? Wait till you hit the ele-
phant stage."

The girl laughed. For the first time, Paige wondered
what it would be like to have a gynecologist like Ian.

"I'll want to do another ultrasound today. But since
twins often come early, I thought we'd go through a few
things about the labor and the birth, and then you can
ask Dr. Kendrick any questions you have about the
babies."

Mary Ellen beamed, making her plain features glow.
"I'm so excited."

"Good. Have you arranged to attend the childbirth
classes I told you about?"

Glancing gratefully at Nora, Mary Ellen nodded. "Uh-huh. Nora's going with me to them."

Breathe, Paige. That's it. In and out slowly...

A frown marred Ian's handsome brow. "I thought your mother was going to be your coach."

"Um, she can't."

"Are you still planning to go home and live with her after the babies are born?"

A proud expression lit the girl's face. "Yes. Mom's getting the room ready now."

Your father and I will clear out the back room, Paige. Daddy will paint it yellow and I'll sew some curtains.

"When will you be leaving Serenity House?" Ian shot a look at Nora—a concerned one this time.

"As soon as the babies are born. My mom can't take care of me now."

Ian's jaw tightened. Paige wondered what was going on.

"All right. Let's talk about getting these babies here first, then Dr. Kendrick can fill you in on what to expect of a newborn."

Do you ever think about her?

Mary Ellen had some questions about epidurals and C-sections, and the dangers associated with having twins. Ian assured her that all her ultrasounds looked good, but if there were problems, he'd be right there to handle them. And he'd delivered several sets of twins, so he was experienced. In fact, he told her, as Paige had told Kari Linstrom, even if he wasn't on duty when she went into labor, she could have him paged and he'd come in to deliver.

After about half an hour, Ian stood. "I'll have the nurse show you to the examining room." He called Cindy Black—one of the part-time nurses—who came and ushered the girl away. Ian closed the door and leaned against it, his big shoulders stiff. "What's going on, Nora?"

Nora sighed. "Her mother drinks. I didn't think she could be counted on to get Mary Ellen to the hospital when the time came, so I convinced her to let Mary Ellen stay at Serenity House until the babies are born."

"I see. Are you sure she's got a place to go afterward?"

I'm only here for a few months, Nora. As soon as my mom and dad get out of rehab, Jade and I can go home.

"Her mother says she wants her back."

We want both you and Jade back, darling. This arrangement is just temporary.

Nora's face showed exasperation. "No, I'm not sure. But I have no say in this, Ian."

Paige straightened. "What do you think's going on?"

"I think Lena Barone plans to use the government assistance Mary Ellen will get for her kids to buy booze." Nora's voice was scathing. "She's got this live-in boyfriend, and there are indications that he put the idea into her head."

Ian swore. "Sorry, ladies. This just galls me."

Paige said, "Isn't there *something* you can do about it, Nora?"

"No. Mary Ellen wants her mother."

I want my mother. Please, I want my mother.

Paige's stomach churned. "It's not right."

Ian stood. "I have to go." He squeezed Nora's shoulder. "We'll take good care of her here, Nora."

When Ian left, Paige stared down at Mary Ellen's chart, but saw, instead, the face of another young, trusting girl.

"This situation hits pretty close to home, doesn't it."

She looked up at Nora. "I don't want to talk about it."

"All right. But let me say one thing. I'm worried about you working here. This kind of parallel is bound to happen a lot, Paige."

"I'm not seventeen anymore, Nora. I have control of my life and my emotions. I'll be fine dealing with girls like Mary Ellen."

"I still can't figure why you're here."

She gave Nora a sideways glance. "Did you ever try to change Ian Chandler's mind about anything?"

Nora laughed. "I see what you mean. But it's unlike you to let a man bulldoze you."

"I really didn't stand a chance against Dr. I'll Get My Way Or Else."

"Still, I don't like it, Paige. I know you don't want to be confronted with your past."

Paige fiddled with the folder and changed the subject. "Is everybody coming for your wedding?"

She rarely asked about the other girls. She didn't want to know what had happened to them after they left Serenity House.

"Dan heard from Anabelle. She's going to make it."

"Where is she?"

"In Seattle." Nora cocked her head. "You want to know?"

"Sure." Paige tried to smile.

"She's a cop."

"Like Dan?" Paige knew there had been a special bond between those two, though she never knew all the details. "How nice."

"Have you spoken with Jade?"

"I caught her on her way out last week. She got your

invitation. She said she'd get back to me, but she hasn't yet.''

"Feeling bad about losing touch with her?''

"No," Paige lied. "I hope she comes home, though, so we can straighten this whole thing out.''

There was a knock on the door. "Come in," Paige called, grateful for the interruption. Cindy entered. Always businesslike, the tall, slender nurse was also warm and friendly. "Paige, Ian wants you to join him in the examining room.''

"Sure." She stood. "Don't worry about me, Nora. I'm okay.''

"I'll always worry about you, sweetie.''

Not liking the ominous reply, Paige headed out to join Ian.

IAN WAS BONE-WEARY as he made his way to his office at the end of the Center's first day. He'd delivered a robust ten-pound boy at noon and had been on the run ever since.

Elliot Emerson and Carol Camp were standing outside Elliot's door when Ian reached it. Elliot said, "We're going for a drink at Rascal's to celebrate the opening. Marcus is joining us. Want to come?''

"Yeah, sure. I'll have to run home and let the dog out, but I can be there. What time?''

"Six."

He glanced at his watch and reached for the door handle to his own office. "Did you invite Paige?''

"Of course." Elliot's eyes showed...interest. "She said no. We couldn't budge her.''

Hmm. Sounded like a challenge to Ian. He could still see her last week filling out her little black swimsuit in all the right places, sipping the merlot, petting his dog.

She'd withdrawn at the end of the evening, but he'd made progress. Twisting the knob, he opened the door to his office.

She was on the phone. Pivoting around in her chair, she looked annoyed to see him.

"I can leave," he mouthed.

"No, that's okay. It's just an answer... Hi, Jade, it's me again. For the fourth time. Please call me back. I'm on my way home. I'll be there all night." She hung up with a bang.

Ian cocked his head. "Jade, as in your sister?"

"Yep."

"Not returning your calls?"

"Nope."

"Wanna talk about it?"

She shook her head. "Nope."

He crossed to his desk, which was on the opposite side of the room. Casually he set down his clipboard and edged a hip onto the surface. "The gang's going to Rascal's for a drink. Come with us."

"No, thanks."

"Paige, it won't hurt to socialize once in a while."

"Go run somebody else's life, Ian." She swiveled around so she wasn't facing him.

"We had fun the other night when you let your guard down."

"It was nice. But I told you not to count on a repeat."

He was quiet a moment. "I don't get it. You're not dating anyone. The message you left Jade said you don't have other plans tonight. Why do you wanna play the hermit?"

Sighing heavily, she turned back to him. "Look, my being here isn't going to work out if you keep badgering me."

He gave her his best choirboy look. "I don't badger."

"Ian, it's your middle name."

He shrugged. "I just don't know why you won't let yourself have a little fun."

"I'm going home to swim. That's fun."

"Alone?"

"Ian…"

"No, I'm not meddling. I'm concerned. You're swimming alone again?"

"I'll ask Darcy to come over. Okay?"

"Well, that's better. If you change your mind, we'll be at Rascal's. I'm going home first to let out Scalpel. He hates being cooped up all day."

"Oh, Scalpel isn't joining you for a drink?"

He chuckled. "No, he's on the wagon. He tied a big one on when this sexy little cocker spaniel down the street dumped him and he hasn't touched a drop since."

Once again Paige couldn't help herself. She laughed.

"That's nice," he said.

"What?"

"That happy laugh."

She shook her head. "Go away, Prince Charming."

They dealt with their paperwork in silence, but Ian's thoughts kept straying to Paige. He didn't understand why she'd want to live her life alone. No family. No boyfriend. Few friends. His mother and father had been an integral part of his life, and he loved his brother dearly. He also had good friends he liked to socialize with. He'd been engaged once and come close a second time. To him, Paige Kendrick was truly an enigma.

When he'd finished his memos, he stood, stretched and glanced over at her. Her back was hunched, her hair lying softly around her shoulders; he was tempted to go over and massage her neck. As he approached her, he saw that she was engrossed in a file. He touched her shoulder.

She jumped. "Damn it, Ian, don't sneak up on me."

He drew back. "Sorry."

Caught unawares, those baby blues were filled with sadness. Was it just Jade? Or Mary Ellen? Something—other than the girl's circumstances—seemed to distress Paige today. But Ian hadn't dared ask her about it.

"I'm leaving. I really wish you'd come with us."

He saw that she was weakening slightly. It seemed natural to reach out and run his knuckles down her cheek. "You can trust me, Paige. I just want to get to know you better. No ulterior motive. No demands. No pressure."

For a minute she allowed the caress, then she drew back.

"I promise. I won't pressure you for anything more. Just a couple of drinks with friends." He almost had her convinced, he could sense it. Again it was time for the big guns. "Let's celebrate the opening of Elsa's center."

"You're incorrigible, you know that?"

"I've been called worse."

"All right," she said. "I'll go home and send Jade an e-mail, then I'll meet you there."

"No way, Rapunzel. If you go back to your tower, you won't leave it."

"But I want to send Jade an e-mail, and I don't have an account on our computer here yet."

Before she could object, he rolled out her chair with her in it and wheeled her over to the computer station. In a few seconds he had his own account called up on his screen. "Send it from here."

"Ian, you really are a bully."

"Send it. I won't look."

Taking several steps back, he waited. She'd just dashed

off the e-mail when the ping for an instant message sounded.

"You have an IM, Ian."

"Don't accept it. I want to get out of here."

"The sender's a woman. Lady Greatlegs. I wouldn't want to interfere with your love life." Under her breath she mumbled, "Two can play at bullying." She pressed the accept button.

He muttered something and came to stand over her. As they waited for the message, he braced his hands on either side of the chair, effectively trapping her between his chest and the desk.

The intimacy of the position hit him instantly and he savored it. He could smell the lemony scent of her hair and see strands of blond in it. He was aware of how slight she was next to him. A primitive male urge went through him.

The message came on. After a moment Paige stiffened, then gasped. He focused on the screen. The note read, "I've been expecting a call from you, Ian, honey. I've tried your house a couple of times and your office downtown. You owe me, handsome, for that information I gave you on Rob Roberts. It's how you got the illustrious Dr. K to work with you. Don't you think you should call me? Love, Marla."

Ian blanched. "Shit!"

YOU CAN TRUST ME, Paige. I just want to get to know you better. No ulterior motive. No demands. No pressure.

She pushed back on her chair and met with a wall of resistance. "Let me up, Ian." Just moments before she had felt safe with his arms braced on either side of her. Now his woodsy aftershave was suffocating.

"Paige I—"

"Now."

He freed her, and she swung around and stood.

He straightened in front of her. "You have to let me explain this," he said.

Taking a deep breath, she forced herself not to over-react. Not to let him see how upset she was. Her throat felt tight and she cursed her reaction. "I don't want to hear excuses."

She was too close to him. The summer sun had turned his cheeks golden. His features were so finely crafted, so angular. But it was the determination in his eyes that sobered her. He thought he could fix this, manipulate this.

He was talking. "...no secret I wanted you for the Center. You're the best. Girls like Mary Ellen need the best doctors, just like slow learners need the best teachers."

"So you tricked me. You and your girlfriend, Marla."

"She's not my girlfriend. We date occasionally. We happened to be out the night you had the problem with Jimmy Linstrom. She asked if Rob Roberts was being considered for the peds position here and told me what happened that day." His expression was sincere. "At least believe that. Marla was *not* telling tales on you. It just slipped out in easy conversation."

In bed, probably.

Paige nodded at the computer. "Her note says otherwise. She says it's how you got me here. Damn it, Ian, I have to deal with this now. Her behavior was unprofessional."

Ian's eyes flared. "Please, Paige, don't blame her. *After* she told me, I laughed and said I'd be forever grateful she'd given me the ammunition to get you to work with me."

"Then why is she bragging about it now?"

His face reddened. The male blush made him even more attractive. "She, um, she wants more from me, I guess. She's using it to get another date."

"How nice for you." Paige tried to edge away, but he grasped her arm. "Let me go, Ian. I'm angry at you." Angry and hurt. And embarrassed. What had she been thinking, letting him in?

"All right, Paige. But first accept my apology. I made a mistake. I shouldn't have used that information to get you here. Like I said, I wanted the best for the Center. And you're the best. I'm sorry. How can I make this up to you?"

"By leaving me alone."

"You're upset."

"Yes, but don't worry, I'll leave quietly. I don't make scenes."

"I'd rather you screamed and yelled and threw things at me."

"Is that what women usually do when they're angry at your machinations?"

His look said yes. Oh, for God's sake. The guy was something else. No doubt he was surprised that he couldn't smooth talk his way out of this. Disgusted, she shrugged off his hand and crossed to her desk. Removing her purse from the drawer, she picked up her briefcase and strode to the door. She'd just reached it when he said, "Are you coming back?"

This was a perfect excuse to quit the Center, she told herself. Say no, say you're done with this place that cuts to your soul and this man who's making inroads to your heart. But an image of Mary Ellen's face came to mind. She pivoted. "Yes, Ian, I'll be back. I'm a person of my word, unlike you."

His eyes widened. He seemed genuinely hurt. No matter, Marla Simmons could cheer him up.

"But understand this. We're colleagues and nothing more. No more crap about trusting you or being friends. Or I will quit."

"All right."

She turned again, and this time she got the door open before he spoke. "Paige?"

Exhaling an exasperated breath, she asked with her back to him, "What?"

"What happened to you to make you this unforgiving, this distrustful?"

Even if she wanted to tell him, she wouldn't know where to start. She left the office without another word.

CHAPTER SIX

CAREFULLY AND WITH PERFECT control—the way she'd lived most of her life since she'd turned seventeen—Paige drove home, parked her car and entered the house. She wouldn't allow herself to think about Ian. She'd swim. Then do some research on the Net for an article she was writing for the AMA Journal. Work, as always, was the best medicine.

Her phone rang just as she reached her bedroom. Dropping onto the sleigh bed she'd ordered from Denmark to match her other teak furniture, she picked up the receiver. "Paige Kendrick."

"Hi, Paige. Surprise. This is your sister."

For some stupid reason, tears misted her eyes. *It's just you and me, Jade.* "Hi, Jade."

Silence. "Are you all right? You sound a little…sad."

Don't be sad, Paige. You still got me. She wondered if Jade's green eyes still sparkled like gems, if her hair was still sun-washed and as straight as her own.

"I'm fine. Just a long day. And some disappointments," she couldn't help adding. After all, that was what Ian's showing of his true colors was. Merely a disappointment.

"Well, maybe this will cheer you up. I'm coming home."

"For Nora's wedding? Oh, Jade, that's wonderful. When will you get here?"

"Sooner than July. I, um…oh, dear, just a second." Jade dropped the phone. Paige heard in the background, "What the…honestly…" Then Jade laughed. Happily. Giddily, almost. Was a man there? When she came on the phone again, there was true joy in her voice. "Sorry."

"What was that all about?"

"You'll find out soon enough."

"Jade, I—"

"I'll be coming soon. I have some business to take care of in Hyde Point."

"Anything I can help with?"

"Yeah, Paige, you can help." Jade's tone was mysterious.

"What do you mean?"

"You'll know when I get there."

Realizing Jade wouldn't say any more until she was ready, Paige decided to concentrate on the good news. Her sister was coming home. "Well, I'm really looking forward to seeing you. I'll get the guest room ready. You haven't even seen my new house. It's huge, plenty of room—"

"I won't be staying with you, Paige."

The hurt she'd kept at bay since the revelation of Ian's trickery surfaced. "You…you won't be staying with me?"

"Paige, are you all right? You sound, I don't know, vulnerable."

I am. But she didn't respond.

"Paige, has something happened to you?"

I just forgot for a little while why I've lived my life alone.

"No, I'm fine. But I feel bad that you don't want to stay here."

"It isn't that I don't want to stay with you, sis. You…won't want me there, is all."

Hope fluttered in Paige's stomach. "Of course I will. Why would you say such a thing?"

"I'm not perfect, Paige."

"I know that. I don't expect you to be."

"Yes, you do. You need everybody and everything to be perfect. You have ever since we left Serenity House." Silence.

"Look, I don't mean to hurt your feelings. We need to talk. About several things."

"Then stay with me. We can do a lot of talking."

A longer silence. "I tell you what. I'll make a reservation at the Carlton Hotel. If you still want me to stay with you after I get there, I will. If you don't, I'll have a place to go."

Paige swallowed hard. *We don't have anyplace to go,* Jade had sobbed a week after the terrible night when their parents had been killed and Paige had given birth. Jade had climbed into Paige's bed, and they'd spent the whole night there, huddled under the covers and afraid. They'd fallen asleep holding hands.

"I told you a long time ago, Jade, you'll always have a place to go."

She could hear her sister draw in a breath. "All right. I'll e-mail you with details. I gotta go."

Her heart clenched. "Jade?"

"Uh-huh?"

"I love you." God, she sounded so desperate.

"I love you too, sis. Take care." Jade clicked off.

Paige fell back onto the silk duvet and sighed. What the hell could be going on with Jade that would keep her away from Hyde Point for three years and then hesitate to stay with Paige?

You expect everybody to be perfect.
What happened to you to make you this unforgiving?
Weary and feeling very alone, Paige closed her eyes.

"ALL RIGHT, all right. Stop yapping at me." Ian rubbed his temples and avoided looking at the big brown eyes that stared up at him with accusation. "I know I was a jerk."

Scalpel barked once again as if confirming the comment, then turned away from Ian and pranced to the door. His big paw scratched at it.

"You can't go out without me, and I don't feel like a run."

The dog gave Ian the canine version of a disgusted look, then sauntered into the kitchen and out to the porch with a huff.

Ian rolled his eyes. Even his dog was mad at him. Man, he'd really blown it. Getting up from the couch, he crossed to the bar and poured himself three fingers of scotch. He wasn't normally a drinker, but he wasn't on call and he'd phoned Rascal's to tell Elliot and Carol and Marcus he wasn't coming. He was feeling like hell about what he'd done to Paige. So he took his drink, wandered over to the windows of his dining room and stared out at the river.

The doorbell rang. He debated whether to answer it, but finally crossed through the house and swung open the door.

Derek grinned at him. "Where the hell is that guard dog of yours, big brother?"

"He's sulking on the porch." Ian looked out past Derek's shoulder. "Did you bring Slide Rule? She'd coax him out of his snit."

"Nope. I was in South Hyde Point to bid on a job, so

I stopped by." He nodded at the drink Ian held. "Rough day?"

"Uh-huh." Ian stepped back, and Derek came in.

Derek's hazel eyes darkened. "The clinic opened today, didn't it?"

"Yes."

"That what's got you tipping a few?"

Ian sighed. "No, it's a woman."

There had never been any secrets between the brothers. Ian had been privy to Derek's whirlwind courtship of his wife Rose and then every painful detail of her death from cancer five years ago. He'd pulled his brother out of many a funk. In return, Derek had seen him through a few dramatic breakups. These days he nagged Ian about settling down and having a couple of kids.

Without asking, Derek crossed to the bar and poured himself a drink. He loosened his tie and unbuttoned his shirt as he sat down. "Hyde Point's Most Eligible Bachelor is down about a woman?"

For a minute the image of a nicely curved bottom and full breasts in black spandex came to mind.

"Want to tell me about it?"

"I behaved like an ass. She's ticked off. It's a professional thing." Ian felt his temper rise at his own stupidity. "I guess I really don't want to talk about her."

Derek studied him. "You sure?"

"Uh-huh." Ian sipped his drink. "Tell me about the job. Is it a house or industry?"

"A house. I'm not doing much industry. It doesn't interest me anymore." Since his wife's death, Derek had changed in a lot of ways. He studied his brother. "So, are you going to help me open the cottage this year? It's already past time."

Ian's insides knotted. "Maybe."

"You gotta do this sometime, bro. Mom and Dad would have wanted us to enjoy the lake. They loved it up there."

"I know. It's...it seems too soon."

"We left it closed all *last* summer."

"I know." Ian ran a hand through his hair. Shrugged. "I just don't want to deal with it now."

Scalpel's nails scratched on the tile in the kitchen. Both Ian and Derek turned. The dog headed right for Derek and nuzzled him. "Hey, Scalpel old boy, what's going on?"

Scalpel crossed to the front door and whined.

Derek stood. "Come on," he said to his brother. "Lend me some of your jock clothes. Let's change and take the dog out for a run. We can talk about this lady who's got you tied up in knots."

"I'm not tied up in knots."

"Whatever you say." He looked at Scalpel. "You wanna go out with Uncle Derek for a run?"

Scalpel barked, Derek laughed, and Ian felt a little better. He wondered if Paige had anyone to coax her out of her mood. He hoped she'd called Darcy.

WHEN SHE WALKED into the Center the following Thursday afternoon for her scheduled work hours, the first thing Paige spied was a big pink bow and an envelope with her name scrawled on it taped to the computer monitor—the one where she'd read Marla's message.

Since her conversation with Jade, she'd been having a lot of second thoughts about what Ian had done—along the lines of, *Yeah, the guy's a real rat, wanting the best for underprivileged women. Women who don't have people like Elsa Moore and Nora Nolan to help them.*

Consequently she hadn't spoken to Marla about the

incident yet, and some of her anger at Ian had abated. Wondering if he was in today, she crossed to her desk, put her purse in her drawer and glanced at the clock. She still had an hour before her first patient. Smoothing down the yellow sundress she wore today—it was hotter than hell for early summer—she crossed to the computer. Tearing off the envelope, she opened it and read, ''Boot up the computer. *Please.*''

She sat down and turned on the machine. After it loaded, Paige shook her head. She should have guessed Ian would pull something like this. Staring back at her was a specially designed screen saver: Ian had put the face of his beautiful black Lab right in the center. Again, the dog seemed to be smiling at her. To the right was a list, which Paige immediately scanned.

Why women prefer dogs to men:
Dogs feel guilt when they've done something wrong.
Dogs admit when they're jealous.
Dogs don't feel threatened by your intelligence.
You can train a dog.
Dogs are already in touch with their inner puppies.
Gorgeous dogs don't know they're gorgeous.
Dogs understand what *no* means.

Once again, as always seemed to happen when she was around Ian and his dog, Paige laughed. He'd even placed asterisks beside a couple of the sayings and indicated that those applied most to him.

Then beneath the list was a note:

Seriously, Paige, I'm sorry. I was wrong to use Roberts to get to you, but please know it was not meant maliciously. I told Scalpel the whole story and he's giving me the cold shoulder. Not only have I lost a new friend, I've lost my best friend. Forgive me? Ian.

Jeez, how was she supposed to resist that?

Leaning back in the padded chair, she closed her eyes. She was making too big a deal about this. He'd only done what was best for the Center. In his place she might have done the same. It wasn't that she didn't forgive easily; it was just that she didn't trust people. After her parents' death and her erstwhile boyfriend's desertion, she'd turned into herself. Jade's cutting off their relationship so abruptly had just added to Paige's isolation.

You need everybody and everything to be perfect. Did she?

From behind her she heard, "Hi, Paige."

Swiveling around, Paige saw Cindy in the doorway. "Hi."

"Your one o'clock came early."

"For a reason?"

Cindy entered the office and handed her the chart. "A three-month-old isn't eating. The mother's overwrought about it."

Paige frowned and opened the folder.

The nurse continued. "I did the vitals, then said I'd see if you were here. The mother's Ian's patient, and he's in with her now trying to calm her down."

Paige read the stats. "This doesn't look good," she said. Standing, she grabbed her lab coat from a nearby coat tree. "How long has this been going on?"

"A few weeks."

"Weeks?"

"She's been to the free clinic in Elmwood, but—"

"Never mind, I'll talk to her."

"She and Ian are in room one of ob/gyn."

Heading there, Paige read the file. Something about this illness sounded familiar, but she couldn't put her finger on it. She was mentally reviewing cases she'd treated and some research she'd done when she knocked on the door to room one and entered.

A frail young woman with a tearstained face sat on a chair, systematically tearing up a tissue. Her clothes hung on her as if she'd lost a lot of weight. Ian stood in the corner cradling a tiny baby in his arms. The image startled her for a minute—he looked so big with the child, yet so competent, so at ease. Glancing up at her, he said, "Hi, Dr. Kendrick." He was all business. "This is Anne Corriddi and this little guy is Sean."

Paige crossed the room. "Hello, Mrs. Corriddi." The mother's lips were bitten raw, so Paige squeezed her shoulder. "Sean has a problem?"

The tears began to fall.

"Anne, I told you Dr. Kendrick's the best. She's going to figure this out. In the meantime, you need to hold it together."

"It's just that he's so sick." There was a quaver in Anne's voice.

Ian sat down on the chair still holding the baby, who lay listlessly in his arms.

"Tell me the history, Anne," Paige said, indicating the chart, "as detailed as you can."

"About two weeks ago he started not eating good."

Paige glanced down. "You're breast-feeding, right?"

"Yes." Anne's eyes darted to Ian, who nodded. "My, um, husband just got laid off from the electronics plant, and I thought it was stress. You know how you get stressed and stop producing milk. My mother-in-law said I should give him solids.''

Not a good idea. "Did you?"

"No, I want to keep breast-feeding him. He's so little. And I read it's good for a baby.''

"It is. You're right to steer clear of solids when Sean's this young. What else?"

"He's been constipated for two weeks.''

"Did you do anything about that?''

"The intern at the clinic in Elmwood said to use baby suppositories.''

Paige made a notation in the chart. "They didn't work?''

"A little bit.''

"Other symptoms?''

"He doesn't want to eat. I can't get him to suck.''

Ian stared down at the baby. His big fingers came up to adjust the collar of the infant's one piece terry-cloth suit. "Oral mucous. Sunken anterior fontanelle. Hypertonia.'' He glanced up. "He can't hold his head up at all now, Paige.'' There was a note of gravity in Ian's voice.

Paige clicked off her pen and closed the chart. "He needs to be hospitalized right away.''

Tears formed again in Anne's eyes, and she looked at Ian beseechingly. "I…we…um, we don't have any medical insurance.''

"That's all right,'' Ian told her. "The center has an arrangement with the hospital.''

Paige checked the clock. "I don't have another patient until two. Let's get the little guy over there now. I'll order the tests in person.''

With Paige expediting the process, it took only fifteen minutes to get the child to an emergency room. After consulting with the head pediatrician on staff, Paige ordered blood tests, urine and stool cultures, and within minutes the baby was receiving IV fluids. That would stabilize him immediately. She also ordered an MRI and an electromography, as well as a thyroid profile. It was near two when she approached Anne, who'd been joined by her husband in the baby's room. "Mrs. Corriddi, I've ordered all the necessary tests. Sean will have them this afternoon." She smiled soothingly. "I've left instructions to be called immediately when the results are in. Until then, we can't do anything but stabilize him."

"St-sta...balize? Could something happen to him?"

"Now that he's on IVs, he's doing okay." She squeezed Anne's hand. "I promise we'll find out what this is."

Paige hurried back to the Center—thank God it was attached to the hospital—and saw her afternoon patients. But her mind kept straying to little Sean Corriddi. Something was familiar about this....

It was five o'clock before she finished with the last child. She'd only seen Ian when he'd poked his head into an examining room to get an update on Anne's baby. He swiveled around from his computer when she entered their office.

"Any news on the tests?" she asked without greeting him.

"A fax for you just came in. But I'll tell you what it says. All Sean's tests have been done. No conclusions could be drawn from them."

"Do you know how the baby is?" she asked.

"I walked over on a break. He's stabilized."

"I'll head there now. I just want to check something." She sat down at the computer. It was only when she hit the space bar calling up the screen saver that she remembered what Ian had done with the machine. Once again, staring into Scalpel's face, she chuckled. "This was cute, Ian."

"I am sorry, Paige."

She didn't look at him. "I know." She thought about Jade's observation about her perfectionism. She thought about Ian's question about being unforgiving. "I overreacted. Let's table it for now, though. I want to do some research on Sean's symptoms. They seem so familiar...."

Ian worked at his desk while Paige visited some medical sites. Food poisoning kept coming up. But the baby was being breast-fed exclusively.

At six she gave up and went back to the emergency room. Little Sean was sleeping soundly in his crib, his face less pinched because of the fluids he'd gotten all day.

Tonight Anne Corriddi's mother-in-law kept Anne company. "My Anthony got a part-time job at the gas station, so I came to sit with Annie." She clutched her rosary beads to her ample chest. "Is the baby going to be all right?"

"I hope so, Mrs. Corriddi." She smiled at Anne. "The tests we've done have ruled out a lot. That's good."

"He's a big boy," the mother-in-law continued. "This breast-feeding, I think it's wrong. In my day, we put babies on cereal right away."

Paige sat down and faced the women. "Well, that was the thinking a while back. But solids for infants are not recommended now."

The elder Mrs. Corriddi looked away, alerting Paige to something. "Mrs. Corriddi, do you baby-sit Sean at all?"

"Annie works at Hannah's Place in the afternoons. I take care of him."

"I leave breast milk, though," Anne explained. "The books say to."

"You should." Paige addressed the issue directly, as they didn't have time to spare. "Have you given Sean solids, Mrs. Corriddi?"

"No, no, she wouldn't." Anne was vehement. "I told her not to."

Mrs. Corriddi reddened. "Just a little cereal. With honey on it so he'd take it."

Honey. It was like finding a crucial piece of a puzzle. Everything fell into place. Paige shot off her chair. "I'll be right back." She strode out of the room and bumped into Ian outside the door.

"What is it?" he asked, steadying her.

"I think I know what's wrong with Sean." She could hear the excitement in her own voice. "Walk with me. I want to confer with the pediatrician on staff." They hurried down the hall. "It's infant botulism."

"Botulism?"

"Yes, it can occur within the first four to six months of life. It's caused by the ingestion of spores that germinate and produce toxins in the gastrointestinal tract. This sort of botulism is quite uncommon and often goes undiagnosed."

"Is it curable?"

"Very much so. I'm starting him on antibiotics right away. Respiratory and nutritional care are the mainstays of the treatment. He might need intubation. But basically, the disease is self-limiting and should work itself out within two to six weeks." She smiled. "Full recovery is expected in three to four weeks if he gets the proper treatment."

Ian's face glowed with joy, and she felt a deep connection with him. Their tiny patient was going to get well.

Paige glanced at the clock. Ian's day should have been long over. "Did you have a delivery here?"

"No, I came because I was worried about Anne and Sean."

"You're a nice guy." She started toward the desk.

"Paige." He snagged her arm. "How did you figure this out?"

"Anne's mother-in-law was feeding Sean cereal with honey. It was the honey." She smiled again. "I ran across a case of honey food poisoning when I was an intern. It was so odd, it stuck with me, but I didn't make the connection here at first, because I thought the baby was only on breast milk."

"So your experience really paid off."

"Of course." She gave him a sideways glance. Gray eyes, set off by his slate-colored shirt, twinkled back at her. "What?"

He shrugged. The tease was back. "Oh, nothing. Just looks like having the best doctor on staff saved the day."

"Don't press your luck, Ian."

He squeezed her arm. "Go talk to the pediatrician, Dr. Lifesaver." He headed down the hall whistling, and Paige watched him till he disappeared.

DON'T PRESS your luck.

Ian tried to remember Paige's warning as, once again, he and Scalpel approached her backyard. But he'd had to come. He could still see her blue eyes sparkling with excitement when she'd figured out the diagnosis. That kind of dedication and joy was more attractive than the sexiest fashion model. It spoke to something deep inside him. All the reasoning in the world couldn't convince him to stay away from her.

At least she wasn't swimming alone. The pool area

was quiet. Her house lights were on, but he guessed she was in the yard. It had been ninety degrees today, and the temperature hadn't dropped much. Over the fence, he saw her. She was staring out at the trees in the back of her property. Her hands were braced on the wooden fence; the whole area was lit by several citronella candles that rimmed the perimeter. Opening the gate, he unleashed the dog and whispered, "Okay, Scalpel, do your thing."

Glad to be free of restraint, Scalpel scampered in as Ian called out, "Hel-lo."

She turned as they crossed to her. When he got closer, he sighed inwardly. He didn't expect this.

"I might have guessed you'd come," she said.

Would she have put on the skimpy hot-pink bikini if she'd known for sure?

Before he could comment, she glanced down at the dog.

Scalpel stared up at her adoringly.

"He brought you a present."

Paige bent over and took the sack out of Scalpel's mouth. She scratched behind the dog's ears enthusiastically. "What'd you bring me, boy?"

He barked and nuzzled her neck. Ian watched that long, slender neck and wished he'd worn more than the navy swim trunks and T-shirt. Surreptitiously, he lowered the towels he carried to cover his lower half.

Standing, she opened the sack. "Champagne?"

"Saying Cristal is only champagne is like calling Everest a hill."

"Ah, I see." Her eyes narrowed on him. "What's it for?"

"You saved Sean Corriddi's life today, Paige. I looked up infant botulism on the Net." He was serious now.

"Delayed diagnosis can be fatal, and it's often misdiagnosed as sudden infant death syndrome."

Paige shuddered.

"You've lost patients, haven't you?"

She nodded. Her big blue eyes were wide with sadness.

"Me, too." He nodded to the champagne. "We should celebrate our successes."

For a moment she studied him, then said, "All right."

Scalpel barked. Her gaze dropped to the dog. "Ian, what's he got around his neck?"

"A towel."

She leaned over and pulled it off him. "Granny's baby," along with a decal of a black lab, was stitched across the bottom of a piece of red terry cloth. "Where did you get this?" she asked.

"My mother embroidered one for Scalpel and one for Derek's dog. She said it looked like she'd never have any human grandbabies so she made these for Scalpel and Slide Rule."

"Let me guess. Your brother's an engineer."

"Close, an architect."

Paige scanned him. "You have your swimsuit on."

"Yeah, well, just in case you invited me and Scalpel to swim, I thought we should be ready."

"He's a regular Mark Spitz, I'll bet."

"And Greg Louganis on the diving board."

Scalpel barked and Paige left to get glasses, shaking her head. Ian had the bottle uncorked by the time she came back out with some strawberries, which she held up. "These bring out the flavor of the bubbly."

"I know."

"Of course you would."

He couldn't take his eyes off her. She'd put on a white

lacy cover-up, but he could still see her curves—more generous than her day clothes revealed.

He poured the Cristal, set the bottle down and raised his glass. "Here's to successful diagnoses." He smiled.

She didn't drink. She just held his gaze. Finally she said, "And to experience. Needed to make those successful diagnoses."

His heart lightened. She'd forgiven him. Maybe even believed he was right to get her to work at the Center.

They sipped the champagne. It was dry, and the bubbles tickled his nose. "Let's sit."

Taking chairs next to each other, they faced the pool. Wordlessly they drank the wine and watched the water. The night was sultry and there were stars out. A sliver of moon cast a mellow glow. It was calming, but somehow sensual. When she bit into a strawberry with white, even teeth, Ian shifted in his chair.

"Tell me about your brother," she said.

Ian filled her in on Derek's life. "Rose's illness came as a shock to us all. Dad felt particularly frustrated by it."

"It was cancer?"

"Yes, cervical. As a gynecologist, he thought he should be able to do something for her."

"I'm sorry your family went through that."

"Me, too. Derek's all right now. He was over the other night." Ian stroked Scalpel, who sat at his right. "But he didn't bring Slide Rule." The dog whimpered. "She's Scalpel's long-time girl."

"I thought Scalpel was involved with a cocker spaniel." At Ian's blank look, she added, "The one who dumped him? So he doesn't drink anymore?"

"Oh, that was just a fling. Slide Rule's the love of his life."

She laughed.

"Did you hear from Jade?" he asked after a while.

Her shoulders stiffened. "Yes, she's coming home for Nora and Dan's wedding."

"Really? She knows them?"

Stiff shoulders became rock rigid. "Yes."

"How?"

"She grew up here."

"You seem close to Nora."

"I am. I've worked with some Serenity House girls. She's a savior to them."

"Still, how does Jade—"

"Oh, look—a shooting star."

Ian got the message. Paige didn't want to share this. He tried a different tack. "Are you close to Jade?"

"I used to be. I haven't seen her in a while."

"Why?"

"It's a long story."

"I've got nothing else to do," he said.

She shook her head.

"Well, I hope it works out for you." He reached over and squeezed her hand. She didn't shake him off or pull away, so he kept their hands entwined. Bathed in moonlight, they drank their champagne.

After a while Paige said, "Jade told me I have to have everything perfect. And she isn't perfect. That, apparently, has something to do with why she's been out of touch."

"Do you? Have to have everything perfect?"

"I don't think so. I hope not." She waited a moment. "And I'm not unforgiving, Ian."

"I'm glad to hear that."

"But I don't like to be tricked."

"Or surprised."

"Promise me something. You won't ever pull a stunt like that again—something underhanded, something manipulative—to get me to do what you want. It will be hard for me to work with you if I can't trust you."

"You can trust me. I won't do anything like that again. I promise."

Scalpel rose and moved close to lick their clasped hands. She smiled at the dog, then at Ian. He smiled back. Her lashes shadowed her cheeks.

He wanted to kiss her more than he wanted to breathe.

Don't press your luck.

Fortunately the moment was lost when she said, "Okay, guys, how about that swim?"

Scalpel barked, and she stood and whipped off her cover-up. "Last one in the pool's a rotten egg."

The dog was at her heels and followed her in with a splash.

Ian just watched them. He guessed he'd lost the game, but damned if he didn't feel like a winner.

CHAPTER SEVEN

RASCAL'S WAS a dim and quiet bar in the Carlton Hotel,
at least until the band started at nine. Frequented by the
older crowd, it was a favorite place for business people
to meet after work. Tonight Ian had enticed everybody
to stop by for a drink to celebrate Marcus's sixty-fifth
birthday, which was tomorrow. No one could refuse his
charming plea, Paige included. They'd been here an hour,
ordered appetizers and drinks, though most were nursing
their first because they were driving.

Around an oval table, Ian argued with Marcus about a
new treatment for endometriosis, Cindy and Carol traded
stories about their children, and Elliot Emerson was putting the moves on Paige. Big time.

He's married, you know.

"Word about your success with Sean Corriddi has
spread through Elmwood." Elliot's smile was sincere. "I
think you're going to be asked to deliver some kind of
paper on the case to the pediatric department."

Paige perked up, thinking about the tiny boy who re-
sponded better every day to treatment. "I'd like that."

"I'll mention it to the dean." Elliot leaned closer.
"Maybe you and I can have dinner some time and discuss it."

Ian's head snapped up from his conversation with Marcus. He glared at Elliot, then at Paige.

Without missing a beat, Paige said, "I'd love to have dinner. Your wife can join us."

A very male smile breached Elliot's lips. "I'm divorced, Paige. It was final six months ago."

From the corner of her eye, she saw Ian's surprise.

"I didn't know." Paige wished she hadn't agreed to dinner. Her comment was meant to make him back off.

Not that she didn't think he was attractive. He was handsome tonight in his pin-striped suit, with his styled hair and animated brown eyes. Very polished and sophisticated, like the men she usually dated.

Quite a contrast to Dr. Cool and Casual in his pressed jeans, open-at-the-throat gauzy white shirt with the sleeves rolled up to reveal tanned, muscular forearms. He'd gone home to let out the dog, had obviously changed clothes, then met them here.

"Happy birthday to you...," came the chorus of a group of waiters approaching their table.

Marcus said, "Oh, my, how nice of you."

As the older man blew out candles, Paige's gaze strayed to Ian's hands, clasped around a bottle of beer. They were big and supple; it had felt good when he'd held one of hers the other night. She'd dreamed about what they'd feel like on her body....

"Paige, when's yours?"

She glanced up. Ian was talking to her. "Huh?"

"We're sharing birth dates. When is yours?"

"September twentieth."

"Thirty...one, maybe?" Elliot said.

"I'll be thirty-three."

"Still a babe." Elliot smiled at her.

When the band started, he grasped her arm. "Dance with me."

There really was no way to refuse. "All right. Then I have to leave."

He was an expert dancer. Holding her close, he spun her around the room. Actually it was fun and made her breathless. When the song ended and another began—a slow one—he didn't let her go. She saw Ian staring at them. Cindy was talking to him, but his eyes never left her and Elliot.

And his face looked like a thundercloud.

After two more songs, he got up and approached them. "You don't mind if I dance with Paige, do you, Emerson?" he asked easily. But his eyes were hot.

"Of course not." Elliot squeezed Paige's fingers, then let go. As he walked away, Paige caught the male look of challenge that passed between the two men.

Great. Just what she needed.

Before she could comment, Ian swept her into his arms and locked her hand with his; he pulled her closer than was respectable and slid his arm around her back possessively; his cheek nestled in her hair.

Paige wasn't prepared for the sensation of being plastered against Ian like a lover. The feel and smell of him triggered something in her, something primal.

Holding on to her, he didn't say anything. And they didn't move much, just shuffled along the floor. She was encompassed by him; he seemed content to hold her. For the first time in recent memory, she let her feelings guide her actions.

It was a while later that she realized there was another song playing, and she and Ian had drifted to an isolated corner of the room, on a part of the dance floor not visible to anyone in her group. When she drew back and looked up at him, he wore a smug smile. "I like that," he whispered to her. His hand cruised lazily up and down her back; she'd worn a lightweight rose-colored shell, and she felt the warmth of his touch.

"Wh-what?"

"You lost track of everything."

"I did no such thing." She had, of course. "I'm sleepy, is all."

"Ready for bed?" he asked.

She swallowed hard. A flash of desire hit her, like lightning zipping through the summer sky. She pictured Ian naked. With her. They'd be sweaty and breathing hard. The image was so real it momentarily stunned her. "Ian, I—"

"Oh, hell."

"What?"

"My pager's going off." He reached to his hip and squinted as he tried to read it in the dim light. "I don't recognize the number."

Grabbing her hand, he escorted her back to the table. Elliot drew her down next to him. Ian gave his colleague a back-off look, then walked to a quieter place to make his call.

Paige decided she'd be wise to leave. She sat down to finish her drink. She'd just wait till Ian got back, then make her excuses.

A few minutes later he returned, his face ashen. He was fishing in his pocket for his keys.

"Is something wrong?" she asked.

"Yeah. That was my neighbor." He raised his chin, and his throat worked as if he was swallowing back some emotion. "Scalpel got out of the screened-in porch where I left him."

"What did he do?" Marcus asked. Everyone at the

Center was well acquainted with his dog's antics. "Make hanky-panky with the pup next door?"

Ian said, "No, he got hit by a car."

IAN'S THROAT felt as if somebody had stuffed a sock in it. Dimly he was aware of comments, questions. "...so sorry...is he all right...do you need a ride...?"

"I'm fine. I'm heading over to the vet's. My neighbor uses the same... Look, I've got to go." Abruptly turning from the table, he strode to the exit. Gripping his keys so tightly they dug into his hand, he pushed open the heavy mahogany door and took the steps two at a time to the parking lot. He reached his car and tried to unlock the door, but his hands trembled so badly he dropped his keys.

"Son of a bitch."

"I'll get them." Paige.

He braced his arms on the hood and briefly closed his eyes. He didn't want her to see him like this, but he couldn't move. In his periphery, he watched her kneel, rummage around under the car and stand up, clasping the keys.

He reached for them.

She brushed his hand away. "I'll drive you there."

"That's not necessary. I—"

"Forget it, Ian. I'm going with you and I won't ride with you driving in this condition."

Damn it, he didn't want her meddling. "I'm fine," he said.

"And I'm the Queen of England." She nodded to the car next to his. It was her BMW. Unlocking the passenger side, she said, "Get in."

He did, then she circled the car and slid into the driver's seat.

Once they were on their way, she asked, "How is he?"

"He's alive. That's all my neighbor knew."

Paige squeezed his arm. "I'm sorry, Ian."

He was glad she didn't offer platitudes. As doctors, they both knew the fragility of life. He stared out the window. Finally he said, "He hates the leash. He's always bucking any kind of restraint. The porch is big; it seemed okay with him. It's screened in and I put all his favorite toys out there." His hand fisted and pounded on his knee.

"It sounds like a nice environment."

"He wanted to come with me tonight. He scratched at the screens and whimpered when I left him." Ian could still hear the sound. "I thought...I thought I latched the door. Must be I didn't. I was in a hurry. I wanted to see you..." His voice faded off.

"This isn't your fault."

"I must have not locked the door."

"Scalpel the Magnificent was bound to figure out how to get out of there eventually."

He smiled at her term. Another long silence. Then he said, "I...I know he means too much to me."

"No. Don't say that."

"Derek and I have talked about it. My parents gave us these dogs on our thirtieth birthdays."

"No wonder they're so important to you."

Paige swerved into the animal hospital parking lot and shut off the engine. Ian bounded out of the car and raced to the entrance. Paige was right behind him. Once inside, the door slammed and the doctor called out, "Ian, is that you? We're back here."

Ian tracked the voice through the reception area to the treatment rooms, and Paige followed. When he reached the doorway of the one with a light on, he froze. Scalpel was stretched out on a table. From where Ian stood, he could see the dog was covered with dirt; there was blood on his lower body and one of his front legs was twisted.

And he wasn't moving. Oh, God.

Ian gripped the doorjamb. "He isn't…is he?"

Dr. Sonya Thompson, owner and operator of the animal hospital, looked up. "He's alive, Ian, but it doesn't look good…"

Ian drew in a deep breath. He felt Paige grasp his arm. He looked at her, and whatever she saw in his face made her slide her hand into his. He gripped it, then turned back to the vet. "Can you do anything?"

"His leg is broken. I'm going to set it as soon as the nurse gets here. I've taken an X ray and, miraculously, they're aren't any internal injuries."

"But…"

"He's unconscious. I haven't even sedated him."

Ian wavered a bit, and Paige leaned in close for support.

"As you know, it's not uncommon. Trauma to the body makes it shut down. Still, it worries me."

He nodded. There was noise outside the office. "My nurse is here." Sonya looked at Paige. "You two can wait in the reception area."

Paige said, "Sure," and tugged on Ian's arm.

"Just a minute." He let go of her hand and crossed to the dog. Up close, it was worse. There were cuts on his face and a lump the size of a golf ball near his eye. Gently Ian ran his fingers over Scalpel's snout, down his ear. "You'll be all right, buddy. I promise. Dr. Sonya's going to fix your leg. I'll be outside." Leaning over, he kissed Scalpel's head. "Get better. Please." His voice broke on the last words.

Paige took his arm and drew him to the doorway. When they reached the waiting room, she led him to a chair and sat him down. Bracing his elbows on his knees, he leaned over and buried his face in his hands. He could feel Paige's soothing touch on his back, but they didn't talk. After a while he sat up and looked at her. "I feel foolish."

"Why?"

"You're probably thinking I'm making too much of this. That he's only a dog."

"No, I'm not, Ian. Scalpel's more than a dog to you. He's your friend. And your parents gave him to you. He's a connection to them. It's all right to feel bad."

The corners of his mouth turned up. "You've got a great bedside manner, Doc."

She smiled. "There's a coffeepot over there. Want me to make you some?"

"Yeah, that would be great." She stood and started to cross the room. He grabbed her hand. "Paige?"

"Uh-huh?"

"Thanks for doing this. Driving me here. Staying with me."

She said, "You're welcome."

Then, like a little boy needing assurance, he asked, "He's going to make it, right?"

"I hope so, Ian."

They'd waited forty-five minutes before Sonya came out. Ian stood up with a start. "What...how did he do?"

"He made it through the surgery, but he's still unconscious."

Ian slumped.

"His vitals are good, though, and he's resting."

"What happens now, Sonya?" Paige asked.

"I'll keep him here. See how he fares."

"All night?" Ian's voice was strained.

"Yes. We're set up for that. The night nurse is on call for these kinds of things."

"Can I stay?" Ian asked.

Sonya shook her head. "That's not a good idea. I have your pager number."

"I want to stay."

The vet looked at Paige. They exchanged a wordless message.

Paige stood. "Come on, Dr. Chandler. Give Sonya your cell-phone number. They can call you if there's any change." Softly she whispered, "You can't stay here, Ian."

Ian's shoulders sagged. "All right."

She fished in her purse, took out one of her cards and a pen. "Give me the number."

Hoarsely Ian recited the number and asked, "Can I see him before I go?"

"Sure."

The women accompanied him back to the treatment room. Scalpel lay on the table as still as death. Ian approached his pet. His head was cocked like it always was in sleep. The rise and fall of his chest was his only movement. There was a clumsy cast on his leg. Ian fingered it. Then he brushed the dog's face with his knuckles and murmured a silent prayer to any canine deity that might be listening.

When he drew back and approached Paige, she was staring at him with an odd expression on her face.

PAIGE GLANCED across the seat of her BMW. Ian was in the passenger side, head back, eyes closed. For as long as she lived, she wouldn't forget how those sculpted cheeks had been wet when he'd turned around and left his dog. Her insides had melted like butter in the sun.

She reached out and shook his arm. "Ian, we're here."

Opening his eyes, he looked around, then saw her and remembered. "I must have dozed off." He squinted through the windshield. "Why are we at my house?"

"I still didn't think you should drive."

"How will I get to work tomorrow?"

"I'll pick you up."

Making no move to get out of the car, he glanced at his watch. "I wonder how he is."

"They'll call. You've got your cell phone turned on."

He stared up at his condo, which loomed big and empty. "I, um…you don't by any chance want to come in, do you? It's only nine o'clock." He gave her a sheepish look. It broke her heart.

Dangerous, she thought. It was very dangerous getting close to this man, caring about him. But she wouldn't let him face his house alone tonight. "For a while, sure."

In the foyer of his condo, Paige looked around. The entryway was spacious with skylights in the cathedral ceiling and beautiful wooden floors that extended to the left into a great room. It, too, was large, complete with fieldstone fireplace, stuffed leather couches, bookcases and long, narrow windows. There were more skylights in there. "Wow, this is beautiful."

Setting his keys on a low table, he smiled sadly. "My mother helped me decorate it."

Elsa had been such a part of his life. He'd lost her, as well as his dad, whom Paige could tell he'd been close to, and now he might very well lose the dog they'd given him.

She squeezed Ian's arm. "You've had a lot of loss in the recent past."

His look said, *Not Scalpel, too.* "Come on in." He ushered her into the spacious room. "Sit down. You want a drink?"

"No, thanks."

"Me, neither."

"What do you want to do?"

"I want to run."

A quick glance at the window, then she said, "I'll go with you."

He scanned her outfit—a sleeveless pink shell and flowered skirt to match. He'd commented on it at Rascal's. That seemed like days ago. "You aren't dressed for it."

"I've got sneakers in the car. Think you can scrounge up something to fit me?"

"Maybe." Again, the male perusal. It was good to see the old Ian return.

In the guest bathroom, a huge area decorated in greens and browns, she changed into the shorts he'd provided, which, he'd told her, had shrunk in the dryer. Still she need pins to hold them up. His navy T-shirt felt soft and smelled like him.

When she exited the bathroom, she found him in gray fleece shorts and a tank, standing at the entrance to the screened-in porch. His hands were fisted on his hips, causing his biceps to bunch.

"I couldn't tell about the lock."

"It's not your fault."

"He *liked* it out here."

She studied the porch. It ran the length of the condo, had a sitting area at one end and plenty of space for a dog at the other. "He's just like you, Ian. He's got a mind of his own."

Pivoting, he looked at her. His gaze was intense. "Thanks." He scanned her outfit. "I have to say, Ms. Jock, you look mighty good in my clothes."

She grinned. "Save it for one of your girlfriends, Mr. Glib and—"

Before she could complete the name, he supplied, "Gorgeous? Mr. Glib and Gorgeous."

She rolled her eyes. "I'm glad you're not conceited. Let's go."

Twenty minutes later they were running along the bike path by the river. The water's soft rush, and the moon's glow was soothing. Though jogging wasn't a favorite activity of hers, swimming had kept her in good aerobic shape.

"They staying up okay?" Ian asked about her shorts. He wasn't even breathing hard.

"Yeah, sure."

"Damn," he said.

When they got back to the condo, they entered through the kitchen and Paige nodded at the stove. "I'm going to make you something to eat."

"You can cook?" he asked, bracing himself against the wall and extending his leg to stretch.

"I cooked for Jade all the time."

"Yeah?" He glanced over his shoulder at her. "Do some stretches, so you don't tighten up. That is, unless you want me to massage your muscles."

"No thanks," she lied, and placed her arms on the wall.

"When's she coming?"

"Tomorrow night."

"You excited?"

His muscles strained against the cotton across his back. His legs, like his taut abdomen and slim hips, were perfectly formed. "Yeah," she said dryly, "I'm excited."

AFTER OMELETS and toast and a glass of chardonnay, they went into the living room. Ian sank down on one of the couches, which had a low table in front of it. "Wanna help me with my puzzle?" he asked, nodding at the jigsaw.

"What is it?" she asked.

"This dynamite little golden retriever. It was Scalpel's turn to pick out the picture." She heard the slight crack in his voice.

So she sat down next to him. For an hour they worked on the puzzle. "Jeez, you're a whiz at this." He frowned, apparently displeased that she'd gotten two or three pieces to each of his.

"What can I say?"

His gaze strayed to the phone. "She'll remember to call when he wakes up, right? Like I said."

"She'll remember, Ian."

"Will she call if he...?"

"You said you wanted to know anything right away."

Abruptly standing, he moved away from the table to the window, where he stared out. "You know, I picked this place because it was quiet and safe for him."

"I'm sorry. Where did it happen?"

"He made it out to the expressway."

A road on which cars traveled more than seventy miles an hour. What were the chances of the dog surviving that? Paige patted the couch. "Come sit." She picked up the remote. "Let's watch TV."

"You can go home, Paige. You probably have early appointments."

Again she patted the couch. "Come on." She flicked on the television. "What do you like?"

"Westerns. Scalpel prefers Lifetime Television for Women."

She laughed. He came to the couch and they both sat back, their shoulders brushing. A romantic comedy was on. Sinking into the sofa cushions, Paige let herself relax. Lulled by the hectic day and the low murmur of the TV, her eyes began to close. She felt something go around her shoulders. Then soft cotton against her cheek. Her hand came up to rest on his chest. And the world faded away.

A RINGING DISTURBED his sleep. He didn't want to move. Paige was lying next to him, all warm and cozy, her face buried in his neck. His hand cradled her head. She snuggled deeper into him, and he was instantly hard.

Then he remembered. His mind registered everything quickly—he wasn't in his bed. Paige was cuddled up against him, gripping his shirt. He saw the cell phone on the table next to them and reached for it. Flicked it open.

"Hello," Ian said hoarsely.

"Dr. Chandler. This is Hyde Point Animal Hospital." He gripped Paige, held her close. "Scalpel?"

"Your dog's awake now. And he seems just fine, though bruised and sore."

"Oh, thank God." He closed his eyes and sighed.

Paige said, "Ian?"

"He's awake," he said. "He's fine." His grip on her remained viselike. He spoke for a few moments to the nurse about arrangements, then clicked off.

Paige smiled up at him. Her hair was mussed, and she still wore his clothes. And all was right with the world. His grin was wide and his body was...wide awake.

"I'm so glad, Ian."

"Me, too."

As if suddenly aware of the intimacy of their position, she tried to pull away. He held her where she was.

"Ian, please. I have to get up. I have to go to work."

"I want to see you tonight," he said simply. "For a real date."

She stared at him, her expression torn. "I'm not sure it's such a good idea to mix—"

He flipped her onto her back and covered her with his body. Blue eyes widened in surprise—then glazed with desire. Every single plane of his body fit each of her curves. He wondered if she was as aroused as he. He glanced down. Her nipples were beaded against the cotton of her shirt.

"Ian." It wasn't a protest.

"If you think for one second I'm not pursuing this relationship after what you did for me last night, you're crazy."

"I did what any friend would do for another."

He pressed into her. "This isn't just friendship."

Her eyes twinkled with humor. "Normal human re-action of the male anatomy in the morning."

His knuckles grazed her breasts. "Is this the normal human reaction of the female anatomy in the morning?"

"Ian—"

"I'm not giving up. So you may as well say yes now." He brushed back her hair. "I always get what I want, Paige."

She swallowed hard, and the vulnerability he saw so-bered him.

"Paige, what's holding you back?"

"I...I'm wary, is all."

"Of?"

"You. Of trusting you."

"You can trust me, sweetheart. I know I blew it with the tactics I used to get you to work at the Center, but I promised I wouldn't do anything like that again." He studied her face, noted the little mole just beneath her chin and the flecks of darker blue in her sky-colored eyes. "I want to take our relationship further, Paige."

She drew in a deep breath. "So do I. Slowly, though, okay?"

His forehead met hers. "I was afraid you'd say that. I'm in overdrive already."

He could sense her smile.

"All right. Slowly." He drew back and cupped her face. "After this."

He lowered his head and covered her mouth with his. She was soft and sweet and willing, though he sensed a certain restraint in her. He brushed his lips over hers, back and forth, back and forth, until she opened to him. His mouth pressed harder and his body sank into hers, making her squirm. Ah, good. He let his tongue lazily explore her. When she returned the favor, passion slammed into him. He gripped her shoulders, felt her grip his. He moaned. She matched it. Her fingers threaded through his hair. The kiss turned wild. He devoured her, nipping her lip, taking tiny bites out of her jaw. Going back to her mouth for more.

He wanted her so badly he thought he might explode.

I'm wary...of trusting you.

Damn. With the willpower of a saint, he wound down the kiss. He almost couldn't pull away, though, when he opened his eyes and saw her face. It was flushed with desire—for him. He stroked her cheek with his knuckles as she watched him with that naked expression. Tenderness, and a little vulnerability of his own, replaced desire.

"Eight o'clock tonight," he said simply.

"All ri— Oh, I can't. Jade's coming."

"Aw, baby, don't do this to me."

"I'm sorry." She kissed his nose. "Soon, Ian. I promise."

CHAPTER EIGHT

IN HER BEDROOM, Paige stood before the beveled mirror and scowled at the blue-flowered sheath she was wearing. "Cool enough, but too formal," she told her reflection. She knew it was silly to be dressing for Jade, but she was excited that her sister was coming to town.

When they were girls, living at home, they fought over clothes. *Mo-om, she took my pink sweater...*

But later, when Paige was struggling to support her adolescent sister...

Here, wear this blouse on your date. It goes with your eyes.

No, Paige, you saved for months to buy that. It's silk.

Doesn't matter, kiddo. We'll be sleeping in silk one of these days.

Paige whipped off the dress and dove back into her closet. There had to be something more appropriate. Her gaze landed on Ian's clothes, which sat in a pile on the floor. She picked up the T-shirt and held it to her nose. His smell encompassed her, causing her mind to drift back to last night, when she'd worn it. Unbidden, her hand went to her mouth. She could still feel his lips—soft at first, then demanding. Her palm went to her chest. *Is this the normal reaction of the female anatomy in the morning?*

It wasn't, of course. She'd been blissfully aroused by his nearness. By *his* arousal. He'd smiled down at her with all that fire reflecting in his eyes, but there was a tenderness there, too, that melted her heart. They'd played phone tag today, but hadn't connected. Instead, throughout the morning and into the afternoon, she'd fantasized about being intimate with him. Somehow she knew making love with Ian would be a lot more than having sex.

With Jade on her way home tonight, Paige felt like some blessed deity had smiled down on her and said, *Okay, let things go right for this woman.*

Settling on a silky rust-colored shorts set with a skinny tank top and unstructured jacket, Paige dressed hurriedly. The outfit reminded her of the one Julia Roberts wore in one of the last scenes of *Pretty Woman*. Paige and Jade had considered that movie so romantic. Paige shook her head. It hadn't taken her long to realize they didn't need—couldn't count on—Prince Charmings to rescue them.

Was Jade still looking for her Prince Charming? What had she been doing the past three years that was so secretive she couldn't tell Paige? Wouldn't even see her?

The doorbell pealed. "Well, you're about to find out." Paige took one more look at her reflection, then bolted out of the room and down the winding oak staircase; by the time she reached the foyer, she was breathless. She whipped open the door.

On her covered porch, flanked by two huge white pillars, stood her sister. It wasn't Jade's low-slung leopard-print skirt and bikini top that halted Paige's words in her throat. It wasn't Jade's hair, that had once been straight and was now a blond mass of curls, that had Paige speechless.

It was the little girl Jade held in her arms. About three, the child's head was nestled on Jade's shoulder, and she was sucking her middle two fingers. Sky-blue eyes—the exact color of Paige's—stared out of a heart-shaped face. Hair, again the same shade as Paige's, rippled down the child's back. She was dressed in a blue flowered sundress and wearing white sandals and a floppy white hat.

The words tumbled out of Paige's mouth. "She looks just like me."

Jade smiled. "She should. Jewel Anderson, meet your aunt Paige." Jade's voice was husky and deep as always. But there was a quaver in it. "Paige, meet my daughter."

"Your *daughter?*"

The little girl nestled more deeply into her mother's arms.

"Your *daughter?*" Paige repeated.

Jade bit her lip.

Don't do that, kiddo. Anybody can tell you're frightened when you bite your lip. You've got to keep up a good front.

The memory warmed Paige. Her love of children and her sisterly heart came to the surface. "Hello, Jewel." She held out her arms. "Come see your aunt Paige?"

Jade's release of breath was audible. After inspecting Paige, Jewel removed her hand from her mouth and reached out. Paige hugged the child close to her. She experienced an immediate connection to the little girl. Paige had to close her eyes to tolerate the emotion flooding her. When she finally looked at Jade, she saw that her sister was staring at them. Her green eyes—she'd been named for them—were misty, like grass glistening in the morning dew.

"Well," Paige said. "This is wonderful."

"You think so?"

"Of course." She hugged the child. "Of *course.*"

Then she reached out and touched her sister for the

first time in more than three years. Jade came forward and embraced Paige so hard that Jewel cried out. ''Mommy.''

Jade pulled back and wiped her eyes. Giving Paige a watery smile, she said, ''You look great.''

Paige smiled. ''So do you.'' She glanced over her shoulder at the shiny new Lexus in her driveway. ''Is he out there?''

Jade cocked her head. ''Who?''

''Your husband.''

At Jade's blank look, Paige said, ''Jewel's father.'' Still no reaction. ''Mr. Anderson.''

It was as if storm clouds had appeared from nowhere to block out the sun. Jade's face darkened. Then, she squared her shoulders and lifted her chin. ''I'm not married to Jewel's father, Paige.''

JEWEL LAY UNDER the covers on the guest room queen-size bed and gazed up at her mother. ''Me sleep with Mommy?'' she asked before stuffing fingers back in her mouth.

''Yes, sweetie. I said you can sleep with Mommy until we get our own place again.'' She reached out and grasped her daughter's hand, kissed it tenderly.

''Lie down now?'' Jewel asked sleepily.

''All right.'' Jade glanced at Paige. ''Sometimes I lie down with her to help her get to sleep. Especially in a strange house.''

''Good idea.'' Paige smiled. ''Can I lie down, too?''

Jade smiled. ''You remember?''

Can I lie down with you, Paige?

All right. It's only been a week since they died.

Just one more night, I promise.

''I remember.'' Paige stretched out on the bed. The

past hour was buzzing in her brain like a thousand little bees waiting to sting. After Jade's admission that she wasn't married, she'd asked Paige to table her questions until Jewel was asleep. They'd given the little girl a snack. Then Jade had bathed her and pulled on her pajamas.

Staring down at the child, whose eyes were already closed, Paige said, "I can't get over how much she looks like me."

"Jewel's father looks a lot like Dad. It's why she's your little clone, I guess." Jade gazed lovingly at her child. "I have baby pictures of you that could pass for Jewel."

Paige smiled and pushed lank bangs from the girl's face.

"She's got your personality, too."

The thought pleased Paige. "Really?"

"Yep. She's a conservative dresser." Of course Jade would state that first. Since they'd grown up, her sister dressed as if she'd stepped off the pages of a Victoria's Secret catalog. "I can't even get her into a pair of jeans. She's meticulous about her things. Her room is a showcase. And she's stubborn and willful."

Paige felt her throat go dry at the blunt assessment. She sounded like one of Cinderella's stepsisters.

Kissing the top of her daughter's head, Jade added, "She's also generous to a fault, kind to every stray she meets—animals and people—and very, very bright." Jade smiled. "Just like Aunt Paige."

"I missed three years of her life, Jade. Why didn't you tell me?"

Jade slid off the bed and picked up the baby monitor she'd brought with her. "Let's go sit. This will take a while."

They stopped in the kitchen, then headed out to the

pool, armed with glasses of wine and the monitor. Jade lounged back in the same chaise Ian had favored when he'd been here. Paige perched on the edge of a chair across from her.

"This is great, sis. You've done well for yourself."

"So have you, kiddo."

"You mean the baby?"

"That goes without saying. I meant financially. A Lexus. Vuitton luggage. Expensive baby clothes." She smiled. "I'm glad for you."

Jade sipped her wine and drilled her fingers on the arm of the chair. "I wish I hadn't quit smoking."

"Did you quit when you got pregnant?"

"Yeah, and I would never smoke around her. Like Mom and Dad did around us."

What do you have, Jade?

Some of their grass.

They'll have a fit.

They won't even know, Paige. They're so burned.

Paige sipped her wine. "I want to talk about why I've missed out on three years of my niece's life."

Slowly Jade lifted her gaze to Paige's. In her face was a determination Paige had never seen before.

"Because of the circumstances of her birth. And what followed."

Swallowing hard, Paige broached a subject she hated to talk about. "Surely you didn't think I'd judge you. After all, I made the same mistake."

Jade's eyes turned frosty. "Jewel is not a mistake."

"You didn't get pregnant on purpose, did you?"

"No, but she's the best thing that's happened to me."

"Okay. I'm sorry it came out that way. In any event, how can you think I'd get on *your* case about her after what happened to me?"

"Because I wanted to keep her."

"Just because you made a different decision than I did doesn't mean I'd be upset about it." She nodded to Jade's perfectly manicured blood-red nails. And her Italian leather sandals. "You've obviously got enough money to buy nice things. You can take care of her."

Jade kicked off her shoes, stood and walked to the edge of the pool. Yanking up her calf-length leopard skirt, she sat down and dangled her feet in the water, making it swirl in the moonlight. "No, Paige, I can't take care of her. At least, I haven't been able to up till now."

Catching the seriousness of Jade's tone, Paige followed her to the water and dropped down on the slate next to her. "I don't understand." She reached out and hugged Jade close. "Honey, you can tell me anything."

"All right." Jade took the quick hug from Paige, then pulled away. "I vowed I'd do this as soon as I got here and I will. Just promise that you'll tell me what you're feeling after you know everything."

"I promise."

"Okay. I was bartending at a place in the theater district in Manhattan when I met Jewel's father."

"At Echo's. I knew where you worked."

"Yes. But you didn't know about him. He produces Broadway shows." She stared out over the water. "His most recent smash was *OnLine*."

"Lewis Beckman? He was on the cover of *Time* a while ago."

"Uh-huh. He's a genius."

He was also older. A lot older than Jade.

"At first it was fun flirting with him. I knew he was married, of course. He'd brought Cynthia into the bar after shows a couple of times. Then he stopped bringing her.'' Jade drew in a breath. ''It was stupid to let him close. But I was lonely, and tired of being by myself.''

''You had a lot of boyfriends.''

''All losers. All uninteresting. Anyway, I fell hard for Beck. Finally I slept with him. It was all fun and glamorous at first. Shows. Parties. No one seemed to care that he had a mistress. New York sophistication, I guess.''

Paige kept her mouth shut. Much as she hated the thought of Jade's affair with a married man, she would never have turned her back on her sister. So why had Jade stayed away?

''When I got pregnant, he wasn't pleased. He and Cynthia had decided not to have kids. He'd had a vasectomy and he thought the baby was someone else's. I knew it wasn't, of course, because I was only sleeping with him—we'd been together a year. So he took me to a doctor, and we had DNA tests. No doubt, Jewel was his. The snip-snip hadn't worked as well as they thought.''

Paige cringed. How could Jade allow that degradation? Paige would have slapped the guy and walked out before she'd have submitted to a test because he doubted her word.

''I cried during the whole test. Ultimately his distrust was enough to kill my feelings for him. I didn't want a relationship with him anymore.''

''Good.''

Jade looked at her then. ''But I needed him, Paige. For Jewel. I couldn't raise her on my salary even if I could keep working.''

''Oh, no, Jade, you didn't.''

''I did. I let him take care of us. Actually I demanded it. I told him I wanted support for Jewel for three years. That was all, then I'd leave town. But I wanted the best of everything for her—a nice place to live, clothes, a good preschool, dance and swim lessons. The whole she-bang.''

So Jade had wanted what they'd never had as children growing up in the projects. Jade wanted what Paige had worked her tail off to achieve.

She reached out and squeezed Jade's hand. "Honey, I would have taken care of both you and Jewel. You didn't have to resort to…*that*.''

Jade winced. "I'd do anything for Jewel. Even *that*.''

"But you wouldn't come to me for Jewel." Paige's words were bitter. "Why?''

"Mostly because you have to have everything perfect—Perfect Paige. You set very high standards for yourself and other people. It started right after we left Serenity House when you turned eighteen. You became so serious and responsible. As if it were a crime to have fun. And it only got worse. I can't live up to your standards.''

What happened to you to make you this unforgiving, this distrustful?

"Is it easier to be a married man's…''

"It's easier for Jewel. Your disapproval would have hurt her." Jade ran a hand through her hair. "Look, I might not be as smart as you, but I read all the stuff on how the first three years of life are the most crucial psychologically. It's why I wanted to be home with her and nurture her and give her everything those first few years." She blew out a breath. "God, I don't want her to be as screwed up as we are.''

Paige stiffened. These days, she never thought of herself as "screwed up.''

"So I told Beck I wanted his support for three years. I wanted Jewel to have everything. Then I'd take responsibility for her. He agreed.''

"Of course he did. He got a young and beautiful bed partner in the process."

Jade's eyes teared up and she looked away. "I knew this was going to be hard. I just didn't think it would hurt so much."

Paige watched her. "I'm sorry. I shouldn't have said that."

"No, you shouldn't have. But not for the reason you mean. It's not accurate. I didn't sleep with Beck again. He came to see Jewel regularly, and frankly we got to be friends. He's a nice guy, outside of all the male/female stuff. And mostly he kept his part of the deal." Her face darkened. Paige could see it in the outdoor halogen light.

"What?"

"When the time came, he didn't want us to leave. He said he loved Jewel. And me, I think, though in a different way from before. We quarreled about my leaving."

"Why *did* you leave?"

"I deserve more than what he was offering. I want a life for us, a real one."

"Good for you."

"So I decided to start making it. Jewel turned three last month, Nora's invitation came, and it was time to bite the bullet and tell you the whole sordid story."

Paige said nothing, her mind whirling. On the one hand, she hated thinking of Jade dependent on a man like Beckman. On the other, she could understand wanting the best for your child. That was, after all, why Paige had given up her own baby.

"You promised you'd be honest with me," Jade prompted.

"I will."

"You disapprove of what I did, don't you."

"Jade, it's not black and white. I think you had alternatives, is all."

"Since when did you start believing in alternatives?"

"What do you mean?"

"After you had the baby, you said there was no alternative but to give it up."

"I couldn't keep her, Jade."

Jade stilled, the glass halfway to her mouth. Finally she said, "You know?"

"Yeah. Darcy let it slip."

"Darcy. As in Shannon?"

"It's O'Malley now. She lives across the street with her two kids."

Jade smiled. "We fought like cats and dogs. Last I knew, she was married and living in Pennsylvania."

"She was. But the guy left her, and she couldn't make ends meet, so she came home to live with her mother."

"Oh, God, not Marian the Librarian." The house sisters had given Darcy's mother the moniker from *The Music Man* because she was so straitlaced. "Darcy must be dying."

"No, she isn't. She's become very respectable."

"You say that with pride."

"Do I?"

"Mmm." Jade stood. "Anyway, Jewel and I will leave the house tomorrow. I can't wake her up now to take her to the hotel."

Paige was confused. "What do you mean?"

"I won't stay here with that disapproval etched all over your face, Paige."

"I don't disapprove. Do I have to agree with what you did for me to be a sister to you and an aunt to Jewel?"

"No. But I will not have Jewel hurt by your prejudices. She's had a good life so far and I'll make it stay good if

I have to work my fingers to the bone. But I won't let anyone hurt her. As far as she's concerned, and everybody else, I was married to an older man when she was born, he died, and we came back home. I've legally changed both our names to Anderson to support the story."

"If you were so sure I'd disapprove, why didn't you tell *me* that same story?"

Swallowing the last of her wine, Jade set the glass down on the table. She wrapped her arms defensively around her waist. "I probably should have. You'd have accepted it without question. But I love you, and I couldn't bear to lie to you. Don't worry, we won't ruin your reputation here. We'll only stay till the wedding. Then we'll go away."

"You said you had business to take care of here. Will you do that before the wedding, too?"

Jade shook her head as if Paige had said something incredibly stupid. "I've just done it, Paige. Tonight."

Paige watched the person she loved more than anyone in the world walk into the house, head high, shoulders stiff.

She almost couldn't contain what she felt inside.

KNOCKING ON THE DOOR of Serenity House, Paige prayed Nora was still awake. She needed to talk to someone. Now.

She'd wanted to go to Ian, to tell him everything, but she didn't want to breach Jade's privacy. If she could have handled this alone, she wouldn't have come to see Nora. But it was midnight and she'd tossed and turned in her bed, so she'd gotten up, thrown on shorts and a shirt, crept downstairs and left her house. Earlier she'd told Jade she was sometimes called out at night, so her sister wouldn't worry if she got up and noticed her absence.

The door swung open and before her stood Charly Donovan, one of the original residents of Serenity House. "Paige, hi."

"Charly? What are you doing here?" She glanced at Charly's nightclothes—simple pajama bottoms and a T-shirt. With her dark hair pulled back in a ponytail, she looked like one of the kids who lived here now.

"I, um, well, it's a long story. Can I help you?"

"I need to see Nora."

I need to see Nora. Now. It was a refrain all the girls had used at one time or another.

"She's out with Dan. I expect her back anytime."

"Oh."

"Why don't you wait?" She nodded to the porch swing. "I'll sit out here with you. Just let me tell one of the girls where I am."

That was odd. Why was Charly reporting her whereabouts to the Serenity House girls? Why was she here, ready for bed?

When they were seated on the swing, Charly smiled at her. "I'm taking over as director of Serenity House, Paige. Right after Nora and Dan get married. She plans to tell everybody when we get together at the lake."

One of Nora's requests was that all the Serenity House "sisters" gather at Dan's cottage on Keuka Lake for a few days before the wedding.

"I can't believe she's quitting."

Charly said, "She waited all her life for this time with Dan. He's retiring next summer, too."

So many surprises. Paige felt herself close down. "What about your life in Elmwood? And Tim?" Charly's late husband had had a son by a former marriage. Charly adored him and had been the World's Greatest Stepmom.

Charly pushed at the floor with her bare foot and the swing started to move. "He's at Cornell, just like his dad wanted."

Lulled by the soothing motion, Paige asked, "You miss Cal, don't you?"

"More than I can say. But I needed to move on. I sat at home for too long and mourned his death." She gestured at Serenity House. "This is good for me. I haven't used my degree in social work in years."

"And you always took care of us."

"No, Paige, you were the caretaker. I was the peacemaker."

Weakly Paige smiled.

"Something's wrong."

"Yes."

A car door slammed. Feminine giggles and male rumbles were heard. "The lovebirds are home," Charly announced with a smile.

Paige chuckled. Nora's happiness was a bright spot in everybody's life. She and Dan strolled up the walkway arm and arm and climbed the steps.

Dan spotted them first. "Well, if this doesn't bring back memories."

Bad ones, Paige thought. *Ones I don't want to resurrect.*

"Hi, Paige." Nora glanced at Charly. "Did we need a doctor? Is something wrong?"

"No. Paige came to see you." Charly stood. "I'll go in." She squeezed Paige's arm. "Take care."

"I'm going, too." Dan turned. "Good night, Charly. Nice to see you, Paige." He gave Nora a sound kiss, headed back to his car and left.

ONCE THEY WERE ALONE, Nora looked at the young woman seated on the swing and was swamped by familiar emotions. Of all the girls in that first group who had come to Serenity House, this was the one she'd helped the least. Because Paige hadn't *let* anybody help her.

Nora crossed to the swing and smiled. All the girls had had their turns out here. Nora had insisted on having one hour with each girl every week to talk, to listen to the birds, to spend idle time together. She sat down and picked up Paige's hand. Paige stiffened, something she hadn't done in years. Nora held on more tightly. "What's wrong?"

Paige rocked the swing. Finally she said, "Jade came home."

It must be really bad if Nora didn't have to pry the problem out of her. "You know why she stayed away?"

"Yes. I can't tell you though. It's too personal."

Jade would tell her, anyway, Nora knew. Paige was the only one who guarded her thoughts as if they were state secrets. "Why are you so upset?"

"Because she didn't tell me." Paige peered over at Nora with wide eyes, the color of the night. "Nora, am I judgmental, inflexible...so unforgiving that my own sister's afraid to tell me things?"

Nora took a breath. "You are fair, flexible and forgiving in your professional life. In your personal life, you expect a lot from people. And it's hard for you to trust."

"I trusted Jade."

"And she didn't trust you to tell you her problems. Instead, she chose to stay away. That must hurt."

Nora knew only too well how girls from Serenity House found it hard to trust. "Sweetie, don't blow this out of proportion."

"What do you mean, blow it out of proportion? My

own sister thinks I'm such a judgmental perfectionist that she refused to see me for years.''

''You aren't that. You're just harder on yourself than anyone else.''

''Jade called me Perfect Paige. Ian said I was unforgiving.''

''Ian Chandler?''

''Yes. He… I…I've just started to…I don't know…''

Nora studied her. ''I've watched Ian with you. He'd be good for you.''

Shaking her head, Paige's eyes narrowed. ''It would be a mistake to let him in.''

''Were you letting him in?''

Paige looked away.

Nora reached over and tilted her chin. ''Paige, were you?''

Slowly Paige nodded.

Tonight she was so much the child she'd been when she'd come here fifteen years ago. She even looked young, with no makeup and her hair pulled back in a ponytail. Well, Nora had made some progress with Paige and had supported her during her pregnancy. But after the birth of her baby, Paige had closed down. ''Then don't back away, Paige,'' she said. ''Ian's a good man.''

''He's a bully.'' Paige said this with such frustration Nora had to bite back a smile.

''Sweetie, no timid simp could handle you.'' She let out the smile and repeated, ''He'd be good for you.''

''I don't know.''

''Think about it.'' Standing, Nora held out her hand. ''Now, come on inside. I'll make you some tea. It always soothed you.''

''It's too warm for tea.''

"Then we'll put ice in it." Nora peered down at her. "Come on, let me baby you tonight."

Paige stared at Nora's hand, then placed hers in it. "All right. For a little while."

THE ROOM WAS DIM, lit only by a small night-light Jade must have brought with her. In its shadows, Paige could see her sister and her niece, cuddled under the bed covers. Jewel was safely tucked in the middle of the bed and had turned to her side, her face nestled against her mother's breast. Paige wondered if Jade had breast-fed her child. God, she'd missed so much of their lives.

Jade slept as she always did, as Paige always did, arms over her head. In the worst of times, when they had been terrified and shared the same bed, she and Jade had clasped hands across the top of the pillow and fallen asleep that way.

Paige missed her sister so much her whole body shook with it.

Oh hell, it was 3 a.m. Leaning over, she kissed Jewel's head and brushed her lips over Jade's hair.

She'd just started toward the door when she heard, "Paige?"

Pivoting, she saw that her sister had awakened. Bracing herself on her elbows, her hair a mass of curls around her face, she looked at Paige through heavy-lidded eyes. "I heard you go out. Is everything all right?"

"Yes." Paige's whisper sounded like a frog's croak. "I'm sorry I woke you." She gave Jade a weak smile. "Go back to sleep, kiddo."

Jade smiled at the old nickname. "Come sit a minute."

"We'll wake Jewel."

"No. She sleeps like Rip van Winkle."

Unable to resist, Paige returned to the bed and sat

down on the empty side. She soothed back a lock of hair that had escaped from Jewel's braid. "It means she's content. Untroubled."

"That's good." Jade studied Paige's face. "*You're* troubled."

What an understatement. Everything was changing so fast in Paige's carefully ordered world. Working at the Center. Ian. And now these revelations from Jade. Paige didn't know what to do with all the turmoil.

"I'm sorry if I upset you." Jade lay back down and watched her.

"No, you were right to say what you did." She scanned the professionally decorated room. The peach walls, white wicker bed and matching dressers seemed to come alive with her sister's presence. Paige hadn't realized how cold everything in her house was. "A lot's been going on in my life lately." The words were wrenched from her.

Propping her head on her elbow, Jade said, "I monopolized the conversation tonight. Tell me about you."

Paige's immediate response was to clam up. She never shared anything with other women, except Nora.

But this was her sister.

And Paige needed to talk.

So she spilled the whole story. How Ian Chandler had crashed into her world and tricked her into signing on at the Elsa Moore Center; what it was like working with girls as troubled as she and Jade had been; Ian's dogged insistence on some kind of personal relationship. She told Jade about the uncannily humanlike Scalpel. She left nothing out, not even the mind-blowing kiss last night.

Jade giggled and rolled her eyes and gave dry comments. She made Paige feel less tense. She used to always do that, something Paige had forgotten.

As the sun started to come up, Paige looked at her sister's face, then at her niece, and suddenly she had her own dawning. There was no way she could let Jade go away again.

"I gotta get some sleep before Jewel wakes up, sis." Jade lay back on the pillows.

"Don't go."

Jade's eyes opened. "What?"

"Don't leave here. Please. Stay with me until the wedding. I promise, I won't hurt Jewel. Or you. I'm so tired of missing you."

A look of old wisdom crossed Jade's face. "I think you miss yourself."

"What do you mean?"

"I think Ian Chandler's ferreting out the old Paige."

"The old Paige is dead, Jade. I killed her. Intentionally."

Sliding down into the bed, Jade said, "I don't think so." She closed her eyes. "Paige?"

"Uh-huh?"

"Get under the covers."

"What?"

"Sleep with us."

And for the first time since…Paige couldn't remember when, tears formed in her eyes. Standing, she shed her shorts, and leaving on panties and T-shirt, she crept under the covers. As she laid her head on the pillow, her arms automatically went over her head.

In a moment she felt Jade's hand cover hers. Paige clasped it and, feeling safe, closed her eyes and slept.

CHAPTER NINE

SITTING ON THE OUTDOOR DECK at Hyde Point Country Club on Sunday morning, Ian looked out over the panoramic view and scowled.

"It's a lovely setting, Ian." Lynne Chandler's tone was dry. "You're staring at it as if the twelfth plague of Egypt were marching down the green."

"I'm not good company today," he muttered, shooting a glare at his brother. "I told you I wanted to cancel." In truth, Ian had been a bear for three days, snapping at everybody except Scalpel, who'd come home from the hospital and turned into the world's worst patient. The dog whimpered and whined and limped around, begging for sympathy.

What a nightmare the whole incident had been. And Paige had been his anchor during it...

He's more than a dog to you... Your parents gave him to you... It's all right to feel bad... It's not your fault...

Not that she'd cared enough to call or come over to see for herself how Scalpel had fared. Or how Ian was feeling. *Soon, Ian, I promise.* Well, she hadn't kept her goddamned promise. And he was good and royally pissed off.

"Now he looks mad," Derek said, sipping his coffee. "I'll tromp him on the tees after we eat." Ian had forgotten about the brunch date and golf game the three of them planned for today until Derek had shown up at his condo earlier.

"In your dreams," Ian said.

"Okay, Tiger, we'll see."

Lynne studied Ian. "It's a woman, isn't it?"

"No. Yes." The brothers spoke simultaneously, but only Derek spoke the truth.

"The one who babied him through Scalpel's accident," Derek teased.

Sometimes Ian wished he knew how to keep his mouth shut. He'd told Derek all about Paige's support because Ian had thought the night he'd spent with her was the beginning of something. But she hadn't called since Thursday, and she'd taken three days off work to be with Jade. He'd tried her at home several times, but the answering machine kept picking up. The last time, he hadn't been at all understanding.

"Where the hell are you, Paige? And why aren't you returning my calls?" Then he relented. *"Come on, baby, I'm dying here."*

"Do you want to talk about her, dear?" Lynne asked.

"No. Let's talk about RTK." He knew discussion of his birth mother's pet project, the Right to Know, would distract her. She made her living at interior design, but helping people find their biological parents or children was her real love.

"We're closing in on our one thousandth match," Lynne said proudly.

"We should do something special to celebrate when we reach that number." Derek took a pad out of his pocket and began to make notes. "When is the *Herald*'s article on us coming out?" he asked.

"Anytime now," Lynne told them. "I didn't check today's paper. It might be in there." Her eyes, the same gray as Ian's, and set off by the slate-blue dress she wore, smiled at the thought.

She reached out and clasped Derek's arm. "Too bad Abby couldn't be interviewed for it."

"They don't have phones in Timbuktu," Derek put in easily. Derek's birth mother was a photojournalist who traveled all over the world.

"The article will be great PR for the Center," Lynne added. "Don't you think, Ian?"

"Yeah, I..." Ian's voice trailed off. His heart started to pound when he spotted a group stepping onto the deck. "Well, what do you know."

First out was Paige, dressed in a sapphire-blue sundress that left her shoulders bare and had ruffles down the front. She wore low strappy sandals and her hair was pulled back in some kind of fancy braid. It showcased her long slender neck and throat. Which right about now Ian felt like wringing.

Next was a goddess. Wearing some kind of green-flowered sarong wrapped around a body with dynamite curves, the woman pranced proudly out from behind Paige on towering white sandals. This must be Jade.

With them was a child, about three, who looked just like Paige; the little girl even wore the same-color outfit and her hair in a braid down her back. For a minute the air backstopped in Ian's lungs. Was she Paige's child? No, of course not. Ian had had contact with Paige for four years. He'd have known if she'd had a baby. The whole idea was ludicrous, but man, they looked alike!

Paige didn't see him. They were seated a few tables away. Jade and the child had their backs to Ian, but he was directly in Paige's line of vision.

"That's her, isn't it, big brother?"

"Yeah," Ian said disgustedly. "That's her."

"Who's the fox with her?"

"My guess is it's her long-lost sister. I don't know anything about the kid." His temper spiked. "I'm beginning to think I don't know anything about her."

You can trust me, Paige. I just want to get to know you better. No ulterior motive. No demands. No pressure.

Lynne reached over and squeezed his arm. "Sending daggers her way isn't going to help anything, Ian."

"It's better than stalking over there and dragging her out by that pretty braid, which is exactly what I *want* to do."

He saw Lynne and Derek exchange surprised glances. Damn, this wasn't Ian's usual style. He was angry that he'd let himself react so strongly to her neglect. What was between them hadn't gone far enough for him to feel this...bereft.

Still simmering, he sat back, crossed his legs at the ankles, sipped his coffee. And waited for her to catch sight of him. He glanced down, trying to remember what he'd put on that morning. A new striped golf shirt that some woman had complimented him on and dark shorts that fitted him well. At least he looked good.

He'd just bide his time until Paige noticed him. Despite his pique, he appreciated how the sun kissed her hair, highlighting its golden strands.

Paige had just been served coffee when she spotted him.

He glared back at her.

Her face was so expressive, when she didn't deliberately shut down. Myriad emotions flickered across it. Joy at seeing him. A little embarrassment. And then, a flash of fear.

I'm wary...
Of?

You. Of trusting you...

She leaned over and whispered something to Jade, who turned to look over her shoulder at him and his family. Then Paige pushed back her chair and stood. Jade and the child did the same. She was wise to bring reinforcements. The three of them crossed to Ian's table. When they reached it, Ian and Derek got to their feet.

"Hello, Ian," Paige said, her voice hesitant.

"Paige." His tone was cut-glass cold.

"This is my sister, Jade. And her daughter, Jewel."

Jade held out her hand, which Ian shook. "Nice to meet you, Ian. I've heard a lot about you."

Jewel mimicked her mother's gesture. Ian knelt down in front of the little girl and took hers in his. "Hi, Jewel. You look just like your aunt Paige."

"She's nice." Jewel sidled over to Paige, grasping her dress.

"Sometimes." Ian stood. "Paige, you've met Lynne. Jade, Jewel, this is Lynne Chandler." No flicker of surprise. Paige must have told Jade everything about him. Nice of her, since she couldn't be bothered to return his calls. His anger resurfaced, and with it his chagrin at feeling so strongly about Paige's actions.

"And you are?" Jade asked Derek.

"Derek Shane." Ian's conservative brother was studying Jade as if she were some rare artifact he'd just unearthed. Beautiful, but totally foreign. "I'm Ian's brother."

Jade smiled at him.

Paige said, "Well, we don't want to interrupt your breakfast. And Jewel's hungry. We just got out of church and we're going to the lake, so..." She was babbling. Good. At least she was nervous. She drew herself up. "Nice to see you again, Lynne. Derek, it was a pleasure to meet you." Warily she turned her sky-blue eyes on Ian. "I'll, um, call you, Ian."

"Yeah? I've heard that before."

She gave a start. In his peripheral vision, he saw Lynne roll her eyes and Derek smirk. Jade bit back a grin.

And Paige was clearly horrified at his candor.

Well, you ain't seen nothin' yet, baby.

Collecting herself, she started to turn away. He grabbed her arm. "Not so fast."

She looked up at him. "Ian, please."

Ian, please. I have to get up. I have to go to work. She'd been under him at the time. The memory charged him.

"You'll excuse us for a minute, won't you, Jade?" He gave his family an unapologetic glance. "I'll be right back."

"Ian, we're ready to order." This from Paige.

"No, that's okay." Jade picked up her daughter's hand. "I'll just take Jewel to the pond to see the ducks. Take your time, Ian," she told him mischievously, and said her goodbyes to his family.

Ian speared Paige with a forceful look. "Let's go down by the pro shop."

"I…"

He started to bark at her, then caught sight of the vulnerability in her eyes. Gently he drew her to the side, away from his family. "Please come with me."

She wanted to refuse, he could tell. "All right."

Stretching out his arm, he never unlocked his gaze from hers. After an interminable moment, she placed her hand in his. They took the stairs to the lower deck, walked out behind the pro shop and over to a bench under a tree. She sat down. He put one foot on the wooden slats, braced his arms on his thigh and stared at her.

She raised her chin. "All right, Ian, what's this all about?"

"Don't play Ms. Coy and Innocent with me. You said you'd call me."

"I did."

"Thursday. I had three deliveries, and by the time I got back to you, all I could get was your goddamned machine."

"Um…" She bit her lip. "Jade came. We talked practically all night."

"You couldn't take one little break?" He shook his head. "I sat by the phone waiting for you to call."

"I doubt that, Ian."

His temper flared. "What's with you? You're acting like Wednesday night never even happened."

She just looked at him.

"And you didn't even take the time to call and find out how Scalpel was."

Her shoulders sagged. "I'm sorry. How is he?"

"Ornery. Cranky."

She gave him a half-smile. "Like his master."

"Both of us have reason to be."

"Is his leg healing?"

"Yeah, but he's having nightmares—the doggy version of post-traumatic stress syndrome. He bit me during one." Ian held up his arm; Lynne had doctored the beefy part of his palm this morning.

Paige touched his hand with her slender fingers. "I'm sure you're taking good care of him." He didn't respond. She rubbed the bandage sensuously. "I'm sorry."

"About the bite?"

He saw her swallow hard. "No, about not calling to check on Scalpel."

His heart clutched. She didn't say anything about him. Again he wondered why he was letting this get to him.

"And for ignoring your calls. It's been an emotional weekend." The catch in her voice alerted him.

"Because of Jade."

She nodded. "And my newly discovered niece."

"You didn't know about her?"

Shaking her head, Paige gazed out at the pond. Ian tracked her line of vision to see Jewel and Jade feeding the ducks. With the morning sun glistening around them, their dresses blending in with the green of the lawn and the blue of the sky, they looked like part of an impressionist painting.

"Jewel was the reason Jade didn't come home for three years."

"Tell me."

Right before his eyes, she withdrew. "I can't."

He straightened. His pride urged him to forget it. To forget her. He didn't need this. But acting on his ego had never served him well in the past. Besides, there was something about this woman… "Paige, you agreed to see me. To give us a chance."

"I know I did."

"Withholding isn't getting off on the right foot."

"I know." She clenched her hands in her lap. "But bullying me and yelling at me isn't, either."

He raked a hand through his hair. "I…I'm not used to having my calls ignored."

That brought a chuckle from her. "No, I don't imagine Dr. Hot and Hunky is."

He snorted. "Don't tease. I've been dying all weekend. I want to see you, Paige."

"We said we'd take it slow."

"Honey, this speed would wear on a tortoise. Can't we pick it up a little?"

"What did you have in mind?"

"Go out with me tonight."

"What about Jade?"

"She can get along by herself. Just for a few hours. I need to be with you."

He raised his hand and ran his knuckles down her cheek. It was smooth and silky, and just touching her made him ache. "Please. I want to talk to you, hold you for a little while. We'll take a drive over to Hyde Point Hill."

"And neck there like teenagers?"

"Sounds good to me." He added, "We'll bring Scalpel along as a chaperon."

"I guess Jade won't mind."

He stiffened; he couldn't help it. Damn it, he needed more than a simple concession from her. Angry again, he drew back and went to stand by the railing of the lower deck. Bracing his arms on it, staring out over the course, he wondered not for the first time if he was going to be able to break down her walls.

He heard her come up behind him. She slid her arm through his and leaned into him. "I wore your T-shirt to bed last night." She whispered the words against his shoulder. "I haven't washed it. It smells like you."

The band of pain around his chest loosened a bit. "That helps."

"I'm sorry. This is hard for me."

"I scare you."

She nodded.

"I'll try not to be so pushy. But I have to have some crumbs, Paige."

"Who are you kidding? You'll insist on the whole banquet."

He grinned wryly. "Tell you what. I'll start tonight with an appetizer. We'll go from there." He raised his hand and ran the pad of his thumb over her lips. "I've thought about kissing you again. For days."

"I've thought about more."

Good. He brushed his lips over hers. "Hmm." Her eyes were slumberous. "That's pretty tasty, Dr. Kendrick."

"Yeah, Dr. Chandler, it is."

"I'll pick you up at eight."

"All right."

Turning, he slid his hand into hers and they headed back to their respective families.

PAIGE FROWNED at her image in the mirror. "How did I let you talk me into this?"

Jade glanced up from where she sat on the bed braiding flowers into Jewel's hair. "You look dynamite in that dress."

"It's too small. I'm taller than you are, and bigger on top."

"Quit bragging."

Biting back a chuckle, she met her sister's eyes in the glass. It was so much fun sharing things the way they used to. "It's not me, Jade."

"Live a little, sis. The halter top will give him easy access to your neck."

Jewel, who sat quietly, dressed in a gorgeous white eyelet bathing suit coverup, asked, "Who, Mommy?"

"Oh, now you've done it." Paige shook her head.

Jade didn't even blink. "Aunt Paige's boyfriend."

An Important Message from the Editors

Dear Reader,

Because you've chosen to read one of our fine romance novels, we'd like to say "thank you!" And, as a special way to thank you, we've selected two more of the books you love so well, plus an exciting Mystery Gift, to send you absolutely FREE!

Please enjoy them with our compliments...

Pam Powers

P.S. And because we value our customers, we've attached something extra inside...

Peel off seal and Place inside...

EDITOR'S
FREE GIFT
SEAL
THANK YOU

How to validate your Editor's
FREE GIFT
"Thank You"

1. Peel off gift seal from front cover. Place it in space provided at right. This automatically entitles you to receive 2 FREE BOOKS and a fabulous mystery gift.

2. Send back this card and you'll get 2 brand-new Harlequin Superromance® novels. These books have a cover price of $4.99 each in the U.S. and $5.99 each in Canada, but they are yours to keep absolutely free.

3. There's no catch. You're under no obligation to buy anything. We charge nothing—ZERO—for your first shipment. And you don't have to make any minimum number of purchases—not even one!

4. The fact is, thousands of readers enjoy receiving their books by mail from the Harlequin Reader Service®. They enjoy the convenience of home delivery...they like getting the best new novels at discount prices BEFORE they're available in stores...and they love their *Heart to Heart* subscriber newsletter featuring author news, horoscopes, recipes, book reviews and much more!

5. We hope that after receiving your free books you'll want to remain a subscriber. But the choice is yours— to continue or cancel, any time at all! So why not take us up on our invitation, with no risk of any kind. You'll be glad you did!

6. Don't forget to detach your FREE BOOKMARK. And remember...just for validating your Editor's Free Gift Offer, we'll send you THREE gifts, *ABSOLUTELY FREE!*

GET A
FREE MYSTERY GIFT...

SURPRISE MYSTERY GIFT COULD BE YOURS _FREE_ AS A SPECIAL "THANK YOU" FROM THE EDITORS OF HARLEQUIN

Visit us online at
www.eHarlequin.com

"Yuck." Jewel stuck her fingers in her mouth. "Don't like boys."

Paige chuckled. Eyeing Jewel, she said, "Do my hair that way, Jade?"

"Not on your life. Men like it down and fluffy. I put those curlers in it for effect. A braid would ruin it." Jade nodded to the dressing table built into the side wall. "Now sit. I'll comb you out."

Ten minutes later Paige was still frowning at herself. Her hair was a mass of waves around her face. The ice-pink dress made her cheeks rosy. And handcrafted black earrings with pink flowers—ones Jade had given her for a birthday—dangled from her ears.

Inspecting her, Jade smiled. "Ian will freak when he sees you."

"He doesn't need encouragement." Paige's frown turned into a scowl. "He was too angry yesterday, considering the circumstances. I don't get it. On Wednesday night, all I said was I'd go out with him. Not calling him back wasn't that big a deal."

"You're pathetic," Jade said from behind her.

"What do you mean?"

"Sis, the guy's hot for you." She spritzed Paige's hair once more. "He ate you up with his eyes."

I'll start with an appetizer.

"He said we'd take it slow."

Jade's lovely green eyes shadowed. Tonight she wore a top in a kaleidoscope of colors with low-slung white shorts that bared her navel. "They really did a job on you, didn't they?"

"Who?"

"Mom and Dad. Ronny."

Paige searched for her lipstick. "As a doctor, I can tell you a child's upbringing affects her forever."

"Well, I'm not as smart as you. But I think—"

Paige whirled around. "Don't do that. Don't put yourself down like that. You're very bright, as well as perceptive and knowledgeable about people."

Stark vulnerability crossed her tough sister's face. "God, I need you back in my life, Paige. Nobody else ever believed in me like you."

Warmed by the compliment, Paige said, "It's all true."

"We go to the pool?" Jewel asked from the bed where she was looking at a picture book.

"Sure, sweetie." Jade squeezed Paige's shoulder. "As soon as I finish Aunt Paige's new hairdo, we'll go wait at the pool for Prince Charming."

The comment bothered Paige. Though she'd meant everything she'd told her sister that first night, the fact that Jade had allowed a man to support her for three years, that she had depended on a man for her survival, for God's sake, was anathema to Paige. No Prince Charmings for Paige Kendrick.

They'd just settled into chairs on the deck, with Jewel in the water—she could swim like a fish already—when the gate creaked.

"Hi." It was Darcy.

Before Paige could respond, Meli burst in with Claire following more demurely. "I just got home," Darcy said. "It's so hot. The kids were driving me nuts. Is it okay if..." Her words died off when she caught sight of Paige's company. "Oh, my God, is that you, Jade?"

"Yeah, Red, it's me."

Darcy scowled at the nickname she'd hated as a teenager. Then she smiled. "Some things never change." She crossed the patio area.

Jade shook her head. "I wouldn't say that. When did you turn into Wall Street?" She gestured at Darcy's prim white suit and turquoise blouse that did indeed make her look like an executive.

"Somewhere along the road to nowhere," Darcy said glibly.

Jade nodded as if she understood.

Darcy turned to Paige. "I'm sorry. I didn't know you had company." Claire had remained by her side, but Meli had gone to the edge of the pool and was gazing down at Jewel, who was doing a pretty good back crawl. "Come on Mel, let's go."

"No need to leave." Jade stood and crossed to Meli. "Hi, I'm Jade."

"Dr. Kendrick's sister," Darcy said, coming closer. "This is my daughter Melanie. And this is Claire."

Jade smiled at Claire and winked at Meli. "That little fish is my daughter, Jewel."

"Pretty name," Claire said.

Jade straightened. "Paige, here, has a hot date, Darce. Why don't you stay and keep Jewel and me company?"

"Are you sure?" Darcy asked.

"Absolutely."

Facing Paige, Darcy smiled. "Who's the lucky guy?"

"Hel-lo."

"See for yourself." Paige's heartbeat was already escalating at the deep rumble of Ian's voice. Jeez.

The gate opened and in skittered Scalpel. The cast on his right front leg slowed him down, but he made a beeline for Paige. She knelt and rubbed his ears, allowing him to lick her carefully made-up face. "Hi, guy. You feeling better?"

Scalpel lifted his injured leg.

"Oh, I know." She kissed the cast, on which Ian had written, "No roads for you."

Scalpel whimpered, nuzzled her some more, and

glanced longingly at the pool, then at Ian. Ian's face was stern. "No swimming, Scalpel. Like we talked about. I mean it."

Paige could swear that the dog sighed. Then his ears twitched and he crossed to the pool where Jewel hung on to the ledge. He watched her for a long time and finally moved his head to look at Paige. Then he turned back to Jewel.

"Yeah, buddy, she's a miniature Paige." Ian's tone was that of an amused father. "Guess you like that, don't you."

Scalpel barked enthusiastically.

Paige studied Ian. He'd obviously taken time with his appearance, too. His long hair was shiny clean and subtle waves framed his face. His steel-blue shirt was rolled up at the sleeves, revealing powerful arms, and opened at the throat, revealing dark chest hair. White shorts and sandals completed the outfit.

Jade came up behind Paige and whispered, "You're dead meat, sis." Her eyes sparkled at Ian. "Nice to see you again, Ian."

As he came closer, his gaze locked on Paige. He barely glanced at Jade. "You, too." Remembering his manners, he looked past them. "Hi, Darce. Meli." He cocked his head. "And who is this?"

Claire backed away. She grabbed her mother's hand.

"This is Claire." Darcy's voice was soft.

"She's a bit shy," Paige said. *Especially around men.*

Scalpel gave a long-suffering whine and everybody turned to him. He'd lain down on the deck and was nose to nose with Jewel. The little girl was petting him and mumbling to him. He seemed to respond. "Uh-oh. I think you've been usurped," Ian told Paige.

She laughed.

After some small talk, Ian asked, "Ready to go?"

Paige picked up a beaded purse. Her hands weren't quite steady. "Yes." She looked at the dog. "Come on, Scalpel."

Scalpel raised his head. He glanced from Paige to Jewel. Damned if he didn't seem torn.

Ian chuckled. "He wants to stay with his new girl."

Paige grinned. "Just like a man."

"You can leave him with us," Jade said.

Ian was amused. "Paige thinks we need a chaperon."

"Ian—"

"All the more reason for him to stay. Meli, Claire and Jewel can swim and Scalpel can watch. Darcy and I will get reacquainted."

Ian said, "It's fine by me."

"Sure." Paige looked at the dog. "Whatever."

Taking her by the hand, Ian linked their fingers. "Good night, ladies." As they started to the gate, he said, "Behave yourself, Scalpel. And *no swimming*."

The dog whined but settled down.

At the car Ian stopped. He angled Paige toward him and scanned her dress, brushed a hand down her hair. "You take my breath away."

"Figures you'd like Jade's clothes."

He ran fingers across her collarbone, raising gooseflesh. "I like what's in Jade's clothes."

She smiled at him. His eyes moved to her lips, then he drew back. "How about some ice cream first?"

First? "I'd love some."

The ride in his convertible was fun. Her curls flew helter-skelter, but the feeling of freedom was just what the doctor ordered. When they arrived at Abbott's, Ian vaulted out of the car and circled around to open her door. Escorting her to the counter, he scanned the offerings. ''Man, Scalpel will have a fit when he finds out they have black raspberry.''

''His favorite?''

''And mine. You'll love it.''

''I don't want black raspberry, Ian. I like chocolate.''

''Chocolate's good. But you have to try this.'' He ordered them both black raspberries.

Too stunned to protest, Paige accepted the cone.

He licked his. ''Hmm.'' He nodded to hers. ''Try it.'' When she just stared at him, he gave her an exasperated, I-know-best look. ''If you don't like it, I'll buy you chocolate.''

She took a bite. It *was* good. ''It's okay.''

He raised his brows. ''I'd love to hear you say I'm right.''

She took another bite.

Lifting his arm, he brushed a drop off the corner of her mouth. The small gesture made her stomach knot. His lips parted.

''Well, isn't this a surprise.''

It was like being awakened from an erotic dream. Paige gave a start, and Ian frowned. They both turned to find Marla Simmons heading for the ice-cream stand.

''Hi, Marla,'' Ian said.

She looked at him. ''Hello, Ian.'' She turned to Paige. ''Hi, Paige.'' When she checked out Paige's outfit, her eyes widened. ''Wow, you look diff—um, great.''

Suddenly self-conscious in the skimpy dress, Paige crossed her free arm over her chest. ''Thanks.''

Marla transferred her gaze to Ian. ''Out for the evening, you two?''

''Uh-huh.'' He licked his cone. ''And we need to get going or we'll be late.'' He took Paige by the elbow. ''Nice to see you, Marla.''

The beautiful blonde's brows knitted at the dismissal. But Ian ushered Paige away before Marla could respond. Once inside the car, he drove at a slower pace so that he could lick the cone. Paige told herself to leave it alone, but she couldn't. "She's your type, Ian."

Staring ahead, he seemed distracted. "Marla?"

"Yes."

"Maybe."

"Did you ever call her after the IM?"

"No." He glanced at Paige. "Did you ever talk to her about it?"

"No. I don't like to mix business and personal stuff."

"She's a nice woman."

"Fine." Paige's tone was clipped. She couldn't help wondering if Ian had slept with Marla. Had he touched her with those wonderful hands, kissed her everywhere?

"What are you thinking?"

"Nothing. Let's drop it."

"Fine." As they drove, he finished his cone, licked his fingers, then placed his hand on Paige's bare knee. She jumped. "My fingers sticky?"

"No."

He began to caress her knee. She moved her leg away.

"I thought we were dropping the subject."

"Of Marla?" He nodded. "We are," she said.

"Then why have you turned into the Ice Maiden?"

Paige sighed. "Why is everything so complicated with you, Ian?"

"Me? You're the puzzle."

"No, I'm not."

He shook his head. "Marla and I were never intimate, Paige, if that's what's got you freezing up on me."

She thought about lying, but she also remembered what Jade had said about the old Paige, so she decided to be honest. "A little, I guess. And seeing Marla reminds me of how you got me to work at the Center. It still makes me uncomfortable."

He pulled over to the side of the road. They'd made it to the foot of Hyde Point Hill. Turning to face her, he said, "I'll apologize again. I'm sorry I broke your trust. Please don't let it spoil tonight. I've been looking forward to this."

"Why, Ian? I don't get it. You can have beauty queens like Marla and Missy Columbo. Debutantes like Tammi Garson."

His face brightened. "You remember my dates' names?"

She blushed, then closed her eyes and sighed. She could feel him lean over, his mouth at her ear.

"I want *you,* lady. No, don't stiffen up. I don't just mean sexually, though being near you in that little slip of a thing sends my blood pressure to the moon. I mean, I want to get to know you. I want you to be my friend. I want you in my life in every way."

"Ian, it's too soon to feel all that."

He drew back, his face as serious as it got when he was studying the chart of a patient. "For you, maybe. Not everybody works to the same timetable. It's okay. I can wait for you to catch up."

Once again she was stunned by his glib certainty, his belief that he was absolutely right. She didn't know what to say.

"Meanwhile—" he licked his lips "—I'm going to enjoy every morsel of the meal." Without warning he took her mouth. It was a firm possession of her lips; he explored her, nipped at her, claimed her. She was breathless when he pulled away.

He started the car again and headed up the hill. Paige reached out to place his hand back on her knee.

BY THE TIME they'd reached a semiprivate parking space on an overlook of Hyde Point Hill, it was dark. The entire valley sprawled down below in front of them, its lights twinkling in the evening. Once they were parked, Ian reached past the gearshift between them and over her lap to pull on the seat mechanism. Paige went back a few inches. "What are you doing?"

"Letting you stretch out." Actually she was just slightly reclined, but the position thrust her breasts out at a delicious angle. His hands curled with need to touch them. He felt himself harden immediately.

All he did, though, was place his hand at her throat. He caressed her there, then ran his knuckles up and down. "Let's talk."

"A-about—" She cleared her throat. In the moonlight, her eyes were glazed. "About what?"

"Anything." His fingertips skimmed along the neckline of her dress. "I just want to get to know you better."

"I can't talk with your hands on me."

His grin was smug and male. "Of course you can."

She groaned when his fingers slid to the low armhole of her dress. They played there, rubbing sensuously back and forth on her tender skin.

"Close your eyes. Feel my touch. But tell me about Jade."

After a doubting look, she closed her eyes. His gaze dropped to her chest, where her nipples thrust against the soft cotton. Mmm.

"She's going to stay with me for a while. We came to terms about things."

"Too personal to tell me, right?"

"Uh-huh."

"I can respect that." He let his hand glide to her waist. It kneaded the indentation there. Leaning awkwardly over the console, he kissed her eyelids. Her nose. He wanted to bathe her in every sensuous delight he could imagine. "Jewel looks just like you, Paige."

"I know."

"Jade doesn't."

"My mother and Jade were two peas in a pod. Apparently Jewel's father looks like my dad."

His hand went lower. When it reached her bare knee, she startled. "Shh. It's okay." His fingers massaged her, then inched up under her dress, slid sexily along the smooth inside of her thigh. The skin there was creamy soft. "At first I thought Jewel might be yours. But I've known you for four years. I would have known if you'd had a baby."

If he hadn't been touching her, if his body hadn't been poised over her, he wouldn't have felt it. But she stiffened slightly.

"Paige?"

"Of course she's not mine."

"You tensed, honey. What's wrong?"

"Nothing." She pushed at his chest. He sank back into his seat—and she followed him. There was a gleam in her eye as she leaned over his lap and pulled at the seat adjuster. Just as she had, he went back several inches. Then she leaned over him, though it was harder for her to get past the gearshift. "Relax, Ian."

"What are you doing, lady?"

"Payback time." She undid a few more buttons of his shirt.

"No fair, I didn't get to touch your bare—" He didn't finish, because he gasped when she kissed him there. His breath started to come in heavy pants as she brushed her nose back and forth on his chest. He gripped her arms when she ran her tongue the length of his sternum. "Paige…"

It only got worse. Or better, depending on how you looked at it.

Skilled doctor hands knew pulse points—at his neck and wrist. They gently examined…under his arm, around his navel…then his ear… Oh God, her tongue there made him jolt off the seat. At one point, as she kept up her torturous ministrations, she whispered, "Practice makes perfect, Ian."

Finally her mouth closed over his. The kiss was carnal, fueled by teasing touches and a sprinkle of moonlight. The mating of their mouths was long and luscious—and completely frustrating.

They left the hill at ten minutes to eleven. When they reached her house, Ian was aroused, but he felt an odd sense of satisfaction even without the natural culmination. He drew her to him after he'd parked the car in her driveway and shut off the engine.

She came as close as she could. "Have enough to eat?"

He nipped at her neck. "For tonight."

She sighed.

"But you know what they say about appetizers?" His gaze was tender.

Her eyes twinkled like the nighttime stars. "What?"

"They make you hungrier for the main course."

She smiled at him.

"I intend to feast, Paige. Soon."

She gave him an arch look. "I guess I'm working up an appetite."

"Good," he said, and went back for one last taste.

THEY REVERTED to their teen years during the following week.

Paige hadn't felt this high since she was Mary Ellen's age and dating Ronny Mitchum, the father of her child. Her relationship with Ian had all the qualities of a high-school romance.

The day after their excursion to Hyde Point Hill, Ian sent flowers to her office. The staff had buzzed about it, and Paige had been embarrassed, but she'd hidden the card in her lab coat. And, like a lovesick teen, she'd sneaked it out several times a day and read it—"Thanks for the taste test. Though I'm no longer famished, I can't wait for the banquet. Eight courses *might* be enough. Love, Ian."

That night, he'd invited himself—and Scalpel—to dinner. Jade had cooked.

"Do you like seafood, Ian?" Jade had asked when he arrived.

"I like all food." He answered Jade but his eyes were on Paige, who wore her tangerine tankini. "I'm a real gourmet."

All evening, he'd devoured her with that blisteringly sexual gaze, and when it was time to leave, he'd grabbed her hand. "Walk me to my car."

Once he'd gotten Scalpel settled in the seat, Ian had backed her into the shadows of her driveway, against the garage door, and took her mouth. "Just a sip," he'd said against her lips. "I've been parched since last night." His kiss was tender for a moment, then turned wonderfully insistent. He'd sworn ripely when he pulled away. "I'm gonna *die*, honey, before you're ready."

They'd had lunch together three times. Just the day before, at his place, they'd taken an hour between appointments at the clinic and gone to his condo. He'd taken Scalpel for a run while she fixed sandwiches, and when they'd returned, he swiped the plates out of her hands and lifted her onto the marble counter.

The cold stone against her bare legs and the hot brush of his hands had been unbelievably erotic.

He'd buried his face in her chest. He'd been increasing the intimacy by degrees, making her crave his touch. And she was ready for more. So she'd pushed him back and unbuttoned her blouse. His eyes had turned molten at her lacy bra, and he'd nuzzled his face into her half-exposed breasts, murmuring, "You are exquisite."

By tonight, in their third midnight swim in the pool, she wanted even more from him. Jade had made a big deal about being *really tired* and how she and Jewel would surely *sleep like the dead,* in case Ian and Paige wanted to know that. They were standing in chest-high water when he released her bikini top and whipped it off. His big hands closed over her breasts in the moonlight, and she delighted in the sensation of the water lapping around her and his hands fondling her. "I don't think I've ever seen anything as lovely as you are right now."

She smiled at him. "You feel so good."

He said only, "Touch me, Paige."

Watching his face, she slid her hands up and down the sides of his torso. His hair was wet, slicked off his forehead, accenting every beautiful angle of his features. His bare chest glistened in the moonlight. When her fingertips flirted with the waistband of his suit, he gripped the edge of the pool; feet spread, his head thrown back, he closed his eyes and sighed.

The sigh turned into a moan when she slid her hands underneath the band and caressed his buttocks. His muscles, firm and toned, tensed.

"Do you like that?"

"Mmm."

She grinned.

Her hands crept around front. Her knuckles grazed him, and he startled. "Ah, Paige..."

She grasped him then. He was firm and full and very hard. "Ian, you're wonderful." She slid her hand up and down his length. "I want to see you."

"Oh, Paige..."

She leaned in close and nipped his ear. "I want to taste you..."

He gripped her shoulders. "Stop, honey, I can't stand it."

"Oh..." she pouted, "I don't want to stop."

Ultimately, he grabbed her hands. "I think you've turned into Ms. Frankenstein. And her timing is lousy."

"Why?"

"Because when we finally do it, I want hours with you, and it's already late." He glanced at the house. "And I want us to be truly alone, to savor every single minute." Taking both her arms, he wound them around his neck and pulled her close. His mouth was in her hair. "Tomorrow night, Paige. We both have the weekend off. Tell Jade you'll be at my place. Stay through Sunday."

"All right," she said.

CHAPTER TEN

PAIGE PACED OUTSIDE the delivery room of Hyde Point Hospital like an expectant father. She tried to rationalize that it was because the about-to-be-born twins were her new patients, but she didn't fool herself. The fact that the mother of these children was a Serenity House resident was what had brought Paige to the hospital with Ian when he'd gotten the call.

The news about Mary Ellen's imminent delivery had come at seven o'clock tonight, just as Paige had arrived at his house. He'd been called into work today to cover for a sick partner and had seemed tired when she'd gotten there. He was still on the phone as he opened the door. He was frowning. "I understand. I'll be right there."

Paige waited for him to click off.

"Damn it," he said.

"What's the problem?"

He slid bare feet into his Dock-Sides and grabbed the keys from the table. "Mary Ellen is in labor. A month early."

"You said she could call you if she was scared."

"It's more than that. Twin B's heart rate has fallen to sixty beats. Rodney Peters is on call. He's good, but inexperienced. He thinks he should do a C-section, but Mary Ellen and Nora want my opinion."

"We should go."

"We?"

"I'm the pediatrician for the babies, Ian."

He smiled as if she'd pleased him, kissed her hard and they left without further talking; they discussed only the medical implications on the way over. Neither mentioned what this premature birth had interrupted.

That had been an hour ago.

Paige turned as Ian came through the delivery-room door. His face was etched with worry. "Mary Ellen's being prepped for a C-section."

"I'm sure that's the right decision." Fifty percent of all twin births were cesarean.

"I want you in there, Paige. I'm worried about twin B, the boy."

"Could the cords be tangled?"

"No, the babies aren't monoamniotic. There are two sacs. But a decelerated heartbeat can mean a thin umbilical cord. That's always dangerous." He didn't point out that when there were complications, the second twin often didn't make it. Paige prayed with all her heart both babies would be all right.

Twenty minutes later Paige watched Ian deliver two squalling infants. The sight caused her eyes to mist. Twin A, the girl, was nearly five pounds. The boy, who indeed had a pencil-thin umbilical cord, was only three pounds. He was whisked away into the neonatal intensive-care unit.

Nora had remained with Mary Ellen throughout the whole delivery. Just as she had for Paige all those years ago.

PAIGE AWOKE the next morning in Ian's bed. Rolling over, she saw him sprawled out on his stomach, wearing only a pair of black boxers. The morning sun played on his back, and she watched the steady rise and fall of his breathing. Just beyond him, the red dials of his clock winked out 7 a.m. She wanted to wake him, but he was exhausted, and obviously in a deep sleep.

They'd stayed at the hospital until after one. Ian had wanted to keep an eye on Mary Ellen, who was experiencing headaches and back pain from the anesthesia, and had freaked out that twin B—now called Sammy—was in intensive care.

Paige had spent time with the neonatologist who'd been called. She was able to report that Sammy was in an isolette, which would regulate his temperature, and he was on a respirator, which would help him breathe. Overall, he was doing okay, but it took a while to convince his mother.

Paige slid out of bed, smiling at the T-shirt she wore. "At least sleep in my shirt," he'd said last night, yawning from a day that had started at six and had ended more than nineteen hours later. "I'll take it back first thing in the morning."

The room was so much Ian that she took a moment to study it. It was about twenty feet square, with two huge windows, framed in light-colored wood, flanking the bed. The view from them was of the rapidly flowing river. The bed itself had a spindled, curved headboard; its covers consisted of navy checked sheets and pillowcases, and a blue-striped comforter. Very masculine. Very Ian.

Grabbing her shorts, she slipped out of the room to find Scalpel on the porch, staring out of the securely locked screen doors. He barked when he saw her. "Shh, boy, Ian's still asleep." She tugged on her shorts. "Come on, I'll take you out. You seem to be managing your cast very well."

The walk by the river was calm and peaceful. Despite

their hellish night, Paige felt serene. "He's good for me, Scalpel. You know that, don't you?"

Scalpel barked, then nuzzled her hand.

"Even though he is a bully." She glanced down at the dog. "How do you put up with it?"

Damned if the dog didn't toss its head, the canine equivalent of a shrug.

"Yeah, 'cause you love him, huh?"

Well, Paige didn't love Ian, but she'd come to like him and respect him immensely. He'd been a savior last night with Mary Ellen, and he'd been a patient, sexy suitor with her. She couldn't wait to get back to him. This morning was going to be…sumptuous.

I intend to feast, Paige. Soon.

It was nearly eight by the time they returned to Ian's condo. Despite the cast on his leg, Scalpel had pulled at the leash and led her around front to fetch the Sunday paper from the porch. She laughed at his antics. All was right with the world.

Inside, Ian hadn't stirred. She decided to make coffee, have one cup, then wake him up with another. He could sleep more afterward. As she sipped coffee, she sat at his butcher-block table and unfolded the newspaper. Leafing through, she came to the Living section.

Still smiling, she read the title of the feature article, "One Big Happy Family." The *Herald* often did human-interest articles on Sunday morning. Mildly curious, she skimmed the second line. Open adoption—nightmare or lifesaver?

Underneath the quote was a picture. Paige froze. She recognized Elsa first, trim and fit, holding Lynne Chandler's hand. Behind them stood Ian. He dwarfed both women, and the resemblance to Lynne was clear. Next to them were Ian's brother Derek, and his father, Tom. In a separate photo was a woman named Abby Shane.

Paige gripped the paper, crushing its outer edges. She forced herself to read the text.

"The Internet organization, Right to Know, is nearing its one-thousandth match. Its founders are shown above. Theirs is a very open, very happy success story. Lynne Chandler and her birth son, Ian, president and vice president of the organization respectively, spoke candidly with us."

Paige swallowed hard. Scalpel came over and nudged her, but she ignored him and read further. Ian was quoted frequently. "My personal opinion is that all adoptions should be open. Birth mothers suffer their whole lives unnecessarily, haunted by what might have happened to their children...so unnecessary. If I had my way, all adoptees and birth mothers would unite...."

Typical of Ian. No middle ground. So sure he was right. Did he have any idea of the arrogance of that statement? Could he possibly fathom the psyche of the birth mother who had chosen a different path?

For a moment anger welled up inside her. His views were so glib. So presumptuous. She scanned the kitchen. God, she'd had such plans for today. It was supposed to be a whole new beginning. Now she felt cheated. Her insides were a jumbled mass of emotions. She couldn't stay, couldn't climb back in that bed with him... Oh, God!

She got to her feet. As she headed for the door, Scalpel barked. "Shh, boy, don't."

He limped over to her and gently grabbed her wrist in his mouth. She smiled sadly. He was trying to keep her here. "No boy, I have to go. I can't..." Her throat closed up. She tugged her arm free, opened the door and left Ian's house.

IAN ROLLED OVER in bed, groping for Paige. In his half-awake state, he remembered she was here. Besides, he could smell her subtle perfume. But his hand came up empty. He opened his eyes. She was not in bed.

Groaning, he flipped onto his back and searched for the time. Eleven o'clock. Damn, why had she let him sleep so long? By now they should be... The thought propelled him out of bed. His body told him to go find her, and he left the room. The smell of coffee hit him as he entered the kitchen.

Scalpel, asleep in a patch of sunlight on the porch floor, heard him, leaped up and barked. "Where is she, boy?" he asked when Scalpel came over and nuzzled him. The dog whimpered. Ian checked his cast. It seemed okay.

"Where's Paige, buddy?"

Scalpel limped to the front door and barked. She was out front? Why? He opened the door. What the hell? Her car was gone.

Slowly shutting the door, Ian faced the dog. Scalpel trotted into the kitchen and barked again. Following him, Ian saw that the paper was open and a cup of coffee sat next to it. He put his hand on the cup. It was stone cold. He glanced down at the paper. Facing up was the article about his family and RTK. Was there something in the report that could have upset Paige? He skimmed it, remembering the day the photo had been taken. He'd just finished his residency, and they were all celebrating. Gently he circled the picture of his mother with his finger. Then the one of his dad. God, sometimes he missed them so much!

Okay, Paige had seen the article. No big deal. True, he hadn't told her about his work in RTK, but there were a lot of things they didn't know about each other.

He grabbed for the phone and punched out her home number. "This is Paige Kendrick. Leave a message." Was she there and not answering? Where was Jade? "Paige, honey, it's Ian. Pick up if you're there." Still no answer.

He decided to try her cell phone. Then he realized he didn't have her number. Damn it, they were going to make love today and he didn't even have her cell-phone number. Anger warred with concern. He stood. He'd shower, stop in at the hospital to see Mary Ellen, then go over to her house. She'd have to go home sooner or later.

Twenty minutes later he reached the hospital. Mary Ellen greeted him with a weak smile. "Hi, Dr. Chandler."

"Hello, Mom." He smiled. "I saw Sammy. He looks good."

"He has to stay here in that little bed." Her eyes teared. "I went down to see him. He's got all those wires on him and a tube in his nose."

"The heart monitor, the feeding tube and the respirator. To help him eat and breathe better."

"They said he's got apnea. You know, where he stops breathing sometimes. Dr. Kendrick explained it to me."

Ian stilled, staring down at the chart. "Oh, really. She was here?" Now his temper collided with his worry.

"Yes."

"Sorry I missed her." Mary Ellen didn't know *how* sorry. "Did she make you feel better about all this?"

"Yeah. But I get to breast-feed Suzy and not him. It's not right."

"Maybe it won't last long."

"I hope not."

After some more convincing, Ian casually asked, "How long ago was Dr. Kendrick here?"

"A couple of hours ago, I think." Mary Ellen frowned. "She looked, I don't know...upset. Said she'd be back later."

Ian spent some more time with Mary Ellen, made notes on her chart, checked the baby in NICU just for his own peace of mind and was in his car, headed toward Paige's house by noon. On the way there, he was once again torn—angry about her leaving him but hoping she was all right. What on earth could have driven her away when he knew damned well she'd wanted to make love with him? And why had she looked upset when she went to see Mary Ellen?

Jade's snazzy Lexus was in the driveway, but not Paige's car, though it could be in the garage. He pulled in behind the vehicle and took the stairs two at a time. Jade opened the door dressed in church clothes.

"Ian?" Her pretty green eyes widened. "What are you doing here?" Her face became terror-stricken. "Oh, no, something's happened to Paige."

"No, no, Jade. Paige left my house early this morning while I was still asleep. I'm sure she's all right. I just can't find her."

The woman sagged like a rag doll. Ian wondered about the reaction. "Come on in." She led him through the foyer into the kitchen. He realized he'd never been in the front part of Paige's house. Its foyer entrance and the soaring ceilings were impressive. Wood and glass were everywhere.

In the kitchen Jade turned to him. "That explains the message she left here."

"Message?" A lump the size of a fist formed in his throat.

She nodded at the phone.

"May I hear it?" he asked through gritted teeth. She'd left her sister a message, but not him.

"Sure." She hit the playback button.

Paige's somewhat husky voice came on. "Jade, it's me. I won't be home for a while. Something's come up. I'll be checking in with my service, but if there's an emergency, call me on my cell. Otherwise, I need some space."

"Son of a bitch."

"I thought it odd. I knew she was with you."

"Yeah, well, she played the disappearing act this morning."

Folding her arms over her chest, Jade cocked her head. "I don't mean to pry, but did something go wrong last night? I know she was dying to…um, looking forward to…being with you."

Ian ran a hand through his hair. "Yeah, well, I thought so, too." He filled her in on Mary Ellen's emergency. "We were exhausted by the time we got home at three. We, um…" Jeez, he was embarrassed. "We decided to get some sleep. When I woke up, she was gone."

Jade shook her head. "Paige is a complicated woman. I worry about her."

"Can you tell me why?"

"Come and sit outside with me. Jewel just went down for her nap." She led him through the kitchen to the outside, stopping to pour them both some coffee. It was another beautiful day with hot sunshine and a pristine sky. He should have been in bed with Paige. Where *was* she?

Once they were seated, Jade didn't mince words. "We had a very hard childhood, Ian."

"I know she raised you."

"From the time I was born."

Ian scowled. "I thought you were fourteen when your parents died."

"I was. But they were more like kids than we were. Paige was always the mother." Jade frowned. "I remember once when I was seven and she was ten, I had a doctor's appointment at the clinic. My parents were off somewhere. Paige took me on the bus."

"Damn. That's why she's so responsible."

"That's why she's so everything. Serious. Diligent. Ambitious. I can't tell you how hard she worked to make her way through college and med school."

Ian stared out over the pool. The water was still and very blue. He remembered their late-night swims, the promises they'd made.

"Did anything happen between you two to send her running?"

He shook his head. "Far as I can tell, she woke up early, took Scalpel out for a walk and made coffee when she came back." He scowled. "The newspaper was open to an article about me and my family, but I can't fathom what could be in there that would spook her."

Jade sipped her coffee. "What was the article about?"

He told her about RTK and his mother and birth mother.

As she listened, Jade's rosy complexion drained of color.

"What is it?"

"I…" She sighed deeply. "I can't tell you, Ian. Paige will have to do that."

"Jade, I'm worried about her. I need to know what drove her away."

"Still, it's not my place to tell. I just can't."

Frustrated by both Kendrick women, he stood. "Fine." He scanned the pool area. "If she comes home, ask her to call me—if it's not too much trouble—and let me know she's okay." He shook his head disgustedly. "She can leave me a message."

Jade rose, too. "Don't be too hard on her, Ian. You don't know the kind of life she's led."

"That's just the problem. I *don't* know." He was halfway to the pool gate when the doors to the kitchen slid open.

He turned to find Paige standing in the doorway.

She looked like hell. Her clothes—the T-shirt he'd insisted she wear last night and her shorts—were wrinkled. Her hair was a mess. But it was her face that got to him.

If he'd ever seen anybody who'd been wrestling with demons, it was Paige Kendrick. His immediate reaction was to go to her, but he held himself back. She'd been pulling away from him since day one of their relationship, and now he needed her to make the first move.

Circling her waist, Paige said, "Hello, Ian."

He folded his arms over his chest, but said nothing.

"I, um, just stopped at your condo."

"How nice."

She raised her chin. "You're angry."

"Yeah, angry. And frustrated. And hurt, Paige."

She glanced at her sister. Something wordless passed between them. "I'll go check on Jewel," Jade said.

Ian shook his head. "Don't bother. I'm leaving."

"No." Paige looked…frightened. "Ian, don't leave. I want to talk to you."

"Well, you know what, Paige? For once, I don't want

to talk to you. I *worried* about you for hours this morning. Now that I know you're all right, I'm out of here.'' He pivoted and strode toward the gate.

She raced after him, reaching him just as he was about to open the gate. She grabbed his arm. ''Ian, wait. Please, don't go.''

His back to her, his fists clenched, he looked up at the sky. ''I'm going, Paige. And this time I won't be back.''

''Don't say that.''

He whirled around. ''Look, lady, I don't know what making love means to you, but it means a hell of a lot to me. You left my bed without a word. You called your sister, not me. You went to see a patient—which is about the only part of this I understand. In any case, my place in your life is very clear. And it's not enough. I won't be an afterthought to you.''

''You're not, Ian. Please, give me a chance to explain.''

''No. I've given you plenty of chances.'' He grabbed the latch and threw it back. ''I can't do this anymore.'' With that, he walked out.

TWO HOURS LATER, Paige stood on the porch of Ian's condo, dressed in a purple-and-pink-flowered jumpsuit. Taking a calming breath, she willed her hands to stop shaking. She bit her lip, remembering his visit.

''If you let him go,'' Jade had said, ''you're crazy.''

And then Paige had done something she hadn't done since her parents died. She burst into tears.

Jade had comforted her. She'd held Paige and stroked her hair while she cried. Then Jade had taken her by the shoulders and given her a firm shake. ''You've got a decision to make, Paige. You've got to let him in. He's tired of coaxing you. Waiting for you to open up.''

"I know. I'd already decided to tell him everything about my past. But now it's too late."

"It's never too late when a man cares about you."

Paige had just shaken her head.

"But you're going to have to fight for him."

"It's too late."

"Nah. Let's go fix you up with some ammunition."

Reluctantly Paige had let Jade run a bath for her and help her dress. Though she felt a little better—Jade's pep talk and fussing had given her courage—she lost her nerve when she arrived at Ian's condo.

Remembering the conclusions she'd come to this morning, she rang the bell. No answer. Damn. Maybe he was by the river with Scalpel. She saw a path leading around back. Slowly she made her way down it.

They weren't at the river. Both Ian and Scalpel were on the porch. Ian must have ignored the doorbell. He lazed in a recliner, watching a ball game on TV. In his hand, he held a bottle of beer, which he sipped occasionally. Scalpel sat at his side.

Paige knocked.

Ian looked up. When he saw her, his whole body stiffened, but he said nothing.

Scalpel stood and barked.

"Don't suppose you could let me in, huh, buddy?"

The dog barked again, then nudged Ian's hand.

"Sit, boy," Ian said. "She's not coming in."

Scalpel sat.

"Ian, please, this is silly."

Still, no answer.

"Please, Ian. Just give me ten minutes."

He actually glanced at his watch, the creep. Rising, he set down his beer, crossed to the door and unlatched the new hook and eye he'd put up high, relatching it when she stepped inside. He crossed back to the chair, sank down and stared at the TV. "I don't want you here, Paige."

Determined, she strode across the room and picked up the remote. She flicked off the TV. "Well, considering how many times the reverse has been true, you owe me."

He seemed surprised. Good. She knew she wasn't going to get him back by being a doormat.

For the first time he really looked at her. His eyes narrowed. "Jade's clothes aren't going to help."

"Actually this outfit's mine."

"Not quite Ms. All Business's style."

"It used to be. I used to dress a lot differently."

He arched a brow.

Clasping her hands behind her back, she focused on her mission. "I went up to Nora and Dan's cottage this morning. I sat on the dock and thought about things."

He was weakening, she could tell. Though he checked his watch again and said, "Eight minutes," there was concern in his eyes.

"I was looking forward to making love with you today. I decided to have one cup of coffee, then wake you up."

He cocked his head. The concern in his eyes turned to warmth.

"I read the article in the paper about you and your family. Your organization."

"I gathered that. Though I can't for the life of me see why that would throw you into such a fit."

"No, you wouldn't. Because I've withheld from you."

"Lady, that's the understatement of the year. I know almost nothing about you. I didn't even have your goddamned cell-phone number."

The hurt on his face gave her the strength to go on. "I'm sorry."

"My mother used to say that sometimes sorry isn't enough."

"Maybe an explanation will be." Taking a deep breath, she crossed to the screen and stared out at the river. After a long moment, her back to him, she said, "I grew up in a dysfunctional home. My parents were hippies—still living in the sixties. They never supervised us, let Jade and me run wild." She wrapped her arms around her waist. "They were heavily into drugs. We practically raised ourselves."

"That must have been hard."

"It was. When I was seventeen, they got busted and were forced to go into rehab in Pennsylvania."

"What happened to you and Jade?" he asked from where he sat.

She drew another deep breath. She had never shared her past with anyone. "We went to live at the newly built Serenity House."

"Paige. I didn't know."

"It was only supposed to be temporary. My parents were going to be in rehab for sixty days. When they got out, Jade and I were going home." She paused. "The day they were released, they made a pit stop at their dealer's. Then, high as kites, they climbed on their motorcycle and sped off. They crashed going eighty miles an hour on a dirt road. Thankfully, they died instantly."

She heard him move to stand behind her, felt him clasp her arms. "I'm so sorry. You must have been devastated."

"I was. So was Jade. But there's..." She had to face him to tell him this. She pivoted.

He took one look at her face and rubbed her arms.

"There was another issue. I was...I was pregnant when I went to Serenity House." She shook her head, stared over his shoulder. She could still see her laughing mother's beautiful face. "When I found out I was going to have a child, my parents were delighted. They said I could keep the baby. That the father could live with us. They had that commune-culture mentality. But it never happened that way."

"I'm so sorry. What did you do?"

"Both Jade and I stayed at Serenity House, and the baby was born there." She shook her head. "Literally. Dan Whitman delivered her. A month early." She sighed. "On April sixth. Do you know what day that is?"

"No."

"It was the day you asked me to be part of the Center. For girls...like I'd been."

"Oh, honey. If I'd known..."

"I gave her up for adoption."

A light dawned in his eyes. "This morning, when you saw the article..."

"I freaked. It had been building, anyway."

"Of course it had. Working at the Center. Finding out I was adopted...meeting Lynne." He shook his head. "I'm so sorry I didn't know. I wouldn't have pushed you so hard to join the Center."

"No, it's all right. I'm glad I'm at the Center. I'm fine about the adoption, Ian. It was the right thing to do. Really, I'm adjusted."

"Was it a closed adoption?"

"Of course. I didn't want to know about it. I didn't even know if the baby was a boy or girl until Darcy let it slip when we were talking about my working at the Center."

"Darcy?"

"She spent a few months at Serenity House, too."

He hugged her close. Kissed her hair. "I'm so sorry. All this with the Center, with RTK...it must kill you."

She drew back. "No. No, it doesn't. I'm all right. It's just that the article threw me. I...I don't know, it just was too much to take in."

"I can understand that."

"But I thought a lot about everything this morning. Trust. Intimacy." She raised her hand to his face. "You. I know I have to trust you. I'm sorry I couldn't tell you this morning, but I'm very cautious, Ian. I had to think it through. Sitting on the dock, I realized I was tired of being alone. Of cutting everybody out. Jade and her situation had already brought that home to me. The article just gave me the final push."

"It must have hurt. That she kept her baby and you didn't."

"No, not that. But her secrecy did. That she could think I'd condemn her because of what she did."

"Paige, you can admit you hurt about giving up your child."

"I don't, Ian. For me, it was the right thing to do. And it's all in the past."

"Still—"

Her hands went to his mouth. "Shh. Please, let's not get into that." She leaned in closer. "I want to make love. I want to start to build this relationship. With trust." She smiled. "With you, Ian."

"Ah, Paige." He raised his hands to her hair. "That's one of the best things I've ever heard in my life." He kissed her softly. His lips went lower and grazed the skin above the strapless top. "I lied earlier."

"About what?"

"This outfit. It does help." He tugged on the material with his teeth. "You look good enough to eat."

She smiled. "I think it's time for that feast, Ian. Please, take me to bed."

He swept her up into his arms.

Scalpel barked as they left the room.

"What did he say?" she whispered against Ian's chest.

"He said, *Bon appetit.*"

WHEN HE REACHED the bedroom, Ian was forced to set Paige on her feet. His hands were shaking badly. What she'd told him had affected him deeply and made him care even more for the complicated, desirable woman in his arms. Gently grasping her shoulders, he leaned down and touched her forehead with his. "Paige," he whispered softly.

She entwined her arms around his neck and aligned her body with his. "Ian."

"I…" He cleared his throat. "I feel so much for you."

"So do I. For you."

Pulling in a breath, he drew back slightly. Her blue eyes were smoky with desire. Yet shadowing that need was a defenselessness that humbled him and gave him the courage to say, "Making love with you is important to me, honey. What if feel is beyond anything I've felt ever before."

She grasped his hand, kissed it. "For me, too, Ian. I'm shaking inside."

It took him a couple of tries to unfasten the snap at the back of her jumpsuit. He swore. She giggled.

He struggled for equilibrium. Slowly he slid the top of the suit to her waist. Her strapless lacy half-bra was a delicate pink. When his knuckles grazed the exposed tops of her breasts and raised tiny pinpricks of gooseflesh, she closed her eyes. Sighed. Moaned. Her pleasure was intoxicating. He unhooked the front closure and she spilled into his hands. He caressed her, cradled her, then leaned over and took a breast into his mouth.

"Oh, Ian..." she murmured.

Kneeling, he removed the rest of her clothes, buried his face in her stomach for a few moments, then kissed his way up her body.

Her fingers went to his shirt and disposed of it. "I love your chest," she said. Then with purposeful intent, she ran her fingers lightly over his abdomen. Slowly and seductively, as if she was savoring every moment, she loosened his belt, released the snap and lowered the zipper of his shorts. When she went down on her knees, his body ricocheted at her bold caresses. "Mmm, Ian," she whispered against his erection, "you taste so—"

He pulled her up fiercely. "I'm gonna lose control, baby," he said as he held her tightly, willing his heart to stop racing. When it finally did, he lifted her onto the bed. He fumbled in the nightstand, made quick work of putting on a condom, then covered her body with his. He brushed her cheek with his fingertips.

"More, Ian," she said raggedly.

"Mmm. Much more." He nibbled on her chin. His tongue trailed along her jaw. His mouth found her breasts, suckled there again.

Sliding his hand down the front of her body, his fingers tangled in her curls. When he found her wet and hot, he inhaled deeply. "I love how you respond. To me."

Paige opened her heart to Ian's words and her body to the insistent probing of his fingers. He rubbed his knuckles against her, and she cried out with the staggering pleasure of the touch. He soothed her with his lips against her cheek. "Let me."

Let him? She was nearly incoherent with desire, and couldn't have stopped him if she... Oh, God, his fingers...

"Ian! Ah, Ian..."

But still he prolonged the caress. He kissed her gently, calming her. Once she relaxed, he became insistent again, exploring her, exciting her.

She grew dizzy with the climb, going higher and higher. Her breath caught as if she was scaling a mountain. Unsure of her footing, she gasped, grabbed on to him. His shoulders were slick with sweat, and the rasp she heard was the rapid escalation of his breathing.

"Now, honey." The words were barely audible. "I have about a minute of sanity left."

"Yes. Now, Ian..."

His entry was strong, sure and powerful. Yet once he was inside her, the groan of satisfaction, the undiluted joy of his possession, turned everything tender again. "This is it, Paige. This is the feast." He kissed her tenderly. "This is exactly what I wanted."

"I want it, too." She did. Though somewhere inside her, she was devastated by what the joining of their bodies meant to her. It left her totally disarmed and exposed, and gave him a control over her that no man had ever had.

Then he began to move.

"Ah..." he groaned.

Thrust.

"Damn it..." he said.

And when he plunged deeper, pushed harder, with unrelenting force and alarming tenderness, she didn't think, didn't hear and couldn't speak for the emotion—and exquisite sensations—that overtook her.

CHAPTER ELEVEN

IAN HAD TO GET a grip. His hold on reality, his professionalism, his sanity, for God's sake, had been slowly eroding all week. And all because of the woman who now entered the hospital room with the brisk efficiency of an OR nurse. "Good morning, Mary Ellen." Paige glanced at Ian without a whit of reaction. "Dr. Chandler."

He nodded. "Dr. Kendrick."

She turned to Mary Ellen, who packed the last of her bag. The girl's shoulders slumped in her denim maternity jumper. As she folded the clothes, her hands were unsteady. She and Suzy were being discharged today. Sammy would have to stay in the hospital a while longer because of his breathing problems.

Ian watched as Paige gave some instructions about the babies. She was Dr. Straitlaced today, wrapped up in her white coat, out of which peeked a summer skirt and matching top the color of daffodils. He knew she wore yellow undies beneath...

Mmm, beautiful, he'd said when he slipped the silk panties on her this morning.

Ian, I can dress myself.

He picked up the bra. *Why would you want to when you have me to do it?*

Later, when she was fully clothed, she went into the

bathroom to tie her hair in a knot at her neck. *Aw, that ought to be illegal.*

She'd looked up. *Spare me.* But there was no sting in her words. And her eyes had glimmered with pleasure.

I'm just going to take it down again tonight....

She'd given him that smile, and he was almost unable to resist telling her he loved her.

He *did* love her, he thought as he watched her gently instruct Mary Ellen on how to care for Suzy's navel. But Ian was afraid to tell Paige how he felt, afraid it was too much, too soon, and he'd scare her with any declaration.

She was facing him. "Any last-minute instructions, Dr. Chandler?" she asked, giving him a where-*are*-you look.

"Already gave them," he said, snapping shut the chart. He eyed Mary Ellen carefully. "Nervous about taking Suzy home?"

Mary Ellen nodded. "A little. I feel worse about leaving Sammy here." Her eyes clouded. Uh-oh. Postpartum hormones were marching front and center.

"We'll take good care of him." Paige sounded confident. "Look at the bright side. You can concentrate on one baby at a time for a few days." Still the girl looked unconvinced. "You'll be visiting Sammy here."

"I guess."

He and Paige exchanged a worried glance.

"Will your mother watch Suzy while you come to the hospital to see Sammy?" Ian asked.

"I...I think so."

"Well," Ian put in smoothly, "give Nora a call if she can't."

"No, she's getting ready for her wedding next week."

"Nora would love to watch Suzy for a bit, Mary Ellen," Paige said. "And it's important that you get to bond with Sammy. You can—"

The door burst open and a woman bustled in. Dressed in spandex black pants, a tight red top and stiletto sandals, the woman had flame-red hair that fell in waves down her back.

"Hi, Ma."

Ma? Oh, great. Was Mary Ellen's mother even over thirty?

"Hi, kid. Listen, Johnny's double-parked outside, so let's get the lead out."

"Ma, don't you want to see Suzy?"

Ian couldn't help himself. "You haven't seen your grandchildren, Mrs. Barone?"

The woman turned frosty eyes on him. Until she got a good look at him. Then her gaze warmed considerably. "Well, hello."

"Hello. I'm Ian Chandler, your daughter's doctor."

Painted lips parted. "You're her gyno?"

"Yes." He crossed to the crib. "And this is Suzanne."

The woman spared the baby a glance. "Only one of 'em's comin' home, right?"

"Yes, Ma. Sammy's too little to leave the hospital."

Mrs. Barone darted a look at the clock and caught a glimpse of Paige.

"I'm Paige Kendrick, the babies' doctor."

"This one isn't sick or nothin', is she?"

Paige folded her arms over her chest. "Suzy's perfect, though a little on the small side. Sammy's got a ways to go. He's having some breathing problems, but that's common in premature babies."

"Oh, sure. Good." Lena Barone turned to her daughter, who peered up at Paige and Ian apologetically. "Let's go, kid," the woman said.

"Did you get the baby seats?"

"The what?"

"The baby seats from Serenity House. The ones the girls gave me. We need a car seat for Suzy, Ma."

"Oh." She glanced at Ian, then Paige. "We'll get it on the way home. Now move. Johnny gets mad if he has to wait."

Ian stepped forward. "I'm afraid you can't do that. Hospital policy says you can't leave without a car seat."

At Mary Ellen's stricken look, Paige said, "I'll call the desk. They may have one you can borrow." She went to the phone and dialed, then faced the Barones. Lena Barone tapped her foot impatiently. Mary Ellen blushed with embarrassment.

"All set," Paige said a few seconds later. "Stop at the desk. It will be ready for you."

After the three left, Ian said, "She forgot the baby seat."

Staring at the door, Paige nodded. "Yeah. Some grandmother." Her voice was raw.

"Paige?"

She didn't move. Instead, she seemed transfixed by the door. He crossed the room and circled around her. Her eyes were wide. And her shoulders were rigid.

"Paige, what is it?"

"We can't do much about this, can we?" she said.

"No. Just take good care of Sammy and keep an eye on the situation."

"Could we call Social Services?"

"Not for a forgotten car seat, honey."

She sighed and murmured, "I hope Mary Ellen knows what she's doing, keeping her children."

He knew he shouldn't push. She'd made it clear several times this week that she resented his probing...

They'd been lying spoon-fashion in bed. "Tell me how

you feel about giving up your child, Paige," he'd asked, and felt her stiffen.

"I already did, Ian. Don't press me on that. I made the right choice for both of us."

"Do you ever wonder about her?"

"Ian, please. I won't stand for your bullying in this area."

He'd nuzzled her neck and wisely shut up. But not long after they'd fallen asleep, Paige stirred and mumbled something he couldn't make out. "Paige, baby, what is it?"

"Ronny?" she asked.

"Oh, great. Three nights together, and you think I'm somebody else."

She jerked awake and stared at him. "I was dreaming."

"Tell me about it."

She'd kissed him, instead. Hard. Her lovemaking had been frantic. It had taken his breath away...

"Ian, did you hear me?"

Wiggling his brows dramatically, he said, "I was thinking about the hot sex we had last night."

She rolled her eyes. "You have a one-track mind."

"*I* have a big appetite."

"That I know."

"And like?"

She gave him that smile again. "And like. However, this is neither the place nor the time to talk about it."

"I'm done at one today."

"I'm done at two."

"Wanna go golfing? We can ask Jade." He knew she felt bad about leaving Jade alone so much. "Jewel can ride in the cart."

Her eyes softened. "You are so thoughtful, Ian."

"Hey, that's me. Dr. Warm and Fuzzy."

They exited the room and agreed to meet at the country club at three.

He indicated the right hallway. "I'm headed this way."

"I need to go to NICU."

"All right. See you later." He wanted to kiss her. Right now. He didn't care how it looked. But he held himself in check, out of deference to her rather Victorian sense of propriety and headed down the hall.

"Ian?"

He turned back. "Mmm?"

"I…"

Love you. Say you love me.

"Thanks."

"For?"

"Being you."

Well, maybe that was enough…for now. He smiled and whistled his way down the hall.

HEAD DOWN, feet spread, shoulder angled in, Paige drew back the driver, swung it down and whacked the ball. It soared over the driving range, hitting the 160-yard marker. Not bad. She fished out another ball and set it on the tee. Looking behind her, she scanned the area for Jade, who'd said she'd meet Paige and Ian here after her own lunch with Darcy. Jewel had wanted to stay with Meli and Claire, so it would be just the three of them.

Paige had been gone most of the week, working at her office or the Center during the day, then spending the nights at Ian's. She hadn't been able to resist Ian's coaxing to stay with him…

What do you mean, you're going home?

I stayed last night, Ian.

He'd nibbled her neck, then turned her to face him. *I want to sleep with you.*

We just had sex.

We just had an orgy. I meant sleep, literally.

Why?

That's what lovers do, honey.

All right, I'll call Jade.

Her sister hadn't seemed bothered by Paige's absence. Jade had been kept busy with her daughter and seemed to be forming a close friendship with Darcy. She'd also mentioned meeting up with an old English teacher, one of the few on staff who'd liked her.

In any case, the process of staying overnight with Ian had been repeated every night this week. It scared Paige, thinking how much power he had over her.

She turned back to the tee. Hitting the next ball—it went a few yards farther—she tried to squelch her worry.

He'd asked her four times to talk about the adoption. She'd counted. Three times she told him gently it wasn't an issue for her now and she didn't want to talk about it. The fourth time, she'd gotten piqued. They'd been walking Scalpel by the water...

"You had another nightmare last night."

"I don't remember."

"You called for her."

"Her? Did I say who?"

"A baby."

"Oh, it was probably Jewel. I miss seeing her. I talked to her on the phone last night."

He'd stopped in his tracks. "It wasn't Jewel, honey."

Automatically Paige had closed down. "Ian, don't start. I'm beginning to wish I hadn't told you about the whole thing. You're making too much of it."

His face hardened. Gone was the teasing lover. "I

didn't make up the nightmares, Paige. Do you have them often?''

''No, actually, just since I started sleeping with you.''

''Which happens to coincide with the birth of Mary Ellen's twins. That should tell you something.''

Exasperated, she threw the ball for Scalpel. Then she turned on Ian. Literally. ''Maybe it tells me that I should be sleeping alone.''

''Is that how you're going to deal with all this? By striking out at me? By shutting me out?''

She swallowed hard. He'd stood before her, looking like some Greek god in white shorts and white shirt. She'd actually thought about telling him yes, she wanted to shut him out. That she didn't want to work at the Center anymore because it was stirring up all sorts of things inside her.

But the truth was she didn't want to shut him out in any way. She wanted to throw herself into his arms and let him make everything all right.

That thought had frightened her even more. Long ago she stopped believing a man could make her life complete. But still, she couldn't let Ian go. So she said reasonably, ''I'm sorry if I struck out at you. I don't want to shut you out. But you make it hard not to. You've got to stop pushing me to look at things like you do.''

He'd recognized her concession. He'd approached her and picked up her hand. ''All right. I'm a bulldozer. I don't want to drive you away. I'm sorry...''

Paige hit another ball and reached two hundred yards.

''Hey, lady, you could give Nancy Lopez competition.'' She turned to find Ian striding up to her. He'd changed into tan shorts and a striped tan-and-white shirt. On his head he wore a baseball cap. He looked fit and healthy and very male. She was hit by a sudden jolt of desire. When he neared her, he stopped and cocked his head. "Don't look at me like that, Paige."

"Like what?"

"You know damn well what, Little Ms. Flirt." He eyed her short white skirt and red spandex top. "Bad enough I have to look and not touch the rest of the day."

"Not touch?" she said, enjoying the byplay. "I don't think so." She turned and faced the range. "I'm having trouble with my swing. I think my stance needs adjusting, but I can't get it right."

He was behind her in a second. Big solid hands gripped her hips. "Well, let me help."

She looked over her shoulder. "I was hoping you'd say that."

"Always here to lend a hand," he said, positioning her hips and not letting go. "This ought to take care of that slice." She'd swung perfectly straight.

"Oh, good."

He ran his palms up and down her hips. "Mmm. Very good."

THEY'D JUST FINISHED dinner, and dusk had fallen. At a table for three, Jade laughed throatily, drawing the attention of the golfers next to them on the deck of Hyde Point Country Club. Ian acknowledged their attention with a smile. Though he only had eyes for one of the Kendrick women, he could appreciate the other's attractiveness. "She's a pistol," Jade finished. "The preschool teacher was never the same after that. I think she was relieved we moved from the city."

"Why did you move?" Ian asked, stretching his legs out in front of him.

Paige tensed.

Briefly Jade looked away. "I wanted to come home.

After Jewel's father died, it didn't seem necessary to stay in New York.''

''I'm sorry you lost your husband. How did he die?''

''A heart attack.''

Paige stood. ''Excuse me, I need to use the ladies' room.''

That was odd, Ian thought. She'd just gotten back from there.

While Paige was gone, Ian asked Jade a few more questions about her life in New York, and then Jade changed the subject. ''So, things okay between you and my sister, Ian?''

''Better than okay. She told me everything, Jade.''

Pretty green eyes darkened. *''Everything?''*

He wondered at the odd note of tension in her voice. ''About how you grew up. About her pregnancy.'' He sighed. ''Does she ever talk about it?''

Jade seemed to relax. ''She won't.''

''That's not healthy.''

''It's a bridge you can't cross with Paige, Ian. I've tried.''

''Still, she should let it out.''

''I don't think you should push her on this. Be grateful you've gotten as far as you have. She's never been as open with any man in her whole life. Not even Ronny.''

Ronny. The dream. ''Ronny?''

''I don't like being discussed when I'm not here.''

Jade's head whipped around and Ian looked up. There was a storm brewing in Paige's eyes.

''I'm sorry,'' Jade said. ''We didn't mean anything by it.''

Paige seared Ian with a doubtful glare. ''Don't pump my sister about my past, Ian.''

''I didn't realize I was. Or that I had to, for that matter.

I thought you and I cleared the air on all this." He gave her a measured gaze, intended to remind her of that night when she'd come to him and promised to be open with him.

It took the wind out of her sails. "Sorry. I'm just touchy about my past."

The air crackled with the tension between them.

Finally Jade said, "So, how you gonna live without her for three days next week, Ian?"

"Live without her?"

Jade looked at Paige apologetically. Damn, Ian thought. Where did all these secrets come from?

Drawing in a breath, Paige turned to him. "I was going to tell you tonight. The six original residents of Serenity House are coming home for Nora's wedding. She asked us to spend a few days at the cottage with her. She wants all of us together again."

Ian frowned. Not because she hadn't told him. He wondered how that reunion would affect Paige.

"Look, I'm sorry I didn't tell you about it."

He reached over and grasped her hand, thinking about those three days for her. "It's all right. I'm just going to miss you."

"You can come up to the lake," Jade suggested. "Taylor's husband is sure to make an appearance. Darcy says Nick Morelli is so smitten with his wife that he'll never leave her be for three days." She smiled. "Come on up, Ian. Paige can sneak out to meet you in the boat-house. It'd be so romantic."

Ian looked away.

Paige said, "Yeah, that's a great idea. Your parents' cottage is only down the road, Ian. You can..." She trailed off when he stood abruptly.

"I'm, um, going down to the bag room. I forgot to ask the kid to clean my clubs for me."

He made it to the lower deck before she caught up with him. They were shadowed by the overhang from the upper deck. "Ian, wait." He stopped. She grasped his arm. "What's wrong?"

"Nothing."

"Ian…"

"You shouldn't leave Jade alone."

"She left. She has to pick up Jewel at Darcy's." Paige pulled him around to face her. "Ian, *are* you angry I didn't tell you about the lake?"

He shook his head.

"What is it, then?"

He blew out a breath and peered up at the darkening sky. "It's stupid."

"Tell me."

"I haven't been to my parents' cottage since they died. We didn't open it last summer because it was too painful. Derek wanted me to help him get the place ready for this summer, but I chickened out."

She leaned into him so her breast grazed his biceps. "Oh, Ian, I'm sorry. I know it must be hard."

"I'm a grown man. I should be stronger by now."

"You can't be strong about everything. I think you're a puppy where your family is concerned."

He shrugged. Looked down at her. "And with you."

She smiled. "Then let me help."

"How?"

"Maybe you should get this over with. Bite the bullet, so to speak. Go up to the cottage and face the ghosts."

"Derek said the same thing. But I couldn't, so he opened it alone."

"Then it's ready for use?"

"Uh-huh."

"Hmm. How about if we go up together? Just you and me."

"When you go for the Serenity House thing?"

"No, tomorrow. We're not working in the morning. We could leave early. It's only an hour's drive. We'd be back by one."

"Tomorrow?" So soon? No, that wasn't good. "I don't think so."

"I do. I think it's best for you."

He gave her a narrow-eyed look. "You trying to bully me into this, lady?"

"Maybe."

He stared out at the darkened golf course, and remembered his father teaching him to swing a club. *You're a natural, Ian. In golf and everything else.*

His mother had laughed from the cart and said his father was spoiling him. The memory was bittersweet. Could he face remembering all the wonderful times they'd had at the lake?

"Just think, Ian. If you *don't* do this, you won't get to see me for three days."

"Oh, God. I'll *starve.*"

"But if we go tomorrow, get this over with, you can come up to Dan's cottage. For a snack." She leaned in closer. "I kinda like the idea. We could make love in the boathouse if you prefer not to go back to your parents' place." She ran her hand up his arm. "Or there's this big oak tree way in the back with a huge tree house. We could sneak out there."

The pressure inside him eased a bit. He could do this, he guessed. With her. "You're pretty good at bribery. And at coercion."

"Really?" she said innocently. "I guess that comes from having a good teacher."

IAN DROVE to Keuka Lake the next morning with Paige next to him, and Scalpel in the rumble seat. The top was down on the Corvette, and her hair flew in her face, as did his. The morning was already muggy with July sultriness. Glancing at her, he noted her denim shorts and pink halter top. He wore denims, too. "You look cute," he said.

She took off her sunglasses. "Why, thank you, sir."

She was trying to keep things light, he knew. "Thanks for coming."

Gently she took his hand in hers, cradled it for a moment, then kissed it. "You're welcome."

Once again—as when Scalpel had been hurt—he was glad she didn't offer platitudes. This trip was going to be hell, opening up this not-quite-healed wound, and they both knew it.

He wished she'd relax, maybe doze off on the drive up. She'd had another nightmare last night—the third since they'd been sleeping together. It involved finding a car seat. After today, he was going to have to deal with the whole issue.

The atmosphere was companionable with some soft background jazz as they drove along the expressway, then turned off and headed toward the lake.

"I love these side roads," she said. "They're such a challenge."

"Mom used to rail at Derek and me as teenagers about going too fast on them. She took my car away for a whole month one summer when the cops stopped me for speeding."

"She was no cream puff," Paige said. "I remember

once when a student cockily informed her that his paper had been unfairly judged and he wanted another opinion.''

He could just picture his five-foot mother turning into Attila the Hun. "What did she do?"

"She got several opinions." Paige was smirking.

"Let me guess. All of them were lower."

"Yeah. She rode him hard all semester after that."

"What happened to him?"

Paige smiled. "He became the head of pediatrics at Boston Medical School just last year. I saw it in a journal. He's reputedly one of the best teachers around. Kids say how *fair* he is."

Ian slowed for a turn. "Mom influenced a lot of lives," he said.

"I know she did mine."

He darted a glance at her. "Tell me more about that."

"One big thing was how she fought for scholarships for me after that first year I worked for her. I had no loans to pay back when I finished med school because of her efforts."

"And your brains, honey."

"She also set it up for me to shadow specialists. I learned a lot from them. She helped me to get published in medical journals, too, my senior year." Paige smiled fondly. "But mostly she taught by example how to love and heal kids."

By the time they pulled into the driveway behind the cottage, Paige had told him many wonderful things about his mother.

Through the windshield, Ian stared at the home Elsa had made with his father. The drive had been newly paved. He stared at the tarred surface.

"Ian?"

"Sorry. I was just thinking about the spring Derek and I blacktopped this driveway. We complained like holy hell, but she made us do it, anyway. Then she brought us breakfast in bed the next morning." He looked up at the gray-sided house. Its black shutters sparkled like onyx in the early morning sun.

Paige reached over and took his hand again. "Want to talk some more before we go in?"

Scalpel, recognizing the cottage, began to bark excitedly. "Shh, boy, you'll wake up the neighbors." Ian leaned around and let the dog nuzzle him, then clipped on the leash. "Scalpel thinks they're here." He forced a smile. "I tried to tell him about their accident, but he's in denial." Ian swallowed hard. "He'll...look for them."

"Maybe we should tie him up outside."

"No, he needs to get used to this, too."

Slowly the three exited the car. There was a patterned brick path that led to the back of the cottage, and another that went around to the front.

"Let's go in from the lakeside." He nodded at the path around the house, then took her hand. Gripping it tightly, he led the way down the sidewalk.

The sight that greeted them was breathtaking. The lake looked gilded in jewels from the rays of the sun, and the air was crystalline. He turned to the house, admired how its trilevel deck wound its way up from the brick patio at the bottom. It was about fifty feet from the shore and had a long span of lakefront.

Ian gestured at the luxurious cruiser out front. "Derek put in the boat." He glanced down at her. "You like boats?"

"Yeah. I waterski."

"Oh, good."

"You're probably a champion on skis."

"Slalom." He glanced up at the house again. "I can do this, right?"

"Yes."

"Okay, come on, boy." He tugged on Scalpel's leash. The dog made his way clumsily up the winding staircase to the second level in front of them. Though it was awkward, Ian kept Paige next to him, instead of going first or letting her precede him. And he moved in close to her.

Quickly and without fuss, he unlocked the sliding doors. Undoing the leash, he let Scalpel go in first. They could hear him travel from room to room, barking, whining, whimpering. Ian remained in the dining area from where he could see much of the first floor.

"This is lovely, Ian." Paige stayed beside him.

"They liked it open. We knocked down walls, remodeled." He waved at the kitchen, filled with gleaming copper pans hanging down over the stove. All the appliances, cupboards and floor were pristine. "This was Dad's pride and joy."

"Your dad's?"

"Yes, Mom didn't cook. She hated it. She either hired someone to do it or got her men to do it."

"Smart woman."

He hugged Paige. "You're so like her in a lot of ways."

"Thank you."

"All right, let's do this." They moved into the living room. Emotion clogged his throat as he studied it. There was a whole wall of family photographs. Paige headed right for the pictures and stared at the twenty-odd portraits.

Ian came up behind her. "Every few years she insisted we get them done."

"Look how cute you were."

He could still hear his mother's sweet—yet often irritated—voice. *Tommy, stop fidgeting with that tie... Derek, if you make a face again, I'm taking away your video games... Tom, come on, you're being a bad influence on the boys.*

"This is a wonderful history of your family. A chronology of your life, really."

Only able to nod, he looked at the pictures. The last had been taken three years ago. Reaching out, he touched his dad's hand, which rested on Ian's shoulder. The photographer had captured a devilish gleam in his father's eye. *Wish you guys were still complaining about the shirts and ties,* his father had joked. *You make me feel old.*

You'll never be old, dear. His mother had leaned over and whispered something in his ear. Probably something naughty, because it had brought that twinkle to his eyes.

Ian coughed and moved away.

They wandered through the rooms, Ian making comments on furniture, Paige asking about trophies or mementos. It took him a while to notice how fascinated she was by it all. Before he could remark on that, they were in front of the closed door to his parents' bedroom, where Scalpel sat whining softly.

The dog was subdued. When Ian approached, he rubbed Scalpel's head. "I told you, boy, they're not here."

Scalpel whimpered and nudged at the doorknob. Ian closed his eyes. "He thinks they're in there."

"Is it...did Derek do anything with their things?"

Ian shook his head. "He planned to, but he said he couldn't follow through on it. I should have come up with him."

"We don't have to go into the bedroom today."

"No, let's exorcise all the ghosts." He reached out and turned the knob.

Scalpel scampered in with Ian close behind. Paige followed them. The suite jutted out from the rest of the house and had glass on three walls. Ian took in the sitting area, where his mother used to read to him, the bathroom and the huge bed where the four had cuddled when the boys were young. Even as adults, Ian and Derek had often come in here to chat. The recollection made his eyes mist.

Scalpel moved from area to area, sniffing and barking.

"Sometimes," he said, going over to the bed and fingering the quilt, "there were summer storms. When we were little, Derek and I would race in here, climb into bed with them and watch the lightning over the lake."

"What wonderful memories. You're lucky to have them."

Gently he ran his hand down the bedspread his mother had made herself. It was an heirloom quilt. "Come look, Paige."

She crossed to him.

His eyes blurred, but he needed to tell her. "That's a piece of her wedding gown," he said, pointing. "And that's one of our baseball uniforms, my dad's varsity letter, Derek's cap and gown, my first lab coat..." When he finished pointing and describing, he simply stared at the quilt.

Moving as close as she could, Paige slid her arms around his waist. "It's the most exquisite thing I've ever seen. Your whole lives are chronicled there. What a treasure."

Scalpel came to the bed then and laid his snout on the quilt. He whimpered soulfully.

Ian couldn't look at the dog. He turned to Paige and

drew her to him. Then he buried his face in her shoulder and cried.

THE RIDE BACK was quiet.

"I'm sorry, we're later than I thought we'd be," Ian finally said as he turned up Spencer Hill. The July air was still hot and heavy, reflecting Ian's mood.

"I don't have an appointment until one. How about you?"

"Um, I'm doing late duty at our practice. Three to nine." Restlessly he raked a hand through his hair.

"Nine, huh? Will I see you after?"

"You want to, lady?"

"I want to, cowboy."

His grin was weak. "There are a couple of babies ready to debut. If they don't come, I'm all yours."

She liked the sound of that. "You okay?" she asked.

"Yeah. You were right. I needed to go up there. The catharsis helped."

"Wow. Scalpel, did you hear that? You're my witness. He said *I* was right."

As they neared her house, he seemed to relax. "I have quite a history displayed in that house. The photos, the quilt."

"I know. Physical reminders are nice to have."

"My past is what made me the man I am."

"You mean arrogant and assuming?"

"Brat!" He ruffled her hair. "I mean confident. Happy. Maybe that's why I'm so pushy."

She didn't respond.

"What are you thinking?" he asked.

"Nothing much."

"You seemed fascinated by all the mementos."

"I was." An uncomfortable shift. "I...don't have any from my own life."

"I had so much more than you."

"Life doesn't treat everybody fairly."

"No, I know. But it treated you worse than most."

"I had Jade."

He smiled and pulled into her driveway.

"I had something else you didn't have—my birth mother's support..."

Please don't let him bring this up now. She tried not to stiffen. He was still raw and didn't need a tiff with her.

"There comes a time," she said rationally, "when you have to put the past behind you."

He brushed back her hair. "I know." He smiled. "I just wanted to say that you're a wonderful, smart, loving woman, and no one gave you much to build that on. I admire you. A lot."

"Why, thank you." She hugged him, held on a moment, then opened the door. "I've got to get going."

She was out on the sidewalk leading to the house when he called out, "Wait a second. I want to tell you something else." Pivoting, she came back to the car. "Two things, really."

Trustingly, she smiled down at him.

"First, thanks for what you did today."

"You're welcome."

He stared at her.

"What's the second?"

"Just this." He cleared his throat. "I love you, Paige."

CHAPTER TWELVE

"HI THERE, little guy. How are you tonight?" Gowned but no longer needing a mask, Paige cuddled Sammy Barone to her chest, taking care not to disturb the heart monitors attached to his chest, abdomen and legs. The smell of baby powder and milk soothed her frazzled nerves.

Laurie, the primary-care nurse and a mother of four, smiled down at her. "He's doing better every day, Dr. Kendrick." Her smile turned to a frown.

"I can see that." Paige rocked back and forth in one of the many NICU rocking chairs. "Why the scowl?"

"His mother doesn't visit enough since she left the hospital." One of the things Paige appreciated about the staff members was their honesty. They were nurturing and supportive in the extreme, but if something was wrong, they confronted it head-on. "You've been here holding him more than she has."

Paige shook her head. "It's hard for her with another infant at home. Without the baby's father to help."

Laurie held up a bottle. "Wanna do this?"

Paige took it. "Sure."

"I wish she could have breast-fed him."

"I do, too. But at least she's nursing Suzy."

"She's too young to have a baby. Let alone two."

"Maybe." Paige watched as little Sammy latched on to the nipple. His tiny features were scrunched into a frown until he got a good hold. He'd been fed with a tube, but now he was taking a bottle once a day, and he was doing great with it.

"He calms really well with you, Dr. Kendrick."

"Years of medical school," she said dryly.

Laurie smiled as she headed for the door. "It's more than that. You have a way with babies." She smiled. "You got any of your own?"

"No."

"Too bad."

Paige managed a smile as Laurie left. She gazed down at Sammy and brushed the tuft of light-brown hair on his head. "So, tell me about your day, buddy." He stared up at her with cloudy blue eyes that kept drifting shut. "Too busy eating? What's that? You want to hear about mine?" Laying her head back on the chair, she sighed. "Nah, my stuff's too grown-up for you. It has to do with a man."

Who'd told her he loved her. This afternoon.

And she hadn't said it back. The moment had been broken when Jewel had run out of the house and thrown herself at Paige, yelling, "I missed you, Aunt Paige."

She'd grasped Jewel and held her between herself and Ian like a shield.

His eyes—those wonderful gray eyes—had shown hurt.

"But what did he expect, Sammy? It's only been a few weeks since we..." Paige sighed. This was stupid. Ian expected *something* in return, rightfully so. But she needed time to mull things over, so when Jade had followed Jewel out, Paige had used her family as an excuse not to respond to the three most important words a man could say to a woman.

Ian had simply driven away. Paige hadn't talked to him

all day; she knew he was working from three to nine, but she hadn't sought him out. As usual she'd been a coward and wasn't in any hurry to face him. Suddenly the door to the neonatal visiting room opened. Paige looked up and saw him standing there.

"I thought I might find you here." His face was lined with fatigue. He wore jeans and a navy polo shirt, and his hair was damp. He must have just showered.

"Have you been at the hospital today?"

"Yes. Two deliveries." He glanced at the clock. "I still need to check on the patients." Taking a seat across the room from her, he stared down at the infant. "How's Sammy?"

She adjusted her arm and angled the bottle. "Better. Gained a couple of ounces."

"How's the apnea?"

"A little better. Only a few episodes today." She looked up at him. "Have you talked to Mary Ellen?"

"Yes. I called her when the NICU informed me she hadn't been in today."

"How is she?"

"Not good. She was having a lot of trouble nursing Suzy, so she stopped. And Lena Barone isn't helping at all. She was supposed to watch Suzy today so Mary Ellen could come here, but she copped out."

"What about Nora?"

"Mary Ellen's adamant about not bothering her before the wedding."

"I'll talk to Nora." She looked down at Sammy. "He needs to be with his mother." Paige transferred her gaze to Ian. "How are you? After this morning?"

"Which part of this morning, Paige?" The gravity of his tone underscored what she already knew.

She sighed. They were beyond denial or avoidance. "I

meant going to the cottage. But I want to talk about what you said, too, Ian.''

''The look on your face says maybe I don't want to hear it.''

That surprised her. ''It's not bad.''

''Okay. Shoot.''

''You surprised me, is all. We haven't been seeing each other that long. It seems early for a declaration like that.''

His expression was one of a man who'd been told he had a serious illness. ''I see. Well, that's a dismissal if ever I've heard one.'' He stood.

''No, it isn't.''

''I'm going to leave. I need time to pick my ego up off the floor and try to piece it back together.'' He crossed to the door. ''I'll call you.''

''Ian—'' She'd spoken too loudly, and the baby began to cry. Paige soothed him. ''Shh, sweetie, I'm sorry.'' When she looked up, Ian was gone.

As she watched Sammy with the bottle, she began to get angry. Damn it, as usual he hadn't given her enough time to explain herself. It was his way or nothing. No middle ground.

She finished with the baby and left the NICU. She needed to talk to Ian. She approached the nurses' station. ''Laurie, do you know if Dr. Chandler's left the hospital?''

''I think he's in maternity. I was getting off the elevator, and he was going up on it.'' She frowned. ''He's always in such a good mood, but he looked pretty upset.''

He is. With me.

After checking at the maternity desk, Paige found him in the lounge. He was doing one of the puzzles. With a very pretty nurse, who was sitting very close to him on the couch.

The sight of him nestled next to another woman made Paige's heart constrict. Her first impulse was to turn around and leave. She got as far as the door and stopped.

Not so fast. I'm not letting him go so fast. She turned back. "Ian, I'd like to talk to you."

He glanced over his shoulder, his face showing surprise.

The nurse looked at her, too. Neither one of them moved.

Paige smiled at the woman. "Could you excuse us?"

"Oh, sure." She touched Ian's sleeve when she stood. "I'll be out at the station, Ian."

When she left, Paige shut and locked the door. She longed to escape, but hell, she had some things to say. She crossed to him and sat on the couch. "I...I know you're upset."

"I'm not upset, Paige. I'm disappointed." He glanced at her. Gone was the teasing lover, the flirt. In his place was a man who had been pushed to his emotional limits today.

"Ian, my feelings for you are deep, but it's early in our relationship and I—"

"Is that what you think—that I expected you to return what I said to you today?"

"I don't know what to think."

"I didn't," he said starkly.

"Then why are you upset?"

"Because I didn't expect you to ignore it, either."

"I didn't mean to ignore it. But Jewel came out, then Jade after her."

"You could have sent them inside. Talked to me about what you were feeling."

"I didn't know what I was feeling."

"That would have been all right." He picked up her hand and brought it to his mouth for a quick brush of his lips. The gesture was so tender it brought tears to her eyes. "I need you to tell me your feelings, honey, regardless of what they are. And just now, up in NICU, I felt like an intern who'd spoken out of turn."

"This is hard for me."

"I know."

Drawing a deep breath, she leaned close to him. "You scared the hell out of me with that declaration."

"I—"

"No, just listen. You want to hear what I have to say, then don't interrupt. I feel things for you I've never felt before. It's more frightening than I can describe. We're different, Ian. I wasn't looking for this with you. It's still hard for me to let you into my life."

He didn't say anything.

"You can talk now."

He sighed. "I'm tired of forcing every issue in this relationship, Paige. It feels one-sided."

"It isn't one-sided, Ian. I'll try to be more open about my feelings. Be patient with me. You're asking me to change the way I've always dealt with people."

"I need to know that there's hope for us."

"Yes, of course there is. I want things to work out between us, Ian. I want a future with you. I'm starting to trust you."

He drew in a breath. "I know how much *that* means to you." He leaned over and kissed her gently on the lips. "Let's go home." He tried to joke, but his voice was still raw. "You can *show* me how you feel now."

She glanced at the door. "No other plans?"

"I hadn't made any yet."

"Good. I want you all to myself."

He laughed and grabbed her hand. "I like the sound of that. Let's go, sweetheart."

"HI, IT'S ME AGAIN." As he spoke into the phone, Ian tapped his fingers on his desk; it was better than kicking the wastebasket. "I've been trying to reach you for a couple of days now. Where *are* you? Call me. *Now*." Realizing how autocratic he sounded, he added, "Please." He clicked off the phone and said, "Son of a bitch."

"Hmm, calling that little nurse?"

Pivoting, he found Paige in the doorway. "Um, no." He glanced guiltily at the phone.

Paige frowned. "Who is she, then? Am I gonna have to beat her up?" It took him a minute to realize she was flirting with him.

"I don't know." He sat on the desk, enjoying this side of her. "She's an older woman."

Closing the office door, Paige leaned against it. "Confess. Or I'll have to torture you."

"Hmm. Handcuffs, maybe?"

"Oh, that's all we need. We tore the covers off the bed last night."

They had. He couldn't seem to get enough of her. "Better watch the flirting, then." He remembered something. "It wasn't just sex that messed up the covers, honey."

She started to close down. He watched her visibly fight it. "Don't, Ian. I can't do anything about the nightmares."

"Paige, you know what's brought these on. They started right around the time Mary Ellen had her babies. Mary Ellen is a Serenity House girl."

The phone rang before Paige could respond. He answered it on the second ring. Scowled at the call from Social Services. After he was done, she changed the subject.

"You still haven't told me who you're trying to reach."

"Lynne. I've been calling for three days. She never disappears like this without telling me. I'm worried."

Paige looked up at him. "That's a little extreme, isn't it?"

"She's all alone in the world except for me."

"She's fifty-five, Ian. She can take care of herself."

He folded his arms over his chest. "You know, I never understood that reasoning. Why would you *want* to take care of yourself?"

"It's safer. You can't be disappointed that way."

"Well, I can accept that you might not want to depend on someone else financially. But emotionally—"

There was a knock at the door. Cursing the interruption, Ian strode over to open it. A tearful Mary Ellen stood at the doorway, holding a crying Suzy. The Center had no more appointments today, and no one was in the outer office.

Paige rose immediately. "Mary Ellen, what's wrong?"

The girl gulped. "I...she won't stop crying. My mother, she keeps yelling. I...don't know..."

Taking the baby from her, Paige felt Suzy's skin. "She's cool. Is she hungry?"

"No, I just fed her." Mary Ellen began to weep. "I think it's the diaper rash."

"Diaper rash?" Paige headed for the door. "Let's go to an examining room."

Ian followed.

Inside the first room, Paige told Mary Ellen, "Undress her while I wash up."

The baby continued to cry.

Mary Ellen did as instructed. Paige crossed to the baby to examine her. "Well," she finally said, "the diaper rash is pretty bad, all right." Reaching into a drawer, she got out a cloth. She soaped it up and bathed the baby. "I told you how to deal with this, honey. Water, not diaper wipes. Air-dry. Zinc oxide." She glanced at Ian, nodded to a cupboard. "There's some prescription cream up there, Ian. Get it for me, will you please?"

Ian found the cream, handed it to her, then sat down in a chair and watched Paige finish. After the baby was diapered, Paige held Suzy close to her chest, protectively. "What happened, Mary Ellen?"

"I...I left her with my mother so I could visit Sammy yesterday. She..." Tears again. "She didn't change Suzy all afternoon."

Paige and Ian exchanged looks. "Maybe you can't leave her with your mom anymore," Ian said.

"What do I do? I have to see Sammy. They taught me this kangaroo thing, where you keep the baby against your bare skin—your chest and stomach."

"Kangaroo care." Paige nodded. "It's very effective with preemies."

"He loves it and calms right away. But it takes time, and I can't do it if I'm not here."

Ian watched Paige. She cradled the baby to her breast. Kissed her head. Held her...like a mother.

"What can we do?" Paige addressed the question to him.

He stood. "Let's talk to Elliot." He faced Mary Ellen. "We have a psychologist on staff who can help you work this out. He has access to some child care, too, to pitch in under unusual circumstances. I'll see if we can get you somebody.''

Mary Ellen swallowed back emotion. "Okay. Thanks.''

"Did you see Sammy today?" Paige asked.

The tears returned. She shook her head.

"Look, as long as you're here, why don't you go over there now? We'll keep Suzy for a bit.''

"Really?''

"Really.'' After Mary Ellen was gone, Paige sat down in a chair across from him and held the baby close. Was she even aware of how motherly her actions were? "The plan's not working.'' Paige's tone was grim.

"It's only been a few weeks. Give it some time.''

"What happens when Sammy comes home? I'm worried about their safety.''

"Can't call Social Services about diaper rash, honey.''

"I know. Just as we couldn't call them about the car seat.''

"I'll talk to Elliot.''

"All right.''

"Oops, there's the phone in my office. Maybe it's Lynne.''

"Ian, you really are…''

But he didn't hear the rest. The caller wasn't Lynne, so he tried reaching her again. She still wasn't home. In the end he left Paige's number—and address in case she needed to see him.

Where the hell was the woman?

WHEN LYNNE WALKED into Paige's backyard, Ian bolted off the chaise and rushed to the gate. From where Paige sat at a table with Jewel and Scalpel, she could see Ian grasp Lynne's arms. "Where the hell have you been?''

Lynne put her hand on her son's chest. They looked so much alike standing there in the setting sun, same sculpted nose, similar bone structure and a similar stubborn tilt to their chins. For the first time Paige wondered if her own child looked like her, then was utterly stunned at her speculation.

With no small amount of frustration, Lynne said, "Ian, really, calm down."

Paige frowned at the unfamiliar yearning she was experiencing. This was Ian's birth mother, who was a part of his life because she'd had the courage to risk an open adoption and the Moores had had the courage to accept one.

"What's the matter, Aunt Paige?"

"Nothing sweetie." It *was* nothing.

"You got the pudding paint all over the table."

Jade had introduced Paige to pudding paint—using chocolate pudding, instead of finger paints, to draw pictures. Jewel loved it, as most kids would.

She heard Lynne, who was clearly exasperated, say, "Ian, I went away with a *man*. It's not exactly something I'd clear with you first."

Ian expelled a breath and ducked his head.

"Now let me say hi to Paige." Lynne strode over with a determined gait. "Hello, Paige." She smiled at Jewel. "Hi, Jewel." Her gaze locked with Paige's. "I'm sorry to disturb your evening, but his phone calls got more and more insistent, so I decided to talk to him in person."

Paige smiled. "He can be overbearing."

Looking chagrined, Ian came up behind Lynne and placed his hands on her shoulders. "I'm sorry. I was just worried."

Paige thought about how Ian had reacted to being at his parents' cottage. He'd lost Elsa and Tom. He was worried about Lynne. She must have realized the root of his concern at the same time. "Nothing's going to happen to me, Ian. Actually I had a wonderful time. Do you want to hear about him?"

"No!" Ian said.

"I do," Paige told her mischievously.

"Come on, kid." Ian smiled at Jewel. "I'll take you for a swim while these women share men stories."

Scalpel barked and followed them to the edge of the pool, though he still had on his cast and couldn't swim.

Paige and Lynne laughed as Ian and Jewel entered the water.

At around ten o'clock, when Lynne had gone and Jade and Jewel were in the house, Paige stared out at the pool.

"Penny for your thoughts," Ian said.

"It was nice getting to know Lynne."

"She's great. She likes you."

"Good, I'm glad." She waited a minute. "Have you always been this close to her?"

"Yes, she's been an anchor in my life."

"Has it been as good for her, having you in her life?"

"Why don't you ask her?"

"No, I wouldn't want her to know..." Paige's words trailed off.

"About the child you gave up. She wouldn't judge you, Paige."

"She made a different choice. And now her life's vocation is matching up birth parents and adoptees."

"She understands both sides."

Paige didn't like where this conversation was going. "No, Ian. I don't want to talk to her about it." Abruptly she stood. "I don't—"

He grabbed her arm before she could leave. "You said

you were beginning to trust me. Show me. Tell me what you're thinking.''

Time froze. Did she really trust Ian? She hadn't even planned to tell Jade about her real reaction tonight as she'd watched Ian and Lynne. But she knew in her heart that Ian wasn't going to accept anything but the truth. He'd expect progress. And somewhere inside herself, she *wanted* to confide in him. ''You're right. I watched you with Lynne tonight and realized I might have had what the two of you have if I'd made a different choice.''

''Honey, you need to talk to someone.''

''I'm telling you.''

''A counselor, maybe.''

She shook her head. ''No, I don't want to talk to a counselor. Do you have any idea how hard it was to tell *you* this tonight?''

''Yes, I do.''

''Then don't push, please.''

He studied her. It was so difficult for him to back off. ''All right. I'll be satisfied that you trusted me enough to tell me as much as you did.'' He pulled her onto his lap and kissed her hair. ''I want you to be happy, Paige. With me and with your life. That's all I want.''

''I know.'' She wound her arms around his neck.

She had him in her life. She didn't need anything else. She didn't.

CHAPTER THIRTEEN

NORA STOOD on the deck of Dan's lake house and peered down at the four young women sunning themselves on the dock. Each had grown into lovely, interesting people. Yet each was—in many ways—still very troubled. Sometimes Nora wondered if she'd done enough that first year Serenity House had opened.

"Hel-lo," Nora heard from behind. Turning, she saw Taylor Morelli and her husband, Nick. They were a good-looking couple. Both dark-haired and dark-eyed. They'd had stunning babies, the last one almost two years ago.

"Taylor, I'm so glad you're here!"

Taylor gave her a hug.

"Hi, Nora," Nick said. He stood back, the way he always did, not quite shy, but reluctant to call attention to himself. Something else he and Taylor had in common. The last of the first batch of residents to join Serenity House in 1987, Taylor had been found on the side of the road, beaten and suffering from amnesia. It still astonished doctors that her memory had never returned.

Nora shook hands with Nick. "So, you're going to let us have Taylor for a few days?"

"I suppose." His smile was self-effacing. "She's never been away from me this long."

"Really?"

Taylor rolled her eyes. "Pathetic, isn't he?"

Nick said, "I'm going to go before I look like even

more of a jerk." He hugged Taylor tightly, kissed her cheek. "Think of me."

She whispered something in his ear.

"You're on, woman." Nick said his goodbyes and left.

"He's a wonderful man." Nora smiled.

Taylor said, "He reminds me of Dan in a lot of ways."

"Me, too."

"Where is the bridegroom, by the way?"

"He went to pick up Anabelle at the airport." Anabelle Crane was the youngest of the first group of residents, and Dan's favorite.

"I can't believe she's coming." Taylor glanced toward the dock. "I can't believe everyone's here."

"You all promised to come back."

Taylor slid an arm around Nora. She was taller than Nora, but there was still a vulnerability about her. "It's because of you. We'd do anything for you."

Nora hoped these three days would do something for the girls, but she didn't say so. "Let's go down. Wait till you see Jade. She's beautiful. And she has a beautiful daughter...."

They reached the dock just as Nora finished filling Taylor in about the four women on the dock. Charly Donovan was talking and didn't see them at first. "...really into more trouble than we were." She stretched out on a blanket next to Darcy. Both wore black one-piece swimsuits. Demure but attractive.

"Oh, come on, Char," Darcy said. "We weren't angels."

"No, but there's something harder about these girls."

"Nothing hard about Mary Ellen Barone." This from bikini-clad Paige, who lay on her stomach.

"Hello, everybody," Taylor said sweetly.

They all looked up. Charly was the first to react. "Hi, Taylor."

Jade stood. In her animal-print thong bikini, she was almost indecent. "I'd hug you, girl, but I'm all greasy."

"You look wonderful."

Jade studied her. "You've gained a little weight. It's good on you."

Taylor's eyes shadowed. Her fragility had bothered the other girls, and they had always tried to fatten her up. "I had a baby twenty-two months ago. Never did lose the weight I gained."

"Well, you look great."

Paige said, "Got your suit on under your clothes?"

"No, I'll go change." Taylor smiled. "I'm glad to be here."

"So are we." This from Darcy.

Nora and Taylor started back up the dock as two people headed down it. One was Dan, tall and handsome and grinning broadly. His arm was around the shoulders of a tall, blond woman.

"Holy hell, is that Anabelle?" Darcy asked.

"It must be," Jade said.

As they neared, Paige eyed Anabelle's dark-green, sleeveless linen dress and matching jacket, which was draped over her arm. "Nice rags. She must be doing pretty well for herself."

Nora noticed that Anabelle leaned in closer to Dan as they approached. The girl seemed as sophisticated as a model, but her body language said she was nervous. They met a few feet from the other women. "Hello, Anabelle."

Anabelle pulled off her sunglasses, revealing amber-colored eyes filled with a world-weariness that belied her thirty-two years. "Hello, Nora."

"The girls are dying to see you," Nora said, giving Annabelle a hug, which was returned stiffly.

"Anabelle." Charly stood. "You look like a million bucks."

Anabelle touched her hair self-consciously and smiled. "You look great, too." She looked down at Paige and greeted her with a warm "Hi."

Paige grinned. "Hi to you, kiddo." Paige had taken an interest in Anabelle, the quietest one at the group home. She'd mothered her. Watched out for her.

Darcy was next to respond. "Anabelle. Wonderful to see you."

"Darcy? God, you haven't changed a bit."

"Don't count on it," Jade laughed. "She's turned into her mother."

"Jade, you look terrific, too."

"So," Jade said saucily, "where has the mystery woman been all these years? We've caught up on everybody except you."

Anabelle waited a beat, then finally said, "I've been somebody else."

"That sounds mysterious," Jade commented.

"I don't mean it to be." Annabelle looked at Dan. "I'm a cop," she said. "Like Dan. Only I do undercover work. Now," she said changing the subject smoothly, "I want to hear all about you guys."

"REALLY, LADIES, I'm far too old for this." Nora's youthful grin and maidenly blush belied her words. With her hair piled up on her head, and a cotton sundress draping her body, she looked about their age. She frowned at the garment in her hands.

"You're never too old for silk underwear, Nora." Slouched in a stuffed chair in the corner of Dan's great room, which looked out at the lake through huge sliding doors, Jade grinned from ear to ear.

"But there's so little of it," Nora said.

"Better not tell Dan you have those under your wedding dress." Jade's voice was all devil. "He won't be able to concentrate on the ceremony."

Nora's blush deepened, obscuring the freckles that had come out after the afternoon in the sun. "Stop."

Paige chuckled, remembering the excursion all six Serenity House women had taken in Charly's van that morning. They'd decided to have an impromptu shower for Nora and wanted *unusual* gifts. "Hey, we held her back in that shop, Nora. You should have seen what she first picked out."

"Where is this shop, anyway?"

"In Elmwood." Paige grinned at the memory of the discreet little store being invaded by six women. "On the outskirts."

"How did you find out about it?"

All eyes turned to Taylor. Shy Taylor, who hid a wealth of secrets. "Nicky took me there to pick out something for our wedding anniversary."

"What'd you get?" Darcy's green eyes twinkled like polished emeralds. Paige had forgotten how much fun Darcy could be.

"None of your business."

"Have some more wine," Jade suggested. "You'll tell us eventually."

"Open mine next," Charly said. She, too, was smiling from where she sat on the floor in shorts and a tank top.

It had been a pleasant two days together and everyone was feeling more relaxed. The only downer for Paige was that she missed Ian. A lot. She'd talked to him several times, but she longed to be with him.

Nora opened Charly's gift. "Charlene Donovan, I'm shocked."

"Well, I know how you like to read," Charly said archly.

"The Kama Sutra?"

"Look on page fifty-six," Jade said glibly. "There are great suggestions for foreplay."

Rolling her eyes, Paige said, "You've read this book?"

"Hasn't everybody?" Jade's innocent expression led to another chuckle around the room.

Paige's present was next. When Nora delicately eased off the paper, she frowned. "You got me a first-aid kit?" She sounded disappointed. "Well, it's—"

"It's got special, um, medicines in it."

Nora must have caught the gleam in Paige's eye. "Is this going to embarrass me, too?"

"I hope so." Paige sipped her merlot.

Gingerly Nora opened the kit. She picked up a bottle. "It's oyster juice."

"Oh, Lord, an aphrodisiac." This from Taylor.

"Poor, Dan. She'll keep him up all night." Jade didn't blink at the pun.

Nora examined the rest of the stuff. "Edible body gel. In several flavors. Massage oil. Oh, look!" she said excitedly. "Body paint for the shower—" She stopped when she realized the girls were laughing at her enthusiasm. Blushing again, she buried her face in her hands.

After a moment Darcy encouraged her to open the next present. "Oh, Darcy, this is beautiful." She eyed the rest of the girls. "And much more demure than all of yours."

"Don't count on it," Jade said.

"What?"

"Nora, look at the lace," Charly instructed.

"It's lovely, dear."

"Ah, look at how strategically it's placed."

Nora examined the garment. "Oh, my."

Darcy giggled. "I tried, Nora, really I did. To buy something sane and sensible. But I couldn't…"

"The old Darcy strikes again," Jade quipped.

There was one present left. Nora eyed it like a snake that might bite. "Anabelle, surely you didn't participate in this shopping trip…"

"As usual, they dragged me along. You know how they always made me do things I never would have done alone." Anabelle sighed dramatically.

Nora opened the box. "Oh, God, girls, please. Dan will—"

"Dan will love them," Jade asserted. "And they're so symbolic. Anabelle's a cop. He's a cop. What better gift?"

She held up the velvet handcuffs. "I'm fifty years old! He's fifty-five!"

"Got a lot of good years left in him, Nora baby," Jade said.

"I'm embarrassed to even tell him—"

"What was that?" Darcy's head snapped around to the screen doors.

"What?" Anabelle asked.

"I heard a noise outside."

Taylor rolled her eyes. "You guys, stop."

Paige remembered how they used to try to scare each other, especially Taylor. Until Nora had explained that wasn't good for Taylor, who spooked easily because of the amnesia.

"No, seriously," Darcy said. "I heard something."

Jade touched her arm. "Honest?"

"Honest."

Anabelle stood. "Everybody, stay right where you are."

Mesmerized, Paige watched Anabelle disappear into the room off to the right, where she was staying. When she returned, she raised one hand to her lips to signal for them to be quiet. In her other hand she held a small revolver.

"Oh, my God, she's packing," Jade whispered.

Paige watched openmouthed as Anabelle switched off the lights and crept to the sliding doors. It was dark; they'd left the deck lights off. They heard a grunt outside. Another noise. Another grunt from the other side of the deck. Paige frowned. More than one person was out there. Her heart started to beat in her chest.

In the next second, lights flooded the deck and the sound of the screen whipping back rent the stillness. In a voice worthy of the FBI head, Anabelle said, "All right, freeze!"

IAN GLANCED over at Nick Morelli, who shrugged sheepishly from the other side of the deck, where he was rubbing his shin. They'd met in the front of the yard and circled around here together. "Sorry we scared you," Ian said.

"You didn't scare us." Jade raised her chin.

Winking at Paige, Ian said, "Why did this one come out armed and dangerous like some police officer if you weren't scared?"

"I *am* a police officer," Anabelle said haughtily. "You're lucky you're still in one piece."

Nick chuckled and Taylor crossed to him. He cuddled her close. "You're a sap, Morelli."

"I know." He held her close. "I'm sorry but I couldn't stand it any longer."

"Me, neither." Ian stalked over to Paige. "Come on, lady."

Shrugging, Paige grasped his hand. "See you later, guys," she called out, and crossed the deck with him.

He pulled her down the steps.

"Ian, slow down. I can't keep up with you."

At the bottom he turned and watched her descend. Barefoot, dressed in simple denim shorts and a striped sleeveless top, her hair back in a ponytail, she looked young and heartbreakingly innocent. When she was on the third-to-the-last step, he picked her up and threw her over his shoulder. "Ian!"

"I can't wait for you, Paige." He glanced at the boathouse. "There? Or the tree house out back."

"The tree. I scouted it out today."

He slapped her bottom. "Hoping I'd come?"

"Oh, yes." She bit his back playfully. "I missed you."

Ian strode to the tree. "You okay? With all the Serenity House group?"

"Of course. Did you bring condoms?"

"A six-pack." He waited a moment. "Any nightmares?"

"Just dreams. About you. Ripping off my clothes and having your way with me."

They reached the tree. "Let's go up first. Then I'll rip your clothes off and have my way with you. Hurry."

Paige clambered up the tree ladder with speed and agility. Ian followed almost as fast. The tree house was about twelve-by-twelve and moderately enclosed. Paige could stand up in it, but Ian bumped his head. She kissed it as he knelt down and undid her shorts. He got them off and nuzzled her. "Oh, God. Lie down, honey."

She did.

On his knees, he took her with his mouth. She climaxed almost instantly. Ian whispered, "Ah, I like that. Shows you missed me." He went back for more. Twice.

"Let me return the favor," she said breathlessly when he was done.

"All right. But later." He pulled out a condom and shucked off his shorts. He was inside her in seconds. "I knew I wouldn't last," he said, just before he exploded.

She was laughing when he collapsed on top of her. "Well, that was a record."

"I'm embarrassed."

"I love it."

He braced himself on his arms and gazed down at her. Moonlight streaming through the opening in the hut caressed her face. "You've gotten prettier."

"I've only been gone for two days."

"Two days too long." He kissed her forehead. "How could I miss you this much?"

"I missed you this much, too."

"I love you, Paige."

"Ian, I—"

He stopped her words with fingers at her lips. "No, don't. I just wanted to say it again." He grinned. "Scalpel misses you, too. He sent along a note. It's in my pocket, though his writing is worse than a doctor's."

She smiled. "You're crazy."

"About you. You sure you're okay?"

"Are you kidding? I came three times."

"No, I mean about the Serenity House reunion. Being here with them."

"Actually it's been fun. Awkward at first, but a little of the old girl in each of us is peeking out."

He kissed her nose. "Really? What's come out in you?"

"Well, this for one. I used to sneak out to meet…"
She trailed off.

He watched her. *Tell me, please.*

"To meet Ronny, my boyfriend. The father."

Thank you, God. "What else?"

"We used to tease Taylor and Anabelle about being shy."

"Are they still?"

"Anabelle's the cop," Paige said dryly.

"Oh, I guess she's not."

"No, she is, despite playing Wonder Woman with a gun." Paige's forehead wrinkled the way it did when she was thinking. "And Taylor still sleeps as poorly as she did back then. I've heard her up a lot in the middle of the night." Paige frowned. "She came to Serenity House with amnesia, Ian. She's never gotten back her memory."

"How sad."

"There are worse things than not remembering."

"Like remembering too much?"

Paige nodded. She waited several moments before she said, "But I'm okay. Honest." She nibbled on his neck. "Except I'm getting hungry again." She pressed her hips into his. "Time for dessert, Ian."

Telling himself to be satisfied with what she'd given him, he said, "My pleasure. Let's get naked this time."

ON THEIR LAST NIGHT together, the Serenity House women sat on the deck around an oval umbrella table, sipping the champagne Nick Morelli had brought on his visit to his wife. The stars glittered above them, and the moon, their only light, cast them in a mellow glow. Nora thought they looked even younger tonight, dressed for bed.

"Let's play FLIP," Darcy suggested. It was a sharing

activity where each participant discussed her *F*eelings, *L*ife priorities, *I*nsecurities and *P*ast regrets.

"Why?" Jade asked. "I remember not liking the game too much back then."

"No, but it always helped us bond."

Nora sipped her champagne. She wondered if the old opening-up activity was the right thing to do now. Would it unearth too much for them? Maybe not. She was a firm believer in unearthing suppressed feelings.

"I'm game," Charly said. She wore a demure night-gown and slippers. "Then again, my life's an open book."

Taylor shrugged. "What the hell, it isn't like we don't all know each other's secrets."

Jade and Paige exchanged looks. They were dressed alike in summer satin pj's Jade had bought for them. "Same rules apply." This from Paige, who liked rules. "No lying. And we can never share what the others say with anyone else."

"Even Dan, Nora," Charly warned. "Or Nick, Tay-lor."

"Or Ian," Jade added.

They all nodded their agreement.

Darcy said, "I'll start since it's my idea. *F*—what I'm feeling now. I'm sad that this time together is nearly over."

They all knew the drill. They went in a circle, then reversed it.

Anabelle was next. "I'm relieved. I was scared about coming."

"I'm happy," Taylor put in. "It makes me feel close to you all again. You're the only memory I have of my adolescence, you know."

Charly reached over and squeezed her hand, then said, "I'm content. I've liked these three days."

Paige confessed that she was surprised it had all gone so well, Jade told them she was shocked a bit by how everybody had turned out. Nora got teary-eyed and said she was ecstatic that everybody had come home just for her.

Nora had to start with *L,* the life priorities.

"That's easy." She wiped her eyes. "The most important thing in my life now is Dan."

For Darcy and Jade it was their kids, who were staying with Darcy's mother. Taylor couldn't decide between Nick or her kids, and Charly said, Tim, her stepson.

Everybody turned to Paige. Nora expected her to say her practice. Instead, she shook her head. "I can't believe this. It's Ian."

The women cheered, but Nora saw surprise on each of their faces that a man was so important to strong, independent Paige.

Paige began the letter *I.* Insecurities. "I hate opening up to people, though this is easier than I thought."

"You still hate opening up to Ian."

"Oh, all right, I'm insecure about trusting him. But I'm trying."

"We all have trouble with trust." This, surprisingly, from Anabelle.

"What's yours?"

"The same. I don't trust men. Except Dan," she said, smiling at Nora.

"I trust Nick. But I'm insecure about him sometimes. When I met him, he was so self-confident. It seems over the years he's become less so. I can't figure it out."

"Do you think it has something to do with *you* becoming more self-assured?"

Taylor shrugged. "Who knows? He won't talk about it."

"Darcy?" Nora watched her. "You okay?"

Darcy had quieted and sipped her champagne with a faraway look in her eyes. "I don't trust that I've really changed. I'm afraid I'll fall back into my old ways."

"Would that be so bad?" Jade asked.

Tears came to her eyes. "It would be horrible."

"I liked the old Darcy."

Darcy became indignant. "You hated me, Jade. We fought all the time."

Jade fiddled with her curls. "I was jealous. Everybody liked you. Especially boys."

"I never knew that." Darcy watched Jade. "What's your *I?*"

"I'm afraid I won't be able to raise Jewel right."

"She's a good kid," Darcy said. "I'm an expert now, and I think you're doing a great job with her."

The others said they'd like to meet Jade's daughter.

Nora dropped her bomb last. She'd been waiting for the right time to say this. "I'm insecure about our new venture."

Paige cocked her head. "Your marriage?"

"No, of course not. Dan and I are opening a boys' group home in Hyde Point. Nathan Hyde's family is providing the start-up money."

Anabelle stood and went to get more champagne. Nora caught the frown on her face.

Finally they were on the last letter, *P.* Past regrets. Nora was really worried about this one. So she used a technique she'd often employed when the girls were young: she told them something that was hard for her to admit. "I wish I'd been able to have more of Dan's life. It was impossible, of course, but I still regret it."

"I regret being such bum gum to creeps." This from Darcy. "I wish I'd attracted better men."

"I regret..." Charly sighed. "I regret not taking more risks. I played it pretty safe. I loved Cal, of course, but thinking back, he was safe."

Anabelle coughed. Her big honey-colored eyes still looked wounded. "I regret not leaving Hyde Point as soon as I got out of Serenity House."

When she said no more, Paige probed. "You worked for the Hydes for a while, didn't you?"

"Yes." She stared at the living room of the cottage as if she were seeing something there. "I wish I'd never met Nathan Hyde."

Nora wasn't shocked, but the girls were.

"Why?" Darcy asked.

"A long and boring story. And very trite. Suffice it to say I was a fool. I regret that."

"He's best man in the wedding, dear." Nora knew Dan had told Anabelle this, but Nora thought she should remind her.

"I know. I can face him. Even though I don't want to." She looked around. "Let's go on to somebody else."

Jade took a gulp of champagne. Nora wondered if she'd be honest. "I regret..." She glanced at her sister, who smiled at her. "I regret that I wasn't able to change Jewel's circumstances, the circumstances of her birth. I wish they'd been different."

"That her father didn't die, Jade?" Darcy asked.

"No. I didn't tell the truth the first day here. Her father isn't dead. I've never been married."

They listened attentively while Jade talked, then all chimed in at once to console or advise her.

When it was her turn, Taylor shook her head. "I can't

talk about regrets. I have no memory of anything in my life. I don't even know who I am.''

''You're a bright, caring woman, Taylor.'' Charly was adamant. ''A good friend. A great mother. A terrific wife.''

''Yeah, but where did I come from? It drives me crazy not knowing. I have nightmares. It's the one thing wrong with my life.''

After commiserating with Taylor, all eyes turned to Paige. Nora saw that she'd gone white and knew why. Everybody had been excruciatingly honest tonight, baring their innermost secrets.

Page bit her lip, and looked so much like the pregnant girl who'd come to Nora. Her hand went to her stomach. She said simply, ''I regret that I had no other alternative than to give up my child.'' Tears filmed her eyes. ''I didn't even know I felt that way until recently. I don't *want* to feel that way.''

Charly said gently, ''We can't help how we feel, Paige.''

''I know. I've tried controlling how I feel, but I can't.''

''Dr. Hot and Hunky put the kibosh on that,'' Jade said.

''He did.''

''Are you glad, sweetie?'' Charly asked.

''Yes, I'm glad,'' Paige admitted.

Nora sighed. Somewhere along the line her chicks had grown up. Judging from tonight, they were doing pretty well with the rotten hands they'd been dealt.

WEDDINGS TURNED everybody into saps, Paige thought as she gazed out over the grounds of Hyde Point Country Club; its sprawling lawns served as a stunning backdrop to the small gazebo where Dan and Nora stood before the minister. As the sun set and the smell of newly mowed grass and wisteria surrounded them, Paige studied the participants and witnesses.

Nora wore her hair up with baby's breath entwined in it; she'd chosen a simple, lacy, white dress which bared her shoulders and fell in a handkerchief hem around her calves. Her face glowed and her eyes were misty as she stared up at Dan. He'd picked a tux of raven black, which set off his salt-and-pepper hair. He peered down lovingly at his wife-to-be, and his voice caught when he answered the minister's questions about honoring and cherishing. Paige guessed they were both only barely aware of the crowd gathered around them.

The honor attendants were closest: Nora's sister, in bright blue, dabbed at her eyes. Nathan Hyde, dashing in his own black tux, stood soberly by, almost wistful, watching the union.

Five of the six original residents of Serenity House were crowded off to the left. Each was dealing with her own emotion; Charly cried openly. In their three days at the lake, Paige had learned how close Charly and Nora had become, but Paige also knew Charly was most likely remembering her own wedding, and her recent loss. Taylor, her husband and three kids flanked Charly. Taylor leaned into Nick, who was dewy-eyed; the man was an absolute dream, from what Paige could tell. Darcy, looking like Ms. Goody Two-shoes in a prim beige suit and low heels, had tears streaming down her cheeks. Jade and Jewel stood on the other side of Paige, both clothed in hot pink; Jade's outfit was a showstopper—a slim-fitting sheath with a flowered crepe overlay. Her face and Jewel's were wreathed in smiles. Anabelle was the only one not standing with the group. Paige caught a glimpse of her in the back, her sunglasses covering her eyes, her classic yellow dress setting off her tall, slender body. She held herself stiffly, and Paige couldn't tell if she was moved by the ceremony.

Paige looked up at Ian. He stood next to her in a light-weight, gray, pin-striped suit, with a gray silk shirt and matching tie. He grasped her hand tightly, and she could see him swallow hard as Nora and Dan took their vows. On a whim, she'd let Ian pick out what she would wear today. He chose the purple-and-pink-flowered silk jump-suit she'd worn the first time they'd made love.

The current Serenity House girls—Charly's charges now—formed a group, too. Paige recognized them all, but kept an eye on one—Mary Ellen Barone. She'd lost a lot of weight since she'd given birth three weeks ago. Her simple pink-and-white dress hung loosely on her. Her hair was lank, and there were smudges beneath her eyes.

Things were not going well at home. Lena Barone constantly berated her daughter, and Mary Ellen was getting little sleep. With Sammy due to be released from the hospital Monday, Mary Ellen's situation would only worsen. Paige had made an appointment to talk to Elliot Emerson about the girl.

"You're scowling, sweetheart," Ian whispered in her ear. "This is a happy occasion."

"I'm happy."

"Hmm." He tucked her arm in his.

When the ceremony was over, the guests gathered on the outside deck for cocktails. Nora and Dan were surrounded by well-wishers. Paige was listening to Ian tell Nick Morelli how upset Scalpel was at not being invited to the wedding. Ian had rented a feature-length *Rin Tin Tin* video to appease the dog.

Paige noticed Dan scanning the small crowd. His gaze

landed on Anabelle, who was once again standing on the periphery. Dan waved her over. But Anabelle didn't move.

"Excuse me for a second." Paige left Ian and Nick and made her way to Anabelle. "Hey, girl, you okay?" Paige asked when she reached her.

Anabelle angled her chin and straightened her shoulders. "I'm fine. I need to go congratulate them." Still, she just stared ahead. When Paige tracked her gaze, she saw Nathan Hyde beside the happy couple talking to the other attendant.

I wish I'd never met Nathan Hyde.

"I'd like to congratulate them, too. Let's go together."

Anabelle removed her sunglasses. Her amber eyes sparked fire. "I don't need anybody to baby-sit me, Paige."

"Who said you did?" She glanced at the couple, then back at Anabelle. "Might be nice to have a friend nearby, though."

"All right, Mother Hen, let's go."

They made their way through the crowd; Dan spotted Anabelle instantly. "There's my girl!" he exclaimed, handing his champagne to his bride and hugging Anabelle. She hugged back and gave Nora a warm embrace, too.

Then Anabelle faced Nathan, who, Paige noticed, had watched her with an inscrutable expression on his face. "Hello, Nathan."

"Hello, Annie."

She stiffened. "I go by Anabelle now."

Nathan didn't respond, just seemed to study her.

"How are you?" Anabelle's voice was remarkably calm.

He cleared his throat. "Fine. You?"

"Good."

"You look different." He seemed to take in the details. "Your hair…"

She touched her French braid. "For work."

"Dan says you're a cop."

"Undercover. Last time, I was a blonde. I kind of liked it."

He smiled. "I do, too."

She was about to say something when Barbara Benton approached them. "Hello, darling."

Nathan acted as if he'd been caught in flagrante delicto. "Barbara." His voice held a trace of irritation.

Paige said, "Barbara, this is Anabelle Crane. A friend of mine."

"Hi, Anabelle." When Nathan remained silent, Barbara added, "I'm Nathan's fiancée."

This did not seem to come as news to Anabelle. "Nice to meet you," she said, and turned away.

Nathan called after her, "Annie, I—"

But she was already out of earshot.

Halfway across the patio, Paige caught up with her. "Anabelle?"

The mask was back. "I'm all right. I need a drink."

"I'll come with you."

"No, I want to be alone. Thanks, though." And she disappeared into the bar area.

Unsure of what to do, Paige watched Anabelle's retreating back. Dan came up behind her. "She okay?" Dan asked.

"I don't know."

"Did Nathan upset her?"

"I don't know, Dan."

Darcy and Jade approached them.

"Anabelle all right?" Jade asked.

"The sixty-four-thousand-dollar question."

A man threaded his way through the crowd toward them. "Wow, who's the hunk?" Darcy asked.

Paige and Jade eyed the guy and said simultaneously, "Wow." He was medium height, had mile-wide shoulders and thick dark hair that brushed the collar of the black T-shirt he wore with slacks; the outfit made him stand out from the other summer-attired guests.

"Oh, my God. I don't believe it." Dan beamed. "I was hoping he'd come."

The man reached Dan. The two of them embraced like long lost buddies. Dan said, "I'm so glad you came, Hunter."

"I wouldn't miss this." Hunter's voice was deep. Paige noticed a scar just under his chin. The word *danger* came to mind.

Dan drew back. He introduced the man to them as Hunter Sloan, but gave no indication of how he knew him. As the two men stepped away, Paige heard Dan ask, "You didn't come all the way to New York on that motorcycle of yours, did you?"

"No, I flew."

"How long can you stay?"

"I'm leaving today. The damnedest thing happened with my ex..." The conversation trailed off.

"He's not married," Jade cooed longingly after the guys were out of earshot.

"Ah, too bad I've given up on bad boys." Darcy's words ended on a sigh.

"How do you know he's a bad boy?"

Darcy snorted. "Other than the James Dean black, the motorcycle and the scars?"

Jade laughed.

"All right, ladies, I'm claiming her." Ian had come up

behind Paige and possessively gripped her shoulders. "You're a bad influence." He nodded in Hunter's direction. "I saw you checkin' out that guy."

Paige laughed, and before Darcy and Jade could comment, Ian dragged Paige to the dance floor, which was off to the side on the far patio.

"You know I only have eyes for you," she said, winding her arms around his neck.

They swayed to the song, and Paige forgot all about Hunter Sloan. She had the best guy in the world in her arms.

After more dancing and some eating at the several food stations set up around the club, Mary Ellen approached Ian and Paige. They were sitting on a bench down by the pro shop. "I've got to go," Mary Ellen said wearily, "but I wanted to say thanks again, Dr. Chandler."

Ian ducked his head. "You're welcome."

"I'm going to stop and see Sammy on the way home." Paige smiled at her. "Tell him I said hello."

As they watched her leave, Paige asked, "What'd you do?"

"Nothing."

"Ian?"

He slid his arm around her and tugged her close. "Nice night, huh? Romantic for a wedding."

"Ian. 'Fess up."

"All right. I got a nurse to watch Suzy a few hours each afternoon so Mary Ellen can go see Sammy."

"How'd you manage that?"

Shrugging, he fussed with his tie. "I hired her."

"On the Center's budget?"

"What does it matter?"

"You're paying for it, aren't you?"

"Maybe." When she just stared at him, he said, "All right. It's not much."

"Ian, that's so generous. Most doctors wouldn't even think of it."

"You would."

"I didn't."

Again the self-conscious shrug.

"You're a nice guy, Dr. Chandler," she said, leaning into him.

"I'd rather be sexy and mysterious."

Paige didn't answer. She thought about the kind of man Ian was. He was a good, compassionate doctor. He was a sexy, unselfish lover. A funny and kind friend. They'd come a long way in the six weeks they'd been seeing each other, and she'd never felt so close to—or so happy with—any other man. In that moment, under the stars, breathing in Ian's woodsy aftershave, thinking about Nora and Dan's vows, everything crystallized for Paige.

"Ian?"

"Hmm?"

She drew back. "I want to tell you something."

He looked down at her. "What?"

"Just that I love you."

He didn't move and his face was shadowed, so she couldn't tell what he was thinking. Finally he asked hoarsely, "What did you say?"

"I said I love you."

"What…" He cleared his throat. "What brought this on?"

"I don't know. The wedding. The tree house. How you hold me at night." She nodded to the exit. "Things like what you've done for Mary Ellen."

"I…I'm speechless."

"Well, that's a first." Still he just stared at her. "Aren't you happy?" she asked.

He met her forehead with his. "Are you kidding? I never really believed you'd say that to me."

"I'm sorry." She fiddled with his tie. "It just takes me longer to process things."

As if it had just sunk in, he smiled broadly and drew her close. "Paige."

The tenderness of the moment overwhelmed her. She let herself sink into him.

"Say it again."

"I love you, Ian Chandler."

Smiling, he tucked her under his chin. "Nothing will ever be the same after this, Paige."

"I don't think I want things to change too much."

"Are you kidding? It's a whole new ball game now. You belong to me, baby, and I'm never letting you forget that."

His phrasing bothered her. Then he hugged her more tightly, and she forgot the fear and simply basked in her feelings for him. As she caught a glimpse of Dan and Nora standing on the balcony, staring up at the sky, she remembered her earlier thoughts.

It seemed like she was a sap for weddings, too.

CHAPTER FOURTEEN

IAN AWOKE to a sharp jab in the ribs. "What the—"

"No! Please give her back. Don't let them take her."

On the other side of his bed, Paige thrashed violently. He switched on a light, leaned over and shook her. "Paige, honey, wake up, you're dreaming." Again.

Tears coursed down her cheeks. The sight broke his heart. "Paige baby, wake up."

"No, nooooooo…"

He shook her harder. Scalpel came in from the living room. He whimpered at Ian, nosed Paige. "I know, boy. I can't wake her up."

Finally, after a few more shakes, she opened her eyes. "Where is she?"

Damn it, he wasn't going to just sit by and let this happen over and over. "Who, Paige?" he said forcefully.

"Her."

"Who's her?"

"My…" She came fully awake then. "Oh, Ian." Raking a hand through her hair, she sat right up. She noticed the dog and petted his head. "Sorry I woke you guys."

"Me, too, Paige."

She raised her brows.

"You can't keep going like this. These last two nightmares have been the worst."

She stared at him with big eyes.

"Don't shut me out now, honey. Part of loving someone is letting him help you."

Wearily she sank back onto the pillows. "I let you help me more than I've ever let anyone."

"I'm not trained for this kind of thing. Even if I was, I couldn't do it. I'm not objective."

"I don't want counseling. I don't want to hack this to death with somebody."

He didn't say anything. He could understand her not wanting to unearth deeply buried pain. But—

"Look, Ian, I've made a lot of progress. These nightmares are the only things wrong with my life. What happened to me affects no other area."

He thought about her attachment to Sammy Barone, and how she'd agonized over Mary Ellen's plight. Before he could comment, she said, "Bear with me awhile. This will pass. It's all the stuff with the Center. With Mary Ellen."

Reaching out, he grazed her cheek with his knuckles. "I'd do anything for you, Paige."

"Then trust me on this. I know what's best for me."

He tugged her close and slid down so they both lay on one pillow. "All right. For now." But he'd be damned if he wouldn't try to come up with some way to stop these nightmares.

"Do you want the truth, Paige?" Elliot Emerson sat behind his desk, all business. In the weeks she'd been working with the psychologist, she'd come to respect his ability. And since she and Ian were so obviously a couple, he'd backed off personally.

"Of course."

"I don't think Mary Ellen's going to make it with the twins. Her mother is not only no help, she's a problem.

She yells at her daughter and screams when Suzy acts up. I fully agree with Nora Nolan that Lena Barone only wants the welfare money Mary Ellen will get for her two kids. With Sammy going home this week, the situation will only get worse.''

Paige felt so sad inside it momentarily silenced her. These were not the words she wanted to hear. ''Can we get Mary Ellen out of the house? Into a place of her own?''

''I'm not sure she can handle that. She's only seventeen. Pretty young to be raising one infant, let alone two.''

''What are you saying?''

''I think she'll end up giving them up for adoption.''

Tears pricked Paige's eyes. ''Maybe it's for the best.''

Elliot took a bead on her. ''You've gotten close to the twins, haven't you.''

''Sammy, mostly.''

''The nurses say you're there a lot.''

''He's so tiny. He needs human contact.''

''You and Ian are something.''

''What do you mean?''

''He's visited frequently, too.''

''Really? I didn't know that.''

''He says the kid needs male bonding.'' Elliot chuckled. ''He'd probably take that damn dog with him if it was allowed.''

Paige smiled. It was so like Ian. She finally said, ''If that's what Mary Ellen decides to do, how would she proceed?''

''Foster care first.'' He picked up a folder. ''I've been looking into it. There's not much foster care in Hyde Point or Elmwood to begin with. It will be difficult to find someone to take infant twins, especially if one of them has problems." Paige was only too aware that Sammy might still need breathing assistance when he was released, which could involve respirators, or at least oxygen.

Paige sighed. "They'll be split up."

"Yes."

"Do you think anyone will adopt them together?"

"It's likely. Though it might take a while longer."

Paige stood and smoothed down the lab coat she wore. "Thanks, Elliot. I appreciate your filling me in."

Elliot rose and crossed the room with her. They stood in the open doorway. "Can I ask you something?"

"Of course."

"You seem unusually attached to this family. Not that there's anything wrong with that. God knows, doctors are human. But I was wondering why."

You need some help with this Paige. Some counseling.

"No reason, I guess."

He placed a hand on her shoulder. "I'm a good listener."

"Of course you are. You're a psychologist."

"A friend, too, I hope. I might be able to help if you have a problem." He angled his head. "Doesn't look like you've been sleeping very well."

Oh, God, it showed. She felt ravaged after those nightmares, but thought she was covering well. Even Jade hadn't noticed she was exhausted.

"I'm fine, Elliot. But thanks for the concern."

He smiled. "Well, pardon the cliché, but the door's always open."

"Thanks." She left his office and headed for the one she shared with Ian. Elliot's observation upset her. She hoped she had time to regroup before she had to face Ian.

She didn't.

As soon as she sat at her desk, Cindy burst in. "Paige, come quick. There's an emergency in the waiting room."

Paige flew out the door behind Cindy. "Julie Jameson's baby is having some kind of seizure," Cindy said as they hurried down the hallway.

Paige grabbed a blanket as she passed a stack of clean laundry. In the waiting room, she found people crowding around a woman holding a child. Tossing the blanket on the floor, Paige took the baby from the young mother. The little boy was stiff. His movements were jerky, his mouth frothy. His lips were blue. "Cindy, tell everyone to give us room," Paige said firmly.

The nurse moved people out of the way.

The baby was not breathing. Paige lay him on his back. Gently she tilted his head, lifted his chin. She covered his nose and mouth with her own mouth, all the while praying, *Please, let this work.* She gave the boy a slow, gentle breath for about one and a half seconds. No response. She waited. Gave another. She was just about to check for airway blockage when she saw the child's chest begin to rise and fall.

Thank God.

She glanced up at the crowd. Everyone was deadly silent, even the kids who were waiting to be seen. And they were looking at her as if she were God and had just brought Lazarus back to life.

She didn't feel like God. She felt like a wet dishrag. Could things get any worse?

They did...at about nine that night when her service telephoned her at home. She and Ian were lounging in the pool, trying to forget the stressful day, which had ended for both of them a couple of hours ago. "Dr. Kendrick?" the operator said. "Mary Ellen Barone is trying to get hold of you. I told her I'd contact the doctor on call, but she's hysterical.''

''I'll call her,'' Paige said, clicking off and punching in the number. ''It's Mary Ellen,'' Paige informed Ian as he climbed out of the water and took the towel Scalpel carried in his mouth for his master.

''What's wrong?'' he asked.

''I don't know.'' She waited as the phone rang. Finally someone answered.

''Hello.'' It was Lena Barone.

In the background, Paige heard yelling. A man's voice. ''Shut up those goddamned…'' A crash. ''I gotta get some sleep!''

''Mrs. Barone, this is Paige Kendrick.''

''Yeah, good.'' The woman didn't cover the phone. Paige heard wailing in the background. She tensed, picturing those tiny babies crying. ''Get your ass over here, Mary Ellen.''

Commotion. Lots of swearing. Paige felt her insides churn.

''Dr. Kendrick?''

''What's happening, Mary Ellen?''

''It's Johnny, my mother's boyfriend. He's mad 'cause Sammy won't stop crying. Then Sammy wakes up Suzy, and they both cry. I can't…I don't know what to do. I woulda called Nora, but she and Dan are on their honeymoon.'' Paige could hear the tears. ''What should I do?''

Two hours later, Paige and Ian were back at Paige's house, sitting, each with a twin in their arms, while Mary Ellen slept on the chaise. At her wit's end with the whole situation, the young mother wanted the kids to be turned over to foster care tonight.

Ian was pensive, but Paige sensed an underlying anger

in him. He gazed down at Suzy. "How can Lena Barone not cherish this beautiful little girl?"

Watching the big man cradle the baby, Paige felt a swell of emotion for him. She hugged Sammy to her chest. Both infants had quieted and were dozing. "I don't know." She gulped back the emotion. "How long will it take Social Services to get here?"

"It'll be a while. Since the family is safe, and we're doctors, the woman on call said she was going to try to find foster homes right away."

Paige felt her eyes fill. "I feel so bad we couldn't do more."

"We did all we could, Paige."

Little Sammy's eyes fluttered open. He stared up at Paige and smiled. "Hi, buddy, you smiling at me?" she asked. He batted her face with his hand.

"He could recognize you," Ian said. "You've spent a lot of time with him."

"He's probably got some gas," she said. "I'm going to miss the little guy."

"I'm sorry, honey."

Paige looked over at Mary Ellen. "Me, too."

Paige was even sorrier when the social worker arrived an hour later. Each of them was still holding an infant. Mary Ellen had already said goodbye to the babies, and Paige didn't want her to get into another emotional scene so she'd sent the girl inside.

The woman's face was lined with fatigue as she led them to the car. "I found people to take them." She smiled at Paige. "Not together, though."

"We figured that." She clutched Sammy to her chest. He smelled like baby powder and milk and curled into her trustingly.

Ian put Suzy in the car seat first. When he had her

strapped up, he kissed her head gently. "Take care, little one."

Paige's throat closed up. He straightened and gently took Sammy from her. "Bye, sweetie," she said, brushing the baby's head with her lips. Her eyes filled.

Ian settled Sammy in, closed the door gently, then thanked the social worker.

They watched until the taillights disappeared, then turned around and walked hand in hand into the house.

PAIGE THREW herself into her work. By Friday she looked ready to collapse, and there was nothing Ian could do about it. Each night she slept less, each day she worked harder. He was beside himself with worry. It was when he was reading his online mail for Right to Know that the idea came to him. An article about a birth mother finding her daughter after twenty years had been forwarded to him. He'd read the story and stored it just as Paige walked into the office; when he saw the dark rings under her eyes in the light of day, he acted on impulse.

"Come here, I want you to see something."

Sighing, she crossed to the computer. A lot of her spunk was gone, and that worried him the most.

He stood up and eased her down. She watched as he clicked on the RTK icon, then called up the article. "Read this."

She skimmed it. He leaned against the desk. Watching her, he wondered if this was the right thing to do. He had a fleeting feeling it might not be, but he was running out of options.

"Do you think Mary Ellen should go for open adoption?" she asked after she finished reading.

"Mary Ellen?"

"Yes. Isn't that why you showed me this article?"

"No, that isn't why. It's because you're looking like Morticia from the Addams family that I showed it to you."

"I don't understand."

He propped his hands on his hips. "Then I'll spell it out for you. I think you should find your daughter. We'll use RTK."

She stared at him.

"You're running yourself into the ground, running *away* from what's been stirred up in you. I can't stand by and watch this any longer."

Slowly, obviously trying to contain herself, Paige rose. She didn't look strong, though. She looked very fragile. "No." She headed for the door.

"Paige, wait."

She stopped, but didn't face him.

"We need to talk about this."

When she pivoted, the ice in her eyes made him shiver. "We won't talk about this. We will *never* talk about this. If you insist on talking about it, I..."

"You'll what, Paige? Run?"

He saw the struggle in her face. "All I know is I won't discuss searching for her with you. It is *not* an option for me." Turning again, she left the room.

Ian stood watching after her for a long time.

"EVER READ Greek drama?" Jade asked Ian as Paige did laps in the water. She'd been in there nearly half an hour. Scalpel, finally freed from his cast, was trying to keep up with her.

Ian crossed his arms over his chest. "Yeah, sure. It's all about guys who gouge their eyes out and consult oracles."

"You know who the Furies are?"

"No."

Jade sipped her lemonade. "The only subject I was ever good in was English. The Furies were the instruments of justice who pursued people until they paid for their crimes." She glanced at Ian. "Until they dealt with what they were running from."

"What are you saying, Jade?"

Tilting her head, Jade nodded to her sister. "She's being pursued by her own personal Furies."

Ian agreed with that. It had been ten days since the Barone twins had gone to foster care. Today Paige had discovered that Mary Ellen had signed an agreement to put them up for adoption, which had brought on this newest spurt of exercise. "What can we do?"

"I'm not sure." Jade shrugged. "She needs some good news in her life. Something to look forward to. Why don't you take her to the Caribbean? Have a romantic vacation or something."

In his heart, though, Ian knew Paige needed more than a trip away. She needed something drastic, something deep and significant that would give her a sense of security that nothing could shake.

That night, as she slept restlessly in his arms after lovemaking that was wild and tumultuous, Ian lay awake thinking. Somewhere near dawn, he made two decisions. When Paige awoke, he was gazing down at her. She came to consciousness slowly, her arms over her head, her eyes sleepy and vulnerable when she opened them.

IAN LOOKED as if he hadn't slept all night. Paige reached up and caressed his jaw. It was scratchy. She let her hand wander down to his chest. Coarse, dark hair curled around her fingers. "Morning."

"Hello, lady."

Yawning, she tried to focus. "You okay?"

"Uh-huh. Just great." He'd angled up his elbow and propped his head in his hand. The sheet draped his hips, making him look very appealing. "I've been thinking."

"Already?" She glanced at the clock. "It's only seven."

"I didn't sleep."

"At all?"

"No."

"Why?"

He grinned. "I had a thought last night, and I wanted to work it through. Look at all the angles."

"Must have been some thought." She watched him, sat up a bit. "Come to any conclusions?"

"Yep. Don't tense up. It's not bad." He brushed back her hair. "You love me, right?"

"You know I do." She lay back on the pillows.

"And I'm crazy about you."

"I like the sound of that."

"You're almost thirty-three. I'll be thirty-nine soon."

"I know how old we are, Ian," she said dryly. "Where's this going?"

"Marry me, Paige. Right away."

It was the last thing she'd expected, and her muddled mind had trouble processing his words. She'd been overwrought by Mary Ellen's situation. The nightmares had been worse than usual. Ian had broached the off-limits subject of her child's adoption, and her first thought had been that he was going to pressure her again about looking into her past.

Gently he massaged the furrow in her brow with his fingers. "You're not supposed to scowl when you get a marriage proposal."

Oh, God, he'd asked her to marry him. Still she said nothing.

"I want to spend my life with you, Paige."

She couldn't take her eyes off him. He looked so dependable, so strong. Then it hit her. This was good. This was what she wanted. Life could be so different; she could trust this man with her heart and with her secrets.

Staring up into gray eyes that glowed with warmth and love, she said, "Yes."

His face went blank. "Yes? Just like that?"

"Just like that."

"I don't believe it."

Playfully she grabbed his wrist. "You can't take it back now."

"I won't. I was prepared to sweeten the pot."

"Yeah?" Happiness bubbled inside her. She ran her hand down his abs, thinking he meant something sexual. "With what?"

His face grew serious. "I want us to adopt Sammy and Suzy Barone."

Paige's heart stopped. "D-do you mean it?"

"Of course I mean it." He gave her a wistful smile. "I kind of like the symmetry of it. My father adopted me from one of his patients. Mary Ellen came from Serenity House. It's like the gods planned this." He tugged her close and kissed her head. "It's the start of a wonderful life, honey. Just like in the fairy tales. I'll be the prince. You be Cinderella."

But she was too moved to participate in his teasing. Instead, she wound her arms around him, moved her body close and held on tight.

TWO DAYS AFTER he asked Paige to marry him, Ian was just about to follow up on another monumental decision he'd made when Congressman Nathan Hyde walked into his office at the Center. "I hear congratulations are in order."

Leaning against the desk, Ian studied Nathan. The man looked tired. "News travels fast."

"This is Hyde Point, Ian." Nathan shook his hand. "When's the happy day?"

"We're trying for next week." Maybe when they were legally wed, those goddamned nightmares would stop. Ian had thought that with commitment, with proof of his love, with something to look forward to, Paige's demons would vanish.

Apparently not.

She'd had a doozy last night. She'd thrashed so badly, she'd awakened with black and blue marks on her arms. He was wondering how to nightmare-proof his bedroom.

Surreptitiously, he glanced at the computer. Maybe, just maybe, there was another way. He had to do something.

"What can I do for you, Nathan?"

"Actually I was looking for Paige."

"She's at her practice on the hill today."

"Oh."

"Anything I can do?"

Nathan gave Ian a questioning look. "Did Paige say anything about Anabelle Crane to you at the wedding?"

"The tall blond cop?"

"That's her."

"No. I did notice Anabelle didn't seem as happy about the wedding as the other Serenity House girls."

Nathan sighed. "I thought the same thing."

"You know her?"

"I did. A long time ago." He glanced at his watch. "I've got a meeting at City Hall on the new boys' home

Nora and Dan are starting. If you see Paige later, tell her I want to talk to her.''

"Nathan, before you go, can I ask you a legal question?''

"Sure.''

"Are birth records sealed in New York State when an adoption is closed?'' He knew, of course, that in New York, like most states, all adoption records were sealed. He wasn't sure about birth records.

"Yes, I think so. I'm pretty sure the Bureau of Vital Statistics seals them at the time of the adoption.''

"So if I want to find out about a baby born in Hyde Point fifteen years ago, I can't do it?''

"Hospital records aren't sealed. As a doctor, you probably could get access to them.'' He paused a minute. "Why?''

"Nothing I care to go into.''

"Well, let me know if I can help. Look up case law for you or anything.''

"Thanks.''

Nathan said goodbye, and Ian sat down at the computer.

All right, he could still do a search for Paige's daughter with the information she'd given him. It would have been better to have birth weight and any distinguishing characteristics, but he could do the search with what he had. And when he found possible matches, Paige could decide whether to go any further. As he clicked into RTK, a voice inside him nagged, *This is not a good idea.*

It was. He pictured Paige's black and blue marks this morning that caused her to wear a long-sleeved shirt to work in eighty-degree weather.

She trusts you.

She didn't know what was best for her. And he loved

her to pieces. He'd do anything for her. Even risk her wrath. Maybe he wouldn't tell her until after their wedding, though. Yeah, that sounded good.

If you're planning to wait until then, you must know this isn't such a hot idea.

But what choice did he have, really? She wouldn't get counseling. Asking her to marry him and adopt the twins wasn't enough to chase away the nightmares. There just didn't seem any other alternative. Jeez, the woman could seriously hurt herself if last night was any indication.

This will seriously hurt her psyche, hotshot.

He silenced his inner self when he got into the RTK folder. In twenty minutes he'd filled out the application with the information he had.

He just wished he didn't feel so uneasy about what he was doing.

CHAPTER FIFTEEN

AT SEVEN THAT NIGHT, the sun had just begun to set, and the pool water glistened with the last rays. Paige stared at the geraniums and impatiens that flowered profusely in her backyard. It was a storybook setting, and she did indeed feel a little as though she was waiting for her prince.

Who'd asked her to marry him.

She hadn't known she could be this happy. For all her adult life, she'd never expected to be able to trust anyone the way she trusted Ian. And it felt wonderful.

Scalpel heralded their arrival with several loud barks. Paige faced the gate expectantly. The dog scampered in just ahead of his master, but Paige only had eyes for Ian. He wore pressed white slacks, a gauzy blue shirt and a movie-star grin. He was happy, too.

At her feet now, Scalpel barked again. Glancing down, she burst into laughter. The dog wore a tuxedolike bow tie, with white cuffs on his front paws. "Don't you two look handsome tonight!"

Whining a bit, Scalpel pawed at his neck.

"He doesn't like to wear ties, but I told him he had to dress formally for the occasion."

"Where did you get the collar and cuffs?"

"At A Dog's Life. It's a great place for shopping. Scalpel's registered there."

Laughing, she stroked Scalpel's head, then studied Ian.

"You look great." Up close, his hair was damp, skimming his collar, and he had a little nick under his chin from shaving. His eyes were sparkling like smoky quartz.

"Not every day a man celebrates with his intended." He reached over and grasped her neck. Bringing her mouth to his, he kissed her soundly. When he drew back, he glanced down at her outfit. "Nice dress, Cinderella." His big hand fiddled with the charm at her throat. "I've never seen this before."

"I don't have the opportunity to wear it a lot. Nora and Dan bought it for me when I graduated from medical school." She fingered the sapphire pendant embedded in white gold. "I forgot I had it until I was looking for something special to wear tonight."

"Hmm. And tonight *is* special."

Scalpel barked. "All right, boy, now's as good a time as any." Ian nodded to the dog. "He brought you a present."

"I already have champagne."

Ian's gaze traveled to the table behind her. "And food."

"Jade fixed cold shrimp and asparagus. And bought the champagne. Then she and Jewel went to Darcy's for the night. All five are having a sleepover."

"How considerate. We've got the place to ourselves?"

Again Scalpel barked.

"Well, almost," she said, kneeling and noticing for the first time the small sack attached to the dog's neck. "What'd you bring me, boy?"

Paige detached the small velvet bag from Scalpel's tie. Standing, she stared at it. And smiled. Her hands trembled a bit as she untied the pouch and shook out a little square box. She looked up at Ian. His gaze was intense. Slowly she opened the box. Inside, on a soft bed of claret velvet, nestled a sapphire and diamond ring. The sapphire was marquis-cut, and the small diamonds surrounded it. They were set in white gold. Paige felt her heart expand. "It's lovely."

"I wanted a ring on your hand right away, so I picked it out myself this afternoon. Well, I had a little help from Lynne." His voice was full and husky. "Diamonds alone just weren't right for you." A blunt-tipped finger brushed her necklace. "Kismet," he said simply.

"Put it on me."

His hands were shaking, too, when he took the ring and slipped it on her finger. It was a little loose. Gently he raised her hand to his mouth and kissed it. "I love you, Paige Kendrick. This is forever. For better or for worse."

"It is."

"Promise?"

"I promise." She looked up from the ring. "I love you so much, Ian."

"This is the best night of my life."

"Mine, too."

"Everything's going to be wonderful from now on." His eyes shadowed briefly. "You'll see."

"I want you to know something else. I trust you, Ian. I really do."

He swallowed hard, said, "I'm so glad, love," and kissed her again. Then Scalpel barked once more. Ian and Paige smiled and drew apart. They poured champagne, sat in chairs under a tree and, having removed Scalpel's dress clothes, watched the dog swim.

Paige glanced up at the sky as it turned darker. And for the first time in recent memory, she thanked the stars for the gift she'd been given. For this wonderful man, whom she really believed in.

LYNNE ANSWERED the door at eight the next morning, looking sleepy and disheveled in a long, white robe. She peered up at Ian worriedly. "Is something wrong?"

Ian stared at her. "Oh, God. I didn't think. Is Romeo here?"

She rolled her eyes and pulled the door farther open. "No, Ian. Come on in." Ushering him through the small house, she led him out to the kitchen. It was bright and sunny and cheerful. "I've just made coffee. Want some?"

"Yeah. I didn't sleep well last night."

Concerned, she glanced over at him from the stove. "Oh, dear. Paige didn't like the ring?"

"No." He fiddled with the place mat on the table. "She loved it. We had a wonderful night."

Setting a cup of coffee before him, Lynne sat adjacent to him. "Then why are you here at the crack of dawn?"

He glanced at her. "Just to tell you how much she liked the ring."

Lynne gave him a knowing smile. "Ian, you've always been an open book. Ever since you were little, when you were up to something, you always had to confess. Elsa said you'd come to her, talk around the subject and finally blurt out what you'd done, or were about to do."

He grunted and sipped his coffee.

"Which is it?"

He studied the brew as if it held answers to life's mysteries. "Both. I've done half of it. I'm about to do the other half." He looked at her. "It involves Paige."

"Tell me, dear."

He drilled his fingers on the table, swamped again by the confusion that had driven him from her bed at three this morning. *I trust you, Ian.* "Lynne, I...there are things you don't know about Paige."

"Do you want to tell me?"

"I can't go into details. They're personal, and she'd have to tell you. But she has nightmares about her past. I think there's a way to stop them." He stood and began to pace. "But she doesn't agree."

"It should be her choice, Ian."

"But she's making the *wrong* choice. The dreams are horrible. I can't stand by and watch them anymore."

"So you've done something."

"Yes, I've put something in the works—or am about to—that I think will fix all this."

"Ian, sit down."

Like an obedient little boy, he stopped pacing and sat back down at the table.

"You can't fix everything, honey. Life isn't like one of your puzzles. Despite what you seem to think, you can't control everything. My guess is you became a doctor because you wanted to fix everything, and that's good. But this controlling streak you have, this insistence that you know the right thing for others, is dangerous." She gave him a half smile. "It's irritating, too, for me. But…it could harm you. It could harm your relationship with Paige."

"So you don't think I should do this?"

"Honey, *you* don't think you should do this or you wouldn't be here."

"It's so hard to watch her suffer when I know I can help."

"Paige is a grown woman. She should be able to make her own decisions."

"We're getting married."

"Yes, and you'll be her husband, not her father." Lynne's tone was dry.

"Oh, hell." He ran a hand through his hair. "I don't want to be her father."

"Then let her make her own decisions. Be there for her. Encourage her. Even fight about it if you have to, but don't betray her trust. I think trust is a big deal to Paige."

"Bigger than you know."

"Is it too late to undo what you've done?"

"Nah, just a little click of the delete button on the computer."

"Then I suggest you go take care of that."

He stared at Lynne. She was so important to him. Paige could be just as significant in her daughter's life. The woman he loved could have so much more and he wanted to give it to her.

But Lynne was right. Paige's trust was more important. He wouldn't search for her daughter without her consent.

PAIGE WAS STILL floating on air when she breezed into the Center that morning. She hadn't told Ian last night—they were busy with other things—but she'd decided to spend half her time at the Center from now on and scale down her private practice. Again she grinned. She was going to have two children to take care of. Mary Ellen had been tickled pink that Ian and Paige were going to adopt the babies, and of course, everything would be done openly.

She thought of little Sammy who'd clutched at her shirt this morning when she'd gone to the foster family to see him before work. And then she'd visited Suzy, who didn't recognize her as easily as her brother, but she soon would. Paige and Ian had filed for foster care of both of them, then would start the adoption proceedings.

Placing her purse in her drawer, she stopped for a second. Was it all too good to be true? She had Ian, and soon they'd be parents to two adorable kids. Could life possibly be this wonderful? Or would something go wrong? Everything was so good maybe the gods were going to get jealous and take away her happiness.

No, that was stupid, she thought as she closed the drawer and rummaged around in her desk for her schedule. People were in control of their own fate, not spiteful deities.

There was a knock on the open door. She turned to find Nathan Hyde in the entryway. "Hello, Nathan. Are you looking for Ian?"

Nathan strode into the room, tall and commanding and just a little intimidating. "No, I was looking for you. Didn't Ian tell you I stopped by yesterday?"

"Um, no." Like a giddy schoolgirl, she held out her beringed hand. "We've been pretty busy."

Nathan studied the ring appreciatively. "Very nice. Congratulations."

"Thanks." She folded her arms. "What can I do for you?"

"I wanted to ask you about Anabelle Crane."

Paige remembered Anabelle's words. *I wish I'd left Hyde Point as soon as I got out of Serenity House... I wish I'd never met Nathan Hyde.* "What about her?"

"I saw her at Dan's wedding. I was wondering...how she is?"

"She's a successful undercover cop in Seattle, Nathan. She's already gone back to her job there."

With his free hand, he fidgeted with his tie and gripped the folder he held in the other. "I know. I was wondering how she was faring personally."

"She seemed okay to me." She'd been a little sad, but it wasn't Paige's place to tell Nathan.

"No big revelations during your powwow at the lake?"

"You know about that?"

"Yes. I had a bachelor party for Dan one of the nights you ladies were up there."

"I see."

"Look, I don't want you to betray any confidences, but I have a vested interest here. I need to know if she's doing well. And Dan won't discuss her."

"As I said, she seems okay to me."

"Any man in her life?" He closed his eyes. "No, don't answer that. I'm going to get out of here before I embarrass myself further." He shrugged boyishly. "I just wonder about her, is all." He turned and headed for the door. Then he stopped. "Oh, I almost forgot." He held up the folder he'd carried in with him. "Can you give this to Ian?"

"Sure."

"It's the case law I found on the question he asked me about birth records."

"Birth records?"

"Yes, it must be for that adoption matching agency he heads. He wanted to know the legality of searching for the birth records of someone who was born fifteen years ago."

Paige swallowed hard. "Fifteen years ago?"

"Yes. Must be trying to match somebody up."

With none-too-steady hands, Paige accepted the folder and said goodbye to Nathan. She stood stock-still in the center of the room, staring at the folder. It could be coincidence, but all her self-protective instincts moved to red alert.

Would Ian do something like this to her? Surely not. But she remembered his overbearingness in every-

thing, how he'd tricked her into working at the Center…
You need some counseling, Paige. Dammit, he'd even
made her try black raspberry ice cream.

Still…

Pivoting, she faced the machine. Swallowed hard
again. Forced herself to think rationally. She crossed the
room, sat down and booted up the computer.

Don't do this, an inner voice warned. *Trust him. Wait
for him to come in and explain.*

But she couldn't. Fifteen years of independence, fifteen
years of protecting herself came to the forefront. She had
to know. Now.

The icons appeared. She searched for RTK and found
it in the left-hand corner, right where it had been that day
Ian had gotten the article for her. After a brief pause, she
called it up. Closing her eyes, she took several breaths,
then looked at the icons that appeared in that folder.

The very last one was labeled PAIGE.

She bit her lip until it tasted coppery. So he'd done it.
All right, might as well get the full dose. She clicked on
PAIGE. Two more icons came up in the folder. BIRTH RE-
PORT. APPLICATION.

She opened the first, and there it was—evidence of
Ian's betrayal. A coldness invaded her.

The statistics: date of delivery, ambulance, hospital admittance. The baby had come early, as Sammy and Suzy
had—almost a month early. Emotion bubbled in Paige's
throat, but she battled it back and read further. So he
hadn't found out the weight, color of her eyes, any distinguishing marks. Maybe he hadn't gone into the hospital birth records yet.

Burying her face in her hands, Paige tried in vain not
to imagine what the tiny infant must have looked like.
Felt like, smelled like.

No, she wouldn't do this! She straightened and clicked on APPLICATION. It was for Right to Know. Ian had already filled it out. Name of birth mother: Paige Kendrick. Father: Ronald...no last name known. Date of birth of adoptee: April 6, 1987. She skimmed the rest.

Again the stark truth hit her in the face, slapping her into sanity. He'd done a search on her child, using the information she'd so foolishly given him.

It was the worst possible kind of betrayal. She sucked in breaths, fast and hard. Her arms banded around her waist, but nothing could stop the blistering pain that fanned out from her stomach to every single part of her.

Why are you surprised? she asked herself. There were so many signs. She remembered his quote from the paper: *All adoptions should be open... Birth mothers suffer their whole lives unnecessarily. If I had my way, all adoptees and birth mothers would unite...no other way for them to lead normal lives...*

You should find your daughter. We'll use RTK.

Ian was a man who did whatever he thought best, no matter what others believed. No matter what he promised.

She glanced down at her hand and saw the sapphire ring sparkling in the sun coming through the office window.

Promise me something. You won't ever do that again— something underhanded, something manipulative, to get me to do what you want.

You can trust me. I won't do something like this again. I promise.

Yeah, sure. She could trust him. Just like she'd been able to trust Ronny. Her mother. Her father.

Overcome by grief, Paige put her head down in her hands. But she didn't cry. She'd cried more since she'd known Ian than she had the past fifteen years. Now, she was done with all that.

She didn't know how much later she heard, "Paige?" His voice sounded husky and concerned.

Immediately she straightened.

"What's wrong?" He crossed to her, and his hand clasped her shoulder. She wanted to shrink from his touch and from the confrontation to come. "Why are you— Oh, shit." He must have seen the screen.

"Déjà vu, isn't it?"

"Paige—"

"Just like the last time. You were standing behind me, I was sitting in this very chair, when we got Marla's instant message." Oh, God, why hadn't she followed her instincts then and run far away from him?

From the man who betrayed her.

He said simply, "I didn't do it."

She cocked her head. "Oh, someone else filled out an application to search for her?" Paige's voice cracked on the last word.

He swung her around and knelt in front of her. His eyes were earnest and intent. "No, I did that. But I didn't send the application in."

"Didn't have time?" she asked bitterly. "Too busy romancing me?"

"All right, I can see why you're upset. But no, I had time—I just decided not to do it. That it would have been too much of a betrayal of your trust."

"Oh, please."

"You don't *believe* me?" He seemed genuinely surprised.

"No, I don't. And even if I did, it was a betrayal of my trust just to fill out the application." She stared into those gray eyes she loved so much. "Do you know you've done the worst possible thing in the world to me?''

"Honey, I'm so sorry.''

"Well, like somebody I know once said, sometimes sorry's not enough.''

"I made a mistake, Paige. I'm sorry for it. But in the end, I didn't betray your trust. I talked to Lynne this morning about it and—''

"You told Lynne about me? After I specifically said I didn't want her to know about this?''

"I didn't give her any details. Just talked about whether I had the right to make decisions for you. She told me I didn't. That it was wrong. I knew I was wrong, I think, from the beginning, but... Anyway, I decided not to do it. I was coming back today to delete the file.''

She shook her head. "Okay, Ian, you were going to delete the file.'' She pushed at this chest; he stood and moved back. She rose and crossed to the other side of the room, her back to him.

"You really don't believe me, do you?''

"It doesn't matter.''

"Of course it matters. We can't start a marriage with this between us.''

Pivoting, she looked at him, standing there, so big, so strong, so sure of himself. She shook her head. Then she peered down at her hand. Slowly she slid off the beautiful ring and set it on the desk. "There isn't going to be any marriage, Ian.''

His face drained of color. "Paige, don't say that. I love you.''

"Unfortunately I love you, too.''

"Then let's work this out.''

"It can't be worked out.'' She turned away, unable to face him. "It's over between us.''

"Paige, please." He strode to her and grasped her arm. "Please, stay. Let's discuss this."

"No."

He moved in close, aligned his body with hers. She felt his warmth in every cell of her body. "Do you remember telling me the nightmares were the only thing wrong with your life?"

"Yes."

"Honey, if you can do this, just walk out on what we have together because I made a mistake, if you can honestly say you don't believe me, there's a lot more wrong with your life than nightmares."

"I don't want to hear this."

"You're going to be alone forever because of your unresolved issues, Paige. If you can walk out on the man who loves you more than anyone's ever loved you, whom you love back..." His voice trailed off.

But she didn't look at him, couldn't stand seeing the pain—she believed it was genuine—in his eyes. "Then so be it, Ian. It's what I learned about life a long time ago, anyway. You were just a detour, that's all."

She tugged her arm free and left the office without a backward glance.

CHAPTER SIXTEEN

THERE WAS NO WEDDING or honeymoon, but Ian still took the week off. He needed the time away; he was afraid he'd make a medical error, or scare his patients to death with his fury. He didn't know if Paige was working or taking some time, too. He hadn't asked anybody about her.

With righteous indignation, he kicked the bucket holding rags and cleaning materials halfway down the deck. He and his dog, who knew what loyalty meant, were washing the boat at his parents' cottage. "How could she not believe me, Scalpel? I made a mistake, which I was planning to rectify."

Scalpel growled, then barked. This time, he, too, was angry at Paige. The dog had been Ian's constant companion for two days, sleeping with him on the deck of his parents' cottage, taking midnight rides on the lake in the boat, running on lake roads until they were both ragged. He sensed Ian's disquiet.

Ian drew in a breath. But he couldn't outrun the image of Paige's face, battered by his betrayal. "We're better off without her, buddy. I'd be afraid the rest of my life that I was going to make another mistake she couldn't forgive."

Scalpel whined in sympathy.

Wiping his brow, Ian sank onto the deck and tossed down the cleaning rag. "But I had such plans." He'd been to see Sammy and Suzy before he left. "I wanted those kids." He glanced at the cottage. "I wanted a life like Mom and Dad's. I wanted *her*." And he'd almost had it all. Except for one little mistake. Well, maybe not so little, but she wasn't perfect, either, damn it, no matter how hard she tried to be.

He was distracted from his self-pity by a boat heading toward his dock. He didn't recognize who was on it until it pulled up close. Dan and Nora. They motored in and tied up. "Hello, Ian," Nora said after Dan's greeting.

"Hi, guys. Aren't you supposed to be on a honeymoon?"

"We are." Nora leaned into Dan. The small intimacy cut to Ian's heart, adding a new layer to the pain already there. He'd never have with Paige what Nora and Dan had with each other.

Exiting the boat, they walked over to Ian. "We need to talk to you."

His insides turned cold. "It isn't Paige, is it?" Nora would know if something happened to her. "She's all right isn't she?"

Nora shook her head. "She's fine physically. But according to Jade, Paige is a wreck emotionally."

"Well, she can join the club."

Scalpel barked for emphasis.

"Let's go up to the deck," Dan suggested. "This might take a while."

When they were seated in chairs and sipping iced tea, Ian said, "I didn't do the breaking up, guys."

"We know that, Ian." Nora's voice was full of understanding. "We're here as friends. And to offer some advice. Jade told us the whole story."

Ian's shoulders sagged. "I wanted this to work, Nora.

But she called me a liar to my face. She doesn't believe I wouldn't have gone through with the search.''

"Paige needs you, Ian. I won't go into the whole she-doesn't-trust-anybody routine. You know it all. But she came a long way with you. Give her some time. She'll get through this, too."

"All the time in the world isn't going to change the fact that she doesn't believe me." He shook his head. "She wants to live her life alone, then fine. Let her."

"Oh, I don't know," Dan said easily. "I think she'll find someone who doesn't demand of her what you do."

Ian sat forward in his seat. "That would be the worst thing that could happen to her."

"Then you'd better regroup fast, buddy. Jade said she's been out with Elliot Emerson three nights in a row."

"Emerson?" He pounded his hand on the table. "Damn."

"Running away up here isn't helping."

"What would help, Dan?"

"Well, I always find that groveling's a start," Dan said with a wry smile.

"I'd do that in a second if it would work." He sighed. "Nothing's going to fix this."

Nora stroked his arm soothingly. "Well, we just thought you should have our two cents' worth."

After Dan and Nora left, Ian sat on the deck with Scalpel and watched the pigeons playing near the water. Were Nora and Dan right? Should he go back? Was she letting Emerson kiss the hollow of her throat, just where she liked it? Was she letting him hold her at night after a nightmare?

He stood. Hell, he couldn't handle the idea of her with another man. She belonged to him. He stalked into the house. Maybe he'd go back for that meeting with the state board at the clinic tomorrow; he'd planned on letting Elliot handle it, but just maybe he *wouldn't* blow it off. He could see what she was up to. Feel out the situation.

One thing was for certain, he couldn't feel any worse.

PAIGE WAS ABLE to function only if she didn't let herself think about what had happened between her and Ian. For three days she'd gone into work at her practice, even though she'd scheduled the time off. She caught up on the details she'd let go over the past few weeks, did paperwork and covered emergencies. She hadn't been back to the Center. But she had spent some time with Elliot. She'd bumped into him at the hospital, and he'd talked her into a late dinner one night, a show the following and a drink the next; he was a good conversationalist, and though she couldn't tell him about her state of mind, he seemed content just to enjoy her company. He'd also asked her to help him run the state board meeting tomorrow at the Center.

She slept fitfully, even though there were no nightmares. It seemed she'd conquered her unconscious.

Tonight, four nights after she'd found out what Ian had done, she dragged herself out of her car to find a snazzy Mercedes in her driveway. She didn't recognize the car. Scowling—she didn't want company—she climbed the garage steps. Inside the house, she called for Jade and Jewel, then heard noises coming from the deck.

Maybe someone had come to see Jade, which was good. She and her sister had not been getting along since Paige's split from Ian. Jade had been vocal about Paige's decision to end the relationship...

Are you out of your mind? The guy's crazy about you.

He went behind my back to find my child.

He thought about doing it, Paige. He admitted it was a mistake. He didn't do it.

How do I know he's telling the truth?

Jade had just stared at her. *He loves you. He only has your best interests at heart.*

I refuse to discuss this further....

Jade had been disgusted, and the two of them hadn't talked about the issue again. Paige had been gone a lot and had clammed up when she was home.

Following the voices to the deck, Paige slid open the door and found Jade stretched out on a lounge chair, wearing the leopard-print outfit she'd had on the day she'd arrived at Paige's just seven weeks ago. Across from her, in a chair, a man held Jewel on his lap while he read something to her. He looked familiar. Paige could tell—by the way he cuddled Jewel, absently kissed her head and smiled when she talked—that he cared about the little girl.

It was with that insight that Paige realized who he was.

"Hi," Jade said sitting up a little straighter when Paige stepped onto the deck. "Come on over, sis."

Paige circled around the pool. Jade said, "Paige this is Lewis Beckman. Beck, this is my sister, Paige."

The man had the same coloring as Jade and Paige's father, as Jade had said, but the resemblance ended there. Beckman was sophisticated from the top of his styled hair—just touched by gray—to his nicely tailored sport shirt and slacks. He wore wire-rimmed glasses and had a lanky runner's build. Except for a few laugh lines around his eyes, he was younger than she'd expected. She noted the Rolex on his wrist. "Nice to meet you, Paige."

"You, too." But it wasn't. She cast Jade a what's-he-doing-here look.

"Beck drove up to see Jewel," Jade said.

"And you." Beckman sent Jade a meaningful look. Oh, great. "I missed both of you. A lot."

"How about your wife?" Paige asked. "Did you bring her, too?"

Shrewd blue eyes focused on Paige. The look in them told her he was not a man to be messed with.

Before he could comment, Jade said, "Jewel, want to go for a walk with Beck? You can show him the pond down the street with the ducks."

Beckman got to his feet, hefting Jewel up on his hip. "Yeah, princess, let's go see the pond."

"Duckies," Jewel said, sticking her fingers in her mouth and laying her head on his shoulder.

"I'll be back," Beckman said to Jade, and without acknowledging Paige, left through the gate with his daughter.

"You were out of line, Paige," Jade said when they were alone.

"Was I? Isn't he still married?"

Jade's expression told her he was.

"What's he doing here, then?"

Raising her chin, Jade said, "He misses us. Especially Jewel."

"Let me guess. He wants you to come back to New York. He wants to install you in your tower where he has access to you."

Jade stood and jammed her hands on her hips. "No, he said he made a mistake letting us go. He wants to come to some kind of compromise."

"Does that compromise involve leaving his wife?"

"We hadn't gotten that far."

"Ten to one he tries to get you into bed with no commitment."

"Paige, what is *with* you? You're acting like all men are pond scum. Beck's a decent guy who makes mistakes like the rest of us."

"Well, you've made a beauty with him."

Jade crossed to her. "You know, if you didn't look like a stiff wind could blow you over, I'd tell you to go to hell. But I'm not going to do that. I'm going to go inside, pack my bags and leave here tonight before we do irreparable damage to our relationship." She started to walk away.

Paige grabbed her arm. "Jade, wait. Don't go with him, please."

Her sister circled around. "I'm not going with him. I'm going to Mrs. Stanwyck's house."

"Mrs. Stanwyck, your old English teacher?"

"Yes, I've rented half of her house. I was going to move out before your wedding. Then when you broke it off with Ian and were so overwrought, I didn't want to leave you. But I'm going now."

"What will you do about *him?*"

Jade shrugged. "I don't know. Things aren't black and white with people, Paige. This relationship with Beck is gray. He loves Jewel. In some ways, he loves me, too. In any case, I'm not going to jump into anything. *I'm* not going to make rash decisions."

"Are you saying I was rash with Ian?"

"Haven't you listened to anything I've told you all week? What you did with Ian is *wrong*. You two were meant for each other." She grabbed Paige's arm. "You could have him, sis, and two beautiful little babies. Whether you ever searched for your child or not, you could have a wonderful life."

"I can't trust him."

"You can't trust anybody. Even me—to make the right

decisions about Beck. To give you good advice. You have a problem, Paige, and you need to deal with it. Preferably soon, before Ian gets sick of your pushing him away and turns to someone who'll accept him just as he is.'' Jade leaned over and kissed her on the cheek. ''I love you, Paige, but you've got to dig yourself out of this one by yourself.'' She straightened. ''I'll be at Mrs. Stanwyck's. She still lives just on the other side of the high school.''

Paige watched her sister walk away, feeling a sense of loss so great she had to sit down. God, what was she going to do now?

Paige had barely recovered from Jade's departure when someone else came around the house to the pool area. She was still sitting on the same chair, watching the moonlight play on the water, when she heard the gate creak.

It was Lynne Chandler, looking young in a one-piece black jumpsuit. Wondering how she would stand this newest onslaught, Paige said, ''Hello, Lynne.'' Then something occurred to her, something so vile she could barely contain it. Her heart thundered in her chest. ''Nothing's happened to Ian, has it?''

''No, except that he's an emotional mess.''

''I'm sorry. I don't want that for him.''

''Well, he's hurting. He came back from the lake tonight for something tomorrow at the Center. I just left him.''

''There's a meeting with the state board for our three-month review.'' She sucked in a breath. ''Did he ask you to come here?''

''No.'' Lynne crossed to the table. ''May I sit?''

''Of course.''

Lynne sat.

"Why are you here, Lynne?"

"Because I can't stand by and watch Ian lose the love of his life without trying to help him."

"How can you help?"

"By assuring you that he was telling the truth. Whatever he was going to do—and he didn't tell me the details in deference to your privacy—he changed his mind. He already knew he wasn't going to do it when he came to tell me about it. He just needed a nudge."

"So he said."

"And you don't believe him."

Wearily Paige pushed back her hair and laid her head on the chaise. "I don't know what to believe anymore."

"Well, believe this. My son loves you more than he's ever loved a woman in his life."

It was the *my son* that did it. Without letting herself think about it, Paige blurted out, "I had a child when I was seventeen. I put her up for adoption. Ian wants me to find her, have a happy ending like you two. He was going to do a search."

Reaching over, Lynne squeezed Paige's hand. "Oh, Paige. How awful. He shouldn't have done that. No matter what the circumstances."

"He was trying to help. I know that. But this…this is the only thing I can't forgive."

Lynne drew back. "Well, then, maybe you're not right for Ian."

It wasn't what Paige expected. "What do you mean?"

"Everybody thinks Ian's such a good catch. And in many ways he is. But he'd be a hard man to live with. He's so arrogant, so confident, so pushy." She smiled wistfully. "He thinks life is like those puzzles he does. Elsa used to say he and his father thought the world was one big jigsaw, and they could manipulate life like they do the pieces on the board.'' She shook her head. ''He needs a strong woman to keep him in line.''

''And you don't think I'm strong enough for him?''

''Not if you can't forgive his mistakes. He's going to make them all his life.''

''Maybe he needs a woman who will let him run her life.''

Lynne smiled wistfully. ''He's almost thirty-nine years old. If he needed that, he'd be married by now.'' She stood. ''I'm sorry this didn't work out with you and Ian. I thought, initially, you were good for him.'' She sighed. ''He's really a wonderful man, but he isn't perfect.''

Perfect.

Jade's words came back to her. *You expect everybody to be perfect, Paige... Beck makes mistakes like the rest of us.*

After Lynne left, Paige thought a long time about what her sister and Ian's mother had said.

WHEN PAIGE WALKED into the conference room the next day for their meeting with the state board, Ian had to turn away from her and catch his breath. He didn't expect the bolt of pain that shot through him at just seeing her. She looked as bad as he felt.

When he'd regained his composure, he took a seat at the opposite end of the table and studied her surreptitiously. Her hair was pulled back in a gold clip; it was limp, instead of vibrant. Her light-blue skirt and top seemed to settle uncomfortably on her stiff body, and it was obvious she hadn't been sleeping.

''Good morning, everybody,'' he said.

Carol, Cindy, Marcus and Elliot all said hello. Paige just stared at him. When she didn't say anything, Elliot got up and walked to the end of the table. He bent over and said something to her. She shook her head. Then he took a seat next to her and squeezed her arm. Ian had to look away from the sight of another man comforting her.

Just then the representative from the State Board of Health came in, and the meeting got under way. The air crackled with emotional electricity the whole time. Paige stared down at the papers Ian had given out, and somehow he suffered through the meeting. It took a little over an hour, but seemed interminable. When the guy was finished and bade them goodbye, everybody rose but Ian and Paige.

Ian's head snapped up when he heard Elliot say, "Come on, Paige, I'll buy you a cup of coffee."

"Actually I'd like to talk to Paige for a bit." Ian fingered the envelope he'd found waiting for him this morning on his desk. Its message had poleaxed him, and he'd chided himself for thinking things couldn't get any worse. "I'm sorry, but this can't wait."

After murmuring something to Paige, Elliot left, closing the door behind him. Paige and Ian were alone together for the first time since their split five days ago. "You don't look good, Paige."

Still seated down the conference table, she faced him. "Neither do you."

"Yeah, well, this is tough."

He thought he saw tears in her eyes. Just wait.

Removing the envelope from his pocket, he stood, strode to the end of the table, pulled out a chair and sat down. He grasped her hand. Up close, she looked even worse. The smudges beneath her eyes were dense.

Still, she didn't try to free her hand, in fact, gripped his.

"Something came this morning." He cleared his throat. "We have to deal with it now."

She glanced down at the envelope. "What is it?"

"The foster-care papers for Sammy and Suzy."

Her grip on his hand tightened.

"We…" Again, he cleared his throat. "We wanted the babies as soon as we were married. I pulled some strings and got the papers fast-tracked." He shrugged. "Too fast, I guess. We've got to tell them right away what we're going to do."

She laced her fingers with his. "This is too hard, Ian. I can't do it."

"I know. For me, too." His voice sounded like sandpaper on steel.

When she met his gaze, her eyes were wet. "If we say no, somebody else gets them?"

He spoke around the huge lump in his throat. "We're saying no, Paige. I don't want to marry you just so we can have Sammy and Suzy. It wouldn't be good for them to have a mother who doesn't trust their father."

Tears leaked from her eyes and ran down her cheeks. He leaned over and pulled her head to his shoulder. His own eyes misted. "I wanted this so badly," he whispered into her hair. "You. These babies. Some of our own."

"Me, too."

"God, this hurts."

"I know." He kissed her hair and let her head stay on his shoulder until she was in control. Finally she drew away. "Let me have the papers, okay?"

"Why?"

She stood and held out her hand. "I don't know. I just want them."

He handed her the envelope. Staring up at her, he couldn't believe this was the end of it.

"I'm going out for a while."

"Well, I only came in for this meeting. I'm heading back to the lake this afternoon."

She nodded.

"You have the number there, don't you?"

"Yes." She straightened her shoulders.

He had to look away. "Fine, call me about this. Soon, though."

"All right." She got to the door, and he prayed she'd leave. She didn't need to see him lose it, too.

"Ian," she called from the doorway.

He didn't look at her. He couldn't. He pretended to make notes on the legal pad he held. "Mmm?"

"I'm sorry."

"Yeah, baby, me, too."

Finally he heard the door close. And none too soon. Like a man who'd lost everything that mattered to him in the world, he put his head down on the conference table.

"HI THERE, little guy."

Sammy's face lit up.

"He recognizes you." Mrs. Barker, the foster mother, grinned. "He recognizes Dr. Chandler now, too. When do you think you'll be taking him, Dr. Kendrick?"

Paige swallowed hard, felt the envelope in her white coat edge into her hip. *Tell her. Tell her you're not taking them.* "I don't know exactly, Mrs. Barker."

"Oh, okay. Well, I'll just let you visit." The woman left and Paige sat down in the rocker with Sammy.

Safely ensconced in the room, Paige took the bottle Mrs. Barker had prepared and brought it to Sammy's lips. She watched him latch on and stare up at her. "How am I ever going to let you go, buddy?"

The baby sighed, but continued to suckle.

I don't want to marry you just so we can have Sammy and Suzy. It wouldn't be good for them to have a mother who doesn't trust their father.

She rocked the baby. "How am I ever going to let *him* go?"

No words of wisdom from Sammy.

"Maybe one of us could adopt you, sweetie." She smiled weakly. "Ian would make a great father. He and Scalpel would hover over you, but they'd let you be your own man."

She thought of Ian heading back to the lake. "He'd teach you to swim, and boat, and waterski."

She thought of him with Mary Ellen. "He'd teach you to be fair, and kind, and understanding."

She thought of him in bed, touching her. "He'd teach you all about girls, how to make a woman feel that she's the only person in the world for you." Paige's voice caught on the memory of Ian's tender ministrations.

"He'd be a better parent than I would. He's fun, and flexible, and carefree most of the time." She raised her chin. "But I'd balance that. I'd teach you responsibility, hard work. Not that he doesn't have those traits."

Lynne's words came back to her...

He'd be a hard man to live with. He's so arrogant, so confident, so pushy. He needs a strong woman to keep him in line.

"But I'm more practical. You need both, Sammy. So does Suzy. She needs to learn how to deal with all the problems society throws at women today." Paige sighed. "Still, he'd be good for you both. He'd—"

Wait a minute. What was she saying here? That she'd trust Ian with Suzy and Sammy? She loved these babies, and she'd trust Ian to raise them? "Oh, God, little guy," she said. "What am I *doing?*"

Sammy, of course, didn't answer. But he did let go of the nipple and, though she knew he was really too little to react, he seemed to give her the biggest toothless grin she'd ever seen.

AFTER A HARD RUN Ian meandered along the lakeshore with Scalpel. "What the *hell* is that woman up to with those papers?" he asked the dog.

Scalpel barked. He didn't understand women any better than Ian did.

Ian had gone back to Hyde Point with some vague notion of trying to hash things out with Paige. Then he'd gotten the notice about the foster care and had been completely immobilized. And Paige had been so overwrought he hadn't known what to do.

She'd left, and he'd come back here. What a mess things were. He stared out over the lake—its glistening surface had always soothed him. He thought of his parents and how they loved the lake. And how they'd died on it.

Life was short. You never knew when it would end. The dog nuzzled him. It seemed so foolish to waste time arguing.

"Thing is, Scalpel, I know she can forgive me. She's got it in her." He threw a stick and watched the dog fetch it. "But she needs reassurance." He thought about her and Elliot Emerson. "Maybe if *I* get some counseling… I can be a stubborn SOB."

Scalpel barked loudly.

"Well, you don't have to agree so fast." He walked farther. "I can change, though. Maybe if I tell her I'll get help for my controlling streak." He sighed. "I'd do anything to get her back."

He started to feel better. He wasn't going to let her go

that easily. He wasn't going to let the babies go. It was true what he'd said about not wanting to be together just for the kids, but at the same time, if they refused the foster care and adoption now, it would be too late when he and Paige finally came to their senses.

Maybe he should blackmail her with that fact.

No, that kind of behavior was what had gotten him into hot water with her in the first place. Dan's words came to him. *I find groveling helps.* He'd be honest, discuss his feelings openly and not give up, no matter how much he had to grovel.

As they neared the cottage, Scalpel halted abruptly; his ears went up. "Hey, boy, what are you— Scalpel, wait!"

The dog darted up the slope to the cottage. At the bottom of the stairs, he stopped, turned and barked at Ian.

"What the hell?" Ian jogged the rest of the way and caught up to Scalpel. "What is it, boy?"

Scalpel grabbed the hem of Ian's damp T-shirt with his teeth and started to drag him up the steps.

"Scalpel, buddy, what is…"

The question trailed off when he saw what had excited the dog. Stretched out in a lounge chair, her arms over her head, was Paige. Fast asleep. "Shh, boy, don't wake her yet." Scalpel quieted and they climbed the rest of the steps silently.

Before he went to her, Ian sucked in a breath and looked up at the cottage. *Hey, Mom and Dad, if you're watching, please help me do this right.* He crossed to Paige and sat down.

She looked even more worn-out up close. Her hair had escaped the clip, and he smoothed it back from her face with loving fingers. The soft rise and fall of her chest told him she was deeply asleep.

Leaning over, he brushed her forehead with his lips.

"Hey, Sleeping Beauty, wake up." He chuckled. He knew now he was no Prince Charming.

Paige didn't stir.

"Wake up, lady. I need to talk to you."

After a few more kisses, her eyes opened. She smiled at him the way she used to when they awoke together. "Ian." Her lids drifted shut again and she sighed. Then her eyes snapped open. "Oh! I—" She looked around. "I fell asleep."

His knuckles trailed down her cheek. It was warm and smooth. "You're exhausted."

"I needed to see you." She grabbed his hand, kissed it, brought it to her heart.

"I needed to see you, too."

She sat up and studied him.

He looked weary sitting there on the edge of the chaise. His mouth was bracketed with lines of stress. He was sweaty— he must have been running—and his eyes were sad. She blurted out, "I love you, Ian. I've been so wrong."

"Paige, I—"

She put her fingers to his mouth. "No, let me finish. I went to see Sammy today after I left you. As I was feeding him, I realized I'd trust him and Suzy with you, even if we couldn't have them together."

Ian's jaw dropped. She hoped he recognized the significance of the statement. In case he didn't, she told him. "It hit me then. If I could trust those tiny babies with you, I could trust my heart with you." She kissed his hand again. "My life."

"Oh, honey."

"I need help dealing with this trust issue. And I need to make some decisions about finding my daughter. I don't know what I'll decide about that, but I've asked

Elliot for some names of counselors." She raised her eyes to the sky. "I should have done this long ago."

His grin was star bright. "Can I talk now?"

"Uh-huh."

"I'd just decided the same thing. That I'd been wrong to expect so much of you. That *I* need some help in dealing with this control streak of mine." He gripped her arms. "I never admitted that before, never saw it as a problem until we got together. But it is a problem, and I'll work on it, baby, I promise." He leaned over and kissed her forehead. "Just don't leave me, please." He felt her crying and drew back. "Why the tears, love?"

"Ian, you didn't have to tell me all that. I told you first I'd compromise. You could have kept what you'd decided to yourself."

Smiling sadly, he shook his head. "I told you that you could trust me, Paige. I don't want to win, here. I just want us to be together. To work this out."

"I do, too."

Scalpel barked. Ian glanced at the dog. "So does he."

As if called, Scalpel scampered over and licked them both until she and Ian were laughing.

Ian inched around and maneuvered them until he and Paige were scrunched in the lounge chair together, with the dog at their feet. They sat that way for a while, just reveling in each other's company.

"We're going to have a wonderful life, Paige," he finally said.

"Mmm."

"Let me tell you about it."

She turned her face into his chest. "No, don't tell me. Let me be surprised."

She felt Ian's deep sigh. As she snuggled into her

soon-to-be husband, she realized she wasn't afraid of surprises anymore. Together, and trusting each other, she
and Ian could take anything the world threw at them.

*   *   *   *   *

*Please turn the page
for an excerpt from*

A Place To Belong

—the next title in Kathryn Shay's new
SERENITY HOUSE *trilogy.*

CHAPTER ONE

January 1987

NORA NOLAN answered the door to Serenity House at eight o'clock at night, her stomach in knots. This admittance would *not* be easy. On the porch, in the chilly January evening, she found her newest client, Darcy Shannon. "Hello, Darcy."

A go-to-hell teenage glare met her greeting.

The girl's mother, Marian Shannon Mason, scowled at the girl, who was a petite five foot two with flame-red hair. "Say hello to Miss Nolan, Darcy Anne."

Still the silent sullenness.

"Well, come on in." Nora reached for the hot-pink suitcase Darcy carried, but the girl snatched it back. Her eyes, the color of wet grass, warned Nora not to invade her personal space, something Nora made a mental note to remember.

Frozen for a moment, mother and daughter stayed on the threshold of the newly opened home for troubled girls. Once they stepped through the doorway, Nora knew their lives—their relationship—would never be the same. A parent admitting she couldn't control her daughter and seeking outside help damaged the trust between mother and child. Nora wasn't sure it could ever be rebuilt. Still, Serenity House filled a vital need, which was why Nora had fought for it in this rather conservative upstate New York town of Hyde Point.

Finally the women stepped inside.

Nora asked pleasantly, "Darcy, would you like to see your room?"

Darcy shook her head, sending her hair into her eyes. She clasped her leather jacket close to her chest. A hot-pink sweater peeked out from beneath it.

"Straighten your shoulders and push your hair back," Marian Mason said.

Darcy clucked her tongue in resentment. Then her gaze was distracted by someone on the stairs. Nora turned to find Paige Kendrick at the top of them.

"Darcy, this is Paige. She and her sister have been here a few weeks. I thought maybe she could show you your room. It's right next to hers."

Panic flooded Darcy's face. It was hard to believe this fragile-looking young girl consistently stayed out all night, shoplifted, often refused to go to school and had recently been caught by the police on top of Hyde Point Hill in the buff, with an equally naked boy.

Paige trundled downstairs. "Hi, Darcy. I know you from school."

Darcy swallowed hard and eyed Paige's six-months-along pregnancy.

"There's three of us here. Me, my sister, Jade, and Charly Smith, who bakes great cookies."

"Well, good," Marian Mason said. "See, dear, you'll like it at Serenity House."

Nora refrained from rolling her eyes. Darcy, however, wasn't so discreet. She gave Mrs. Mason an are-you-nuts look.

"So, I'll be going." The woman fidgeted with her purse. "I'll call you, Darcy, tomorrow."

Darcy wouldn't look at her mother. Marian didn't touch her daughter, simply said goodbye, nodded to Nora and opened the door. She reached the porch before Darcy yelled, "Mom!" and bolted after her. In the darkness of late winter, Darcy threw herself at her mother, grasping her around the waist. "Please, don't leave me here." Hiccups. "I promise I'll be good. I'll change. I'll be what you want." Tears. "Just don't leave me in this place."

Paige sidled in close to Nora, and Nora slid her arm around the girl.

Reluctantly Marian placed her hands on Darcy's shoulders. And pushed her away. "I can't, Darcy. You won't change. The authorities think this is the best. It's only for a few months until you learn some discipline."

"Please."

The woman said coldly, "No."

Darcy yanked herself away. "Fine. Go take care of other people's kids." Nora knew that Marian ran a day care in town with her new husband, Jeremy Mason.

Angrily Darcy brushed back her bangs, revealing furious eyes. She straightened her shoulders and said in a voice like death, "I'll never forgive you for this."

Mrs. Mason paled. "Don't say that, Darcy."

The girl raised her chin. "I won't forgive you. Ever."

Nora knew that truer words were never spoken. Sixteen-year-old Darcy would be affected well into womanhood by her mother's decision to put her here.

With quiet dignity now, Darcy stepped back, entered Serenity House and said to Paige, "You can show me my room now."

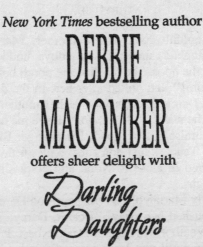

Welcome to Bloom's
where food is love and everybody *loves* food

JUDITH ARNOLD

Love in Bloom's

The Blooms have run the family deli for generations, and Grandma Ida isn't about to let a culinary mishap change that. So when her son, the president, meets an untimely demise, the iron-willed matriarch appoints her granddaughter Julia to the top seat. Nobody is more surprised than Julia. But no one says no to Ida. And once Julia's inside the inner sanctum of Bloom's, family rivalries, outrageous discoveries and piles of delicious food begin to have their way with her.

Life at Bloom's is a veritable feast.

Available the first week of June 2002
wherever paperbacks are sold!

MIRA®

MJA918

Visit us at www.mirabooks.com

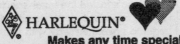

If you enjoyed what you just read,
then we've got an offer you can't resist!

Take 2 bestselling love stories FREE!
Plus get a FREE surprise gift!

//

Clip this page and mail it to Harlequin Reader Service®

IN U.S.A.	**IN CANADA**
3010 Walden Ave.	P.O. Box 609
P.O. Box 1867	Fort Erie, Ontario
Buffalo, N.Y. 14240-1867	L2A 5X3

YES! Please send me 2 free Harlequin Supperromance® novels and my free surprise gift. After receiving them, if I don't wish to receive anymore, I can return the shipping statement marked cancel. If I don't cancel, I will receive 6 brand-new novels every month, before they're available in stores. In the U.S.A., bill me at the bargain price of $4.05 plus 25¢ shipping and handling per book and applicable sales tax, if any*. In Canada, bill me at the bargain price of $4.46 plus 25¢ shipping and handling per book and applicable taxes**. That's the complete price, and a saving of at least 10% off the cover prices—what a great deal! I understand that accepting the 2 free books and gift places me under no obligation ever to buy any books. I can always return a shipment and cancel at any time. Even if I never buy another book from Harlequin, the 2 free books and gift are mine to keep forever.

135 HEN DFNA
336 HEN DFNC

Name	(PLEASE PRINT)	
Address	Apt.#	
City	State/Prov.	Zip/Postal Code

* Terms and prices subject to change without notice. Sales tax applicable in N.Y.
** Canadian residents will be charged applicable provincial taxes and GST.
   All orders subject to approval. Offer limited to one per household and not valid to
   current Harlequin Supperromance® subscribers.
   ® is a registered trademark of Harlequin Enterprises Limited.

SUP01   ©1998 Harlequin Enterprises Limited

HARLEQUIN *Super* ROMANCE®

One of our most popular story themes ever...

Pregnancy is an important event in a woman's life—
and in a man's. It should be a shared experience,
a time of anticipation and excitement.
But what happens when a woman is
pregnant and on her own?

**Watch for these books in our
9 Months Later series:**

***What the Heart Wants* by Jean Brashear (July)**

***Her Baby's Father* by Anne Haven (August)**

***A Baby of Her Own* by Brenda Novak
(September)**

***The Baby Plan* by Susan Gable (December)**

Wherever Harlequin books are sold.

HARLEQUIN®
Makes any time special ®

Coming in June 2002...

THE RANCHER'S BRIDE

by

USA Today bestselling author

Tara Taylor Quinn

Lost:

His bride. Minutes before the minister
was about to pronounce them married,
Max Santana's bride had turned and
hightailed it out of the church.

Found:

Her flesh and blood.
Rachel Blair thought she'd
finally put her college days
behind her—but the child
she'd given up for adoption
haunted her still.

**Could Max really
understand that her future
included mothering this child, no matter what?**

Finders Keepers: bringing families together